A Daring Escape

A Daring Escape

Tricia Goyer

HARVEST HOUSE PUBLISHERS
EUGENE, OREGON

Cover design by John Hamilton Design

Published in association with Books & Such Management, 52 Mission Circle, Suite 122, PMB 170, Santa Rosa, CA 95409-5370, www.booksandsuch.com.

Unless otherwise indicated, Scripture quotations are from the King James Version.

The quote from Psalm 23 on page 65 is from S. Kohn, *Gabriel: A Story of the Jews in Prague* (London: Forgotten Books, 2017), 32. Originally published in 1869.

A DARING ESCAPE

Published by Harvest House Publishers
Eugene, Oregon 97408
www.harvesthousepublishers.com

ISBN 978-0-7369-6514-9 (pbk.)
ISBN 978-0-7369-6515-6 (eBook)

Library of Congress Cataloging-in-Publication Data

Names: Goyer, Tricia, author.
Title: A daring escape / Tricia Goyer.
Description: Eugene, Oregon : Harvest House Publishers, 2018. | Series: The London chronicles ; 2
Identifiers: LCCN 2017028152 (print) | LCCN 2017030410 (ebook) | ISBN 9780736965156 (ebook) | ISBN 9780736965149 (softcover)
Subjects: LCSH: World War, 1939-1945--Fiction. | BISAC: FICTION / Christian / Historical. | FICTION / Christian / Romance. | GSAFD: Historical fiction. | Christian fiction. | Love stories. | War stories.
Classification: LCC PS3607.O94 (ebook) | LCC PS3607.O94 D37 2018 (print) | DDC 813/.6—dc23
LC record available at https://lccn.loc.gov/2017028152

Printed in the United States of America

17 18 19 20 21 22 23 24 25 / BP-GL / 10 9 8 7 6 5 4 3 2 1

— Prologue —

Ústín, Czech Republic
September 20, 1993

Condensation dripped from stone-hewn walls as Charles lowered himself down into the dry well, seeking the treasure his grandfather had tucked away just days before the Allies sacrificed the Sudetenland to Hitler's death squad like a lamb to the slaughter. The rock walls and the earthy, wet smell reminded him of medieval dungeons and secret tunnels he had read about as a child, and of tales of adventurers hunting treasure.

The harness Charles wore was connected to a rope and attached to a pulley—his father's idea. Knowing that fifty-five years prior his grandfather had had no such contraption, he wondered how the man had managed to get down here and hide the treasure. *If there is family treasure.*

Even though he'd heard the story all his life, Charles wasn't sure whether what his grandfather had told Charles's father was true or just a distraction from the mounting war right outside their home. He would soon find out.

At his father's insistence, they had come to search out the

treasure. His great-grandmother's land and country house had been returned to their family as restitution a few months prior. It had taken his father, a retired Christian minister born a Jewish son of a storekeeper, only a few weeks to book flights to the place that had never left his mind or his heart.

Yesterday, as they'd descended the airplane's stairway after arriving at the Prague airport, Charles had a feeling his father had come not only to seek the treasure but also to lay to rest his past and find some direction for his future.

This is my story too, Charles whispered within his heart. No one from their family would be alive if it hadn't been for others risking their lives, especially a special woman his father swore never to forget.

"Do you see initials in the stone?" The older man's words echoed down the well. Even though this was the first time he'd been back in his home country since he'd ridden away on the kindertransport in 1939, his Czech accent was still strong. Most people knew that Ondřej Šimon, or Andrew Simon as he was known in the United States, was of European descent, but few understood what he'd faced during the war. It had been hard for Charles to understand as well until he'd come here. His father seemed to come alive when they arrived, as if landing on his home soil had been the key to unlocking the emotions hidden deep inside.

Standing before the astrological clock yesterday in Prague's Old Town Square, his father—who'd given a hundred talks about his experience in the war without shedding a tear—had wept, leaning heavy on his son for support. Then, as if remembering the Nazis' rigid march pounding down the cobblestone streets, he'd clutched Charles's hand and urged that they return to the quiet of their hotel room. Side by side, they'd walked with quick steps, memories trailing his father like hunting hounds.

It had been a miracle that his father had escaped Czechoslovakia in the first place. The majority of Jewish boys his age had become ashes in the crematoriums of Terezín, Sobibór, and Auschwitz.

"I'm looking for them," Charles called back up, pushing his tangle of thoughts down to the well's depths, forcing his attention back to the task at hand.

Charles placed his hands on the moist rock wall and turned himself slowly as he dangled just below the opening. He supposed his grandfather had tied a rope to a nearby tree to lower himself into this place. Had he expected his young son to do the same?

His headlight illuminated the gray stone. Halfway around his slow circle, he spotted something. He sucked in a breath, cool air filling his lungs. A carved stone with the letters "A.S." sat eye-level, undisturbed for the last fifty-five years.

"I see it!" he called up to his father.

Charles reached into his back pocket and pulled out the long iron file his father had brought from his workshop in Michigan. He inserted the end of the file under the stone and was amazed by how easily the rock slid out and how light it was in his hand. It was rectangular, no more than four inches thick—the size of a small box of cereal. Charles discovered next that it was a mere cover for a secret compartment behind it, and his respect for the grandfather he never knew grew. Had Abram Šimon also been fascinated by medieval tales and hidden treasure as a child?

Charles was amazed that his grandfather had come up with such a clever secret compartment and that the man had recognized the threat the Germans posed just outside their country's gates. Not only had he known, but he had the forethought to hide something of value and then tell his young son its location. And now through the stories—and whatever was held within this hidden chamber—Abram Šimon's legacy would live on.

"I have the cover off. What do you think, Dad? Should I reach inside and see what I find?"

"Is that a real question?" Nervous laughter flowed down the well, echoing around Charles. "Why have you not done it yet? Are you waiting for me to have a heart attack right on this spot?"

Charles reached into the opening, his fingers brushing against something soft and wet. Was something alive in there? He quickly pulled back his hand and then focused his headlamp to illuminate the space. A dark form filled the opening. A black velvet bag. And reflecting off his headlamp was an intricately stitched Star of David, sewn upon the velvet, and Hebrew lettering he couldn't decipher.

Charles reached in his hand and pulled. The bag was bulky—larger and heavier than he thought. He had to wiggle it to and fro to get it out of the spot. Finally, he was able to release it, though it almost slipped out of his hand and into the depths of the well.

"I have it!" he called up to his father, trying to balance the heavy bag in one hand and the stone in the other.

"Ready to be pulled up?"

"Wait a minute. Let me put the stone back."

"*Ne!*" his father called, slipping back into the Czech language as he often did when thoughts of his home country filled his mind. "Bring that up too. I need to see it."

Need to see it. Need to feel the connection with his father. Need to be reminded how he was cared for and loved.

"Okay then, pull me up!"

Charles allowed himself to be lifted to the surface by his father's slow pulls, much the same way he'd allowed himself to be pulled into his father's stories throughout the years. Many survivors refused to speak about what they'd experienced, but his father had been the opposite. For as long as Charles could remember, his father visited schools and organizations, telling about his daring escape and how his life had been spared.

The gold star of David embroidered on the velvet bag spoke of times past and a family Charles had never known. It spoke of his grandfather, who'd found a way to offer a gift to those left behind, even after his death. But mostly it was a tangible reminder of who his father was and the miracle that had saved his life in a war-torn world, where heroes had emerged from the most unlikely places.

ONE

London, England
Monday, December 12, 1938

Amity Mitchell shivered slightly despite the warmth of the small coal-burning stove inside the conservatory. Across from her sat her student, poring over her books—or at least pretending to for her tutor's sake.

Even though Christmas was just a few weeks away and white flakes of snow fell, fifteen-year-old Celia, her pupil and friend, insisted on doing her studies within the glass-walled greenhouse attached to the large London family home. It was bad enough to Celia that she and her father came to their London home for the winter, leaving their Somerset estate for the season, but the young woman couldn't bear to be within the stuffy walls of the brick manor while doing her studies. The chilly conservatory was a compromise.

Celia craved the wide-open countryside. She longed for fresh air, for freedom. This glass cage was as close as Amity could offer. Little did Celia realize that all of England had become a glass cage to Amity. A place to view the cold world beyond the United Kingdom's rocky shores. A fragile protection that Amity guessed would shatter the moment Adolf Hitler, chancellor of Germany, raised his fist in force against her adopted country. The world had already witnessed Germany's hate and violence against the Jews. The *Kristallnacht* pogrom on November 9, when Jewish homes, shops, businesses, and synagogues were destroyed, showed what would happen to anyone Hitler wished to destroy. It was said hundreds of Jews had been murdered and thousands arrested. Did the English believe they were beyond such fate?

Don't have such dreadful thoughts, Amity scolded herself, but it didn't work. With the recent signing of the Munich Agreement, permitting Nazi Germany's annexation of portions of Czechoslovakia, she was starting to see a threat on every corner, a German spy behind every smile—just as in one of Celia's father's novels.

Amity needed to focus her mind on educating one young woman instead of allowing her thoughts to cross borders and fret about foreign issues over which she had no control. *At least for today.* But what about the holiday to come? She was considering actually crossing borders and traveling deep into the heart of Europe. Would leaving for a time, at her brother's request, jeopardize her position here? Worries crowded in again.

Do your job and do it well, and perhaps Clark will choose to extend your contract, she reminded herself. It wasn't every American who was offered a chance to enjoy London society the way she had been. But was there something more for her?

Like Celia, Amity enjoyed her employer's country house—a Georgian manor near the village of Templecombe named Cartwright Manor. But the city house was nothing to sneeze at either. It was grander than any home she'd been in back in the states and was situated on The Drive, one of the most beautiful parts of London in the South Woodford district. Amity had her own large bedroom with an en suite bath, and most of the time she felt more a part of the family than an employee.

And yet the year was almost over, and Clark had not brought up her terms for the upcoming year. Did they still want her around? Celia was a bright girl. Did her father feel it unnecessary to hire a tutor to continue preparing Celia for university but was afraid to tell her so? Amity could understand if that was the case.

Amity enjoyed the flexibility and freedom that came with being a private tutor. If only she'd been allowed to explore and to dream when she was Celia's age instead of being the one to care for her mother and stepfather while her half-brother, Andrew, moved abroad.

Andrew's father was a British sea captain, and he had met and married their mother after meeting on holiday. After his death from a shipwreck, their mother had returned to America and married a second time, and that's when Amity had been born. Five years her senior, Andrew had been a doting brother, and her heart had been broken the day he decided to leave. Adored by his British grandparents, Andrew had moved to London as a teen and had done well for himself.

After her parents' death in an automobile accident, Andrew had sent for her, and a few years after her arrival he had introduced her to the bestselling author Clark Cartwright, a widower who was in need of a young, interesting tutor who could maintain control of Celia, yet also not be too uptight about her fanciful ways.

"School the child without shattering her imagination in the process," Clark had urged. Amity attempted to do her best with both.

Amity rubbed her hands together now, fighting off the chill, and Celia lifted her gaze from the history book in front of her.

Her eyes widened as she looked out the window beyond Amity's shoulder.

"Oh, look, Ami!" Celia jumped to her feet and pointed to a bird that hopped around the base of the shrubbery. "It's a thrush. And look, he's carrying a red berry. What a cheeky little thing, isn't it?"

Amity blew out a sigh. How would she ever be able to keep this young woman focused on her studies when her soul ached to be out in the winter gardens exploring?

"Very cheeky indeed." Amity forced a smile. "Tell you what, let's finish our history, and then we'll bundle up and take a stroll. Maybe you can use the camera you received for your birthday."

"I'd rather watch the birds than photograph them, but it *was* a thoughtful gift from Father. But really, do we have to finish this chapter? There's always tomorrow." Celia winked.

Amity slid Celia's book closer to herself, scanning the pages they'd already covered. "Well, how about you answer two questions, and if you get them both right we'll finish the rest of the chapter tomorrow?"

Celia straightened in her chair and tucked a strand of silky black hair behind her ear. Her hair was opposite of Amity's own auburn locks, which were neither straight nor silky.

Celia clapped her hands together. "Two questions. I'm keen on that." She wore a dark blue dress and white sweater, and the young woman looked more like a lady with each passing day—except for moments like these, when the little girl inside wanted to explore and play.

Amity tilted up the book so her pupil couldn't see the answers and flipped back a few pages. She cleared her throat. "First question: What fierce invader was labeled 'the scourge of God'?"

"Are you talking about the fourth century or today?" Celia

smirked. "Because after the annexation of the Sudetenland, Daddy thinks Hitler is just getting started, and Grandfather has called the Germans the Huns since the Great War. So, if that's who you mean..." She let her voice trail off, humor in her gaze.

Amity lifted an eyebrow, wondering how much longer she'd be able to keep up with her pupil's intellect. "I agree with your father about Hitler—and yes, the Germans were often referred to as the Huns during the war—but I was discussing the *fifth* century, thank you very much."

"Then that would be Attila the Hun, of course." Celia studied her nail cuticles as if bored by the question. Then she perked up, shifting in her seat with excitement. "But speaking of the invader, did you hear there is a new novel called *The White Stag* about the Huns and Attila's sweep through Europe? I can't imagine the drama. I assume it's downright brilliant, and Daddy promised to get me a copy the next time we're at the bookshop. He's heard good reviews despite the fact it's from an American author."

Amity placed a hand on her hip. "*Despite* the fact?" She narrowed her gaze, pretending to be offended.

"Second question," Amity started before Celia could launch into reviews of other new books she hoped to read. "What was the name of the pope who stopped Attila just outside of Rome and obtained from him the promise that he would withdraw from Italy and negotiate peace with the emperor?"

Celia rose and smoothed her hands down her skirt. "Pope Leo I. Can we go out now?"

Amity closed the history book. "Yes. You've done well. Bravo." Then she pointed to the scattering of papers and books on the worktable. "But first put away your things. I'll never hear the end of it from Mrs. McGovern if you leave your papers askew."

"Oh, I have no doubt about that." Celia gathered up her books in a pile. She grinned. "Sometimes I wonder who really is the head of this household, my father or our stodgy head housekeeper."

"Shh." Amity covered her lips with her finger. "The walls seem to have ears here." Then she helped by gathering up the loose papers and pens.

As they cleaned up, Amity couldn't get the young woman's comment about Hitler off her mind. She hadn't heard anyone compare the German dictator with the Hun destroyer before, but something deep inside told her it was a fair comparison. After listening to Hitler's speeches on the BBC, she'd be surprised if he stopped at the Sudetenland. Even though both France and Britain were intent on avoiding war, Amity suspected it would come to that.

Once the cleanup was complete, Celia wasted no time and took hurried steps toward the cloakroom.

"One more question," Amity called out as she rose from her spot at the table.

Celia swung around, placing her hands on her hips and swishing her skirt from side to side as she pouted. "But you said two questions only."

Amity nodded. "This isn't so much a question as something to ponder. Would you have done it? Would you have dared to approach someone as vicious as Attila the Hun?"

Celia lifted her face to the conservatory's glass ceiling and focused on the falling snow. She stood quietly, and for a moment Amity was certain she'd forgotten the question and had again become lost in her thoughts. Amity was about to ask again when Celia met Amity's gaze.

"I suppose if I knew God was on my side I would dare to stand up to a Hun invader. Surely Pope Leo I felt that He was."

"But he could have died," Amity commented, following Celia to the cloakroom to grab their wraps.

"We're all going to die, aren't we?" Celia's voiced softened, and she suddenly seemed older than her fifteen years. Her face fell, and the joy of the earlier moment was gone. Amity had no doubt the young woman was thinking of her mother, who'd died little more than three years ago. "It's a good question though," Celia continued. "What if Leo hadn't gone? What if he'd been too scared?"

Amity slipped her arms into her wool coat, and a strange sensation settled in her chest. "Rome would have been conquered, and the world as we know it would have been different."

It still might be different yet, a nagging fear inside Amity's gut suggested. Despite the festivities of this season—the Christmas lights of Oxford Street and the Trafalgar Square tree—this century's own Attila seemed to be on the move, first annexing Austria and now the Sudetenland.

"Peace for our time," Chamberlain had declared after signing a nonaggression treaty with the German leader, but who really believed Hitler would hold up his side of the bargain?

Hush now, it's none of your concern, she scolded herself. Even though Andrew now worked for the British Home Office, which oversaw immigration in the United Kingdom, they were both American citizens and could leave the UK at any time. Attila wasn't storming at her own country's gates. At least not yet.

Amity considered the telegram she'd received from her brother at lunchtime. It was a cryptic note, one she didn't fully understand.

Please visit me in Prague for the holiday. Need assistance with Jewish welfare work. Send date of your arrival. Room will be waiting for you at Hotel Evropa. STOP.

It was just like her brother to demand so much and send so little information. Did he expect her to drop everything and come? To buy a ticket and travel to a part of the world in crisis? What would Clark think about that? What about Celia? Amity couldn't just leave the young woman behind, could she?

Then again, what was this Jewish welfare work? Surely it had to be important for her brother to send for her. Even without more information in the telegram, Amity understood the context behind her brother's message. With the recent occupation of the Sudetenland, the Jews who'd lived in that part of Czechoslovakia had been pushed out of the newly annexed area, either by Nazi terror or Nazi threats. Were the streets of Prague now filled with refugee families? It would make sense if they were. But if that was the case, why had Andrew requested her? She was no Pope Leo I. What could she offer in the face of Hun invaders?

~ Two ~

Afternoon shafts of light slipped across the sky, and a fine snow hung suspended in the air. From the second-story window of his study, Clark Cartwright watched his daughter's tutor, Amity Mitchell, walking in the misty depths of the garden with Celia. A pain struck his heart, and he swallowed down emotion. Celia was taller than Amity now, and the shining image of her mother. Gwen would have loved to see how their daughter had grown. Celia's love for life could not be shaken, and he had Amity to thank for that.

Dear Lord, what would we have done if she had not come? Clark shook his head, not wanting to consider such a thing. *Amity has rescued Celia...rescued us both from a life of mourning.*

The two outside paused, turning their faces up to catch the snowflakes falling from the sky. Then, with a smile brighter than beams of sunlight, Amity lifted gloved hands into the air and began to twirl in a slow circle. Her laughter carried to the window, shimmying through the glass and wrapping around Clark's heart.

In that moment Clark was struck again by what he'd known for the last year. *I love Amity.* Not in the same way he'd loved Gwen, but with a new, tender love he couldn't shake.

If only he didn't struggle with these feelings. He felt like a fool for having them, for even entertaining the idea that Amity would care for him a fraction of the same way. *What a foolish old bloke you are. Get on now with your feelings before you lose her for good.*

The problem was Amity was closer to Celia's age than his. At twenty-five years old, she was twelve years younger than he. *Why would such a beautiful young woman care for an old man such as myself?*

"What luck to find such a fine tutor," Clark's editor had said upon meeting her and seeing the effect she had on the whole family. But luck had nothing to do with. While Clark wrestled with God after his wife's death—like Jacob at the River Jabbok—he had no doubt God's hand had brought the young woman to them.

The Lord gives, the Lord takes away. The words slipped into his mind unwelcome.

No, not again. Please not again. He pushed that thought from his mind. He didn't think they could bear it if Amity was taken from them too.

For the first two years after his wife's death, it was the *taking away* that had kept Clark up at night, stretching his hand across his bed to find only cold, empty sheets next to him.

Yet in the last year a shift had happened, and Clark had started to look at his life differently. He'd started to consider more what he'd been given—what he and Celia had both been given. Amity's joy, friendship, and care for others was of high value, something he never wanted to take for granted. Yet fear kept him from sharing his true feelings.

He didn't want to ruin their professional relationship by sharing his heart, and he didn't want Amity to laugh in his face. He was also afraid Hitler's antics would cause her to run back home to the States. He'd even been afraid to bring up the conversation of next year's contract, fearful that she wouldn't want to stay. How could he handle the disappointment, the ache, if she decided to leave? And what would Celia do?

Why would such an amazing young woman remain in Europe when she could go someplace safe, like America? How many others wished they had an American passport and could travel there now? Thousands—tens of thousands—would love to escape, especially Jews and Communists, men, women, and children Hitler was sending to camps, or so rumors reported.

With the ache expanding in his chest, Clark turned his back to the window and approached his desk. He sat and opened a newspaper before him yet was unable to focus on the words on the page. He flipped to the next section, but still it did no good. Surely God wouldn't rob him of Amity too.

He glanced at the paper—a *Chicago Tribune* from two days prior—and the third page headlines were like a slap to the face:

HITLER PREPARES TO OPEN HIS DRIVE EAST NEXT SPRING: ASKS RULERS OF IRAN AND AFGHANISTAN TO PARLEY

And the next headline seemed even more unbelievable.

NAZIS BREAK UP HOMES OF JEWS WED TO ARYANS: COUPLES MARRIED MANY YEARS MUST PART

By Sigrid Schultz

BERLIN, Dec. 9

Nazi organizations are bringing pressure to bear on Aryans married to Jews and half-Jews to compel them to obtain divorces. Thousands of Aryan

> men have been ordered to divorce their Jewish wives under threat of losing their jobs. This pressure is being exerted despite the fact that no official decree has been issued ordering the dissolution of such marriages.
>
> Couples who have been married thirty or forty years are being ordered to dissolve their unions. Elderly men who are faced with the prospect of living without their lifetime partners are desperately seeking a way for their elderly wives to leave Germany. They have no financial means of supporting them abroad, and in most cases the women, who never held professional jobs, are too old to support themselves.

Clark pressed his hand against his forehead and shook his head. No doubt the British Home Office was being flooded with immigration inquiries. Yet what country would ever be willing to take on immigrants unable to support themselves? As painful as the truth was, Great Britain had enough of her own homeless and jobless to consider. Unemployment and depression in Britain seemed significantly more important to the people than the fate of foreign Jews. There was a time for compassion and a time to protect one's own...wasn't there?

He glanced to the sepia-colored photo of Celia on his desk, and a new thought hit him. What about the children born to these couples? Even the grandchildren. Surely the German people would let their chancellor go only so far with his so-called racial cleansing.

Clark also wondered what part Amity's brother, Andrew, had in making decisions about the influx of requests. Was the Home Office entertaining the idea of helping such cases?

Clark had read recently that the Refugee Children's Movement—a subsidiary group of the Central British Fund for World

Jewish Relief—was trying to pull together various organizations to organize Operation Kindertransport. And most recently there was a fund set up to aid victims not of flood or famine but of "man's inhumanity to man."

Picking up the framed photograph of his daughter, Clark tried to imagine how a father would feel if he knew his young one was considered impure and unworthy in Hitler's eyes. *A shame, a disgrace, all of it.*

Hopefully someone would do something to help those caught up in the whole mess, although he had no idea what actions could be taken. Germany was a force to be reckoned with, and even Britain and France had chosen to give in to Hitler's demands for the northern, southern, and western areas of Czechoslovakia, which were inhabited primarily by ethnic German speakers, rather than risk another world war. How many lives would be lost if things came to war? Pitiful war veterans were still all too common on the streets of London, not to mention lives lost. Thankfully, matters like this could efficiently be handled by the Home Office by capable people like Amity's brother.

Clark had met Andrew only a few times at social gatherings and on Andrew's rare visits to the manor to see his sister. Andrew seemed kind and trustworthy, with a decent head on his shoulders. He was thankful Andrew had suggested that he hire Amity as a tutor. Although it was a battle at times to convince Mrs. McGovern that Amity's American ways should be tolerated, Clark thought she brought a breath of fresh air to their otherwise stuffy home.

Turning the newsprint page again, Clark tapped the tip of his pen on the crossword puzzle, but even that was incapable of holding his interest. Laying down his pen, he rose from his leather chair and moved to his desk, flipping through a stack of letters and dinner invitations. He frowned. Something was missing. He made a mental note to talk to his head housekeeper about it later.

In the pile among the bills was an invitation to his publisher's house for a cocktail party, and another one for a reading for a local group of mystery lovers. Yet he couldn't attend either because they'd ask the same question—"How's the next novel coming along?"

Dare he tell them that he hadn't finished one page on his next novel that was due in six months? He'd crumpled up every page he'd started, tossing it into the wood burner. At least the large black stove radiated a pleasant warmth.

Surely with all the drama happening in the world he could come up with an idea for a simple spy novel. Then again, perhaps that was the problem. Maybe because there was so much drama, his fictional attempts seemed unimaginative in comparison.

He glanced at the typewriter, with one blank sheet of paper propped up within the rollers, and shook his head. He hadn't written a decent story since Gwen's death. And that was the problem. His publisher was giving him one last chance before they backed out of their contract, taking with them Clark's income.

As much as he'd adored his father, the elder Cartwright had been land rich yet penny poor. It was only because of the success of Clark's books that he was able to keep and maintain both properties. And if he couldn't pull off the next novel? Clark shuddered at the thought, but the country house would have to go. He couldn't imagine Celia's despair if that happened.

Good job, old chap, Clark thought, running his fingers through his short-cropped brown hair. *Worrying about finances, fretting about crushing your daughter's spirit by selling the country house, and a possible war. Three more ways to kill the muse.*

The footsteps of Mrs. McGovern were barely distinguishable

on the wooden hallway outside the door. She paused, no doubt checking for the clacking of the typewriter keys before knocking, but she needn't worry.

Clark turned toward the door and rubbed his brow. "Mrs. McGovern? No need to knock."

The thin wisp of a woman opened the door, a large bunch of yellow chrysanthemums in one hand—a touch of spring in the clutches of winter. Celia would be pleased. With her free hand, the older woman pushed the gray hair back from her forehead.

"Yes, sir?"

"I was certain I noted a telegram delivery today. Do you know where it was placed? It wasn't with my other mail."

"Yes, sir, I placed the telegram on Miss Ami's bureau, seeing's it were for her."

"For Amity?"

"Yes, from her brother in Czechoslovakia, sir. She mentioned it to Celia as they were dressing for the out of doors. She is planning to speak to you at dinner. It seems she's considering taking holiday there."

In Czechoslovakia? Clark cocked an eyebrow. "Well, it appears she'll not have to broach the subject now, will she, considering you have already done that for her."

Mrs. McGovern shifted her weight between her feet, as if unsure to how to answer. "I suppose not, sir, but if I have the liberty, a holiday in such a place doesn't seem wise, does it now? Especially with Hitler's troops claiming part of that country for themselves. I shudder at the thought of the scourging that's already taking place."

Why, of all times, was Andrew in Czechoslovakia, and why would she want to join him there? Surely it wasn't truly for holiday.

After all, who would choose to visit such a place now? Did it have to do with those who were being forced to leave, just like what was happening in Germany?

"Thank you, Mrs. McGovern," he stated to dismiss her, and then he remembered she'd come to see him. "Oh, and did you wish to speak to me?"

"Yes, sir. It seems the flower shop down the street is closing. The owners are immigrating to Canada, sir, although why someone would want to move to the wilds of Canada is beyond me."

"That is interesting, and I have no doubt that as rumors of war grow we'll be seeing more people fleeing."

"I believe so, sir, but I wanted to ask...there is another shop a mile beyond. Do I have permission to use your car and driver every week or so to place an order? It's a nice shop, although their flowers are a bit more pricey."

"Of course." Clark smiled and hoped the head housekeeper didn't see the worry in his eyes. Each month he calculated the cost of the upkeep of the properties, and each month he saw his accounts dwindling. Yet a few pounds more for flowers wouldn't break the bank. Celia did love fresh flowers in their home.

"Do what you must, Mrs. McGovern, but thank you for asking. Also, do you plan on purchasing poinsettias this year? Miss Ami mentioned they were a favorite that reminded her of her mother."

"Yes, sir, in next week's order. Oh, I do hope Miss Ami will still be here for Christmas."

Clark clucked his tongue. "No need to worry. Amity has a good head on her shoulders. Why don't you double that poinsettia order as a surprise?"

Mrs. McGovern's eyes widened. "I will, sir, with delight." Then she hurried out of the room.

Clark turned his attention back to the window and saw that Amity and Celia had moved from the garden to the badminton area. He smiled, remembering the summer days the three of them had spent playing the game.

Although Celia was fifteen, and Amity ten years her senior, today they laughed and talked like schoolgirl friends, their words volleying back and forth like the feathered shuttlecock—a streak of white in the fading golden light.

"Czechoslovakia," he said under his breath, already considering what arguments he would use to urge Amity not to travel there. No woman had any business traveling to Czechoslovakia, especially with Hitler's troops rattling its gates.

Clark picked up his pen again and tapped it on his lips. The softest smile played there as he imagined Amity squaring her shoulders and lifting her chin in defiance, voicing her reasons for why she wished to travel.

Then another thought came to mind—maybe a change of scenery would conjure new book ideas. Surely an American woman shouldn't travel Europe alone, especially with Hitler on the rampage. But then again, he couldn't leave Celia, and he couldn't take her with him. His mind became quite muddled with all the unanswered questions.

— THREE —

Olomouc, Czechoslovakia
Monday, December 12, 1938

Konrád Hanak strode over the cobblestone streets of Olomouc, heading to the main square, recently renamed Adolf-Hitler-Platz. Just ten days ago he'd stood not twenty yards from Adolf Hitler in this very square. With fist held high, Konrád's voice had raised in unison with fellow countrymen as they proclaimed, "Heil Hitler! Heil Hitler! Heil Hitler!" The fervor of the crowd had been electrifying. In all his days he'd never forget that moment when he looked into his savior's face. The cries of unity and devotion continued until Konrád was certain he'd lose his voice. Finally, motioning to the crowd to quiet, Hitler had approached the microphone.

As he spoke, the Führer's eyebrows tipped down and his mouth straightened into a thin line as he cried out with conviction about his continued hope for a united German people. The Führer had met Konrád's gaze, and his voice had risen in fervor as he spoke of racial cleansing.

Can Hitler sense the blood on my hands? he'd wondered.

Konrád's heartbeat quickened with a knowing that this was just the beginning of his fight. He would be a willing participant to any of the Führer's plans. The German people had suffered long enough. Now it was their turn to show the world their strength and power.

Today, though, the fervor of the previous week had been replaced with the raw tension that came with the new occupational forces. Uniformed German soldiers milled around the Holy Trinity Column and up and down the streets. Their eyes swept the roads and alleyways for any sign of resistance.

In contrast, Czech students, professionals, lay workers, and housewives hurried along, carrying their bundles pressed tight to their chests. One middle-aged woman, with a grocery sack in hand, urged her young son to quicken his steps so they could make it home before curfew fell.

Not too many years before, the opposite had been true. At only five years old, and raised solely around German-speaking people, he'd not understood then that the country's boundaries had been redefined. Overnight the part of the world he'd lived in had been placed under Czech control.

Konrád remembered the first time he'd been shooed home by a Czech police officer after the collapse of the Austro-Hungarian empire. He hadn't understood the new language, and after not responding to the Czech officer's strict demands, Konrád had been rewarded with a whack over his head with a stick. Tears had streamed down his eyes as he ran home, mixing with blood from the gash on his forehead. Yet instead of running into his mother's arms and seeking comfort, he'd come upon his parents packing up their apartment. Their own tears and heartache kept them from providing comfort to their son. That night he'd fallen asleep on a pallet on the floor, with all his things in crates. All he knew as he drifted off to a fitful sleep was that a dark road lay ahead of him, filled with the unknown.

With the memory, a familiar ache tightened Konrád's gut, but he pushed those feelings of helplessness down. He was no longer a defenseless five-year-old boy. He—not they—now held control. Glancing around, Konrád appeased himself by noting large red banners bearing swastikas hanging from windows and balconies. The fabrics writhed and turned as if having lives of their own as they fluttered in the icy breeze.

Such disgrace will never be upon our people again, he told himself, which calmed his spirit.

They will be repaid for their mistreatment of my people. A half smile curled up his lips. The Greater German Reich was now a reality.

He tightened the scarf around his neck and gave a slight shudder at the cold breeze that carried with it the aroma of coffee from a nearby café. Konrád still had time before he was due to meet friends at the pub. He moved to the nearest bench and sat, his frosty breath clinging to the air around him. Despite the cold that seeped through his coat, he wanted to enjoy his last day in this city, to revel in the transformation before he moved on.

Just two years prior, Konrád had joined the *Kameradschaftsbund,* an organization of Nazi-supporting Germans who were preparing themselves for leadership roles in a possible future with an independent Sudetenland. Konrád had volunteered his time to stand guard over their meetings. His forward thinking had done him well. Many of these men were now in control, chosen by the Nazis for their dual language skills and their understanding of the Czech people. And in a matter of days, Konrád would be starting a new position. Even though nowhere on paper would he be listed as part of the Gestapo, he would still be on their employ. More than that, he'd be reporting in Prague, and he'd do so knowing his family had once again reclaimed what they'd lost.

He stood and strode toward the pub. He would be celebrating with his friends in the *Kameradschaftsbund* today. It was the last day they would lift their glasses together before most of them were transferred to various positions in Germany, around the Sudetenland, and beyond.

With the joining of the Sudetenland, the new nation's birth certificate had been signed. Austria and the German-speaking areas of Czechoslovakia were united with the motherland. Overnight Konrád had become as a native son. Joy flooded his soul as he realized he was just as much a part of the German nation as those in Berlin, Munich, Hamburg, and Vienna. The German youth to come after him would never again have to face such disgrace—living in a world of prejudice, being ruled by a weaker people, living apart from one's true home.

Twenty years ago, after the end of the Great War in 1918, the Austro-Hungarian Empire had been divided, and many ethnic Germans found themselves living on Czech soil. Overnight, Germans in positions of authority were out of jobs, including his father. Instead, Czech soldiers, policemen, and bureaucrats rushed in to take their place. Like everyone else, Konrád had to learn a new language and follow new rules.

The new foreign policies were bad enough, but then it was declared that expanding the Czechoslovakian government would overcome social injustice through the redistribution of wealth. Konrád's grandparents were one of many families who had portions of their land turned over to Czech peasants. And not long after that, the country fell into a state of depression. There were no jobs, not enough food, no hope.

Previously dependent on foreign trade with Germany, thousands of men lost their jobs and homes. Konrád knew the pain. His family had been one of the first to lose their home...to a

Jewish family who could pay the mortgage that his family could no longer afford. Every day as Konrád walked to and from school, he witnessed the Jewish boy playing in *his* yard, running through *his* front door. Konrád seethed over knowing the boy was sitting in *his* kitchen, sleeping in *his* room.

Konrád's fingers curled around the pistol handle at his hip as new memories surged up to replace the old. It brought extreme satisfaction knowing that Jew-boy—grown into a man—would never run, never laugh, never breath again. Konrád had seen to that.

On the evening of the *Kristallnacht*, the Night of Broken Glass, only a month prior, Konrád had done his part to make sure there were three fewer Jews in the Sudetenland. The terror on their faces as they dug their own graves was still fresh in his mind, as were Abram's pleas.

"I am a husband, a father now. Please have mercy on me. We—my family—will give the apartment back to you. We will leave the area. Just give us the chance, Konrád."

Hearing his name on the Jew's lips had caused anger to surge through his veins, and even though the November night was cold, Konrád had felt hot all over.

Even now, on the walk to the pub, the memory filled him with heat inside. An older woman strolled by with a shawl heavy on her shoulders. Noting Konrád's uniform, she lifted her fist in a "Heil Hitler." The next instant her worried, wrinkled face broke into a smile. Konrád lifted his arm straight out, returning the gesture. Yet even as he saw the old German woman before him, another face filled his mind, that of Abram's mother. Instead of crying, instead of pleading, she'd stood at her husband's side with her arm wrapped around his shoulders, as if accepting her fate. There was even pity in her gaze as she looked upon Konrád, who had drawn his pistol. The pity only fueled his anger.

"I will pray for your mother, Konrád," Rebekah Šimonová had stated simply. "She always was kind to me."

The Jewess's words had pushed him over the edge, and she'd received the first bullet. Her husband's anguished sobs had erupted in the forest and filled the night, so his death came next. In the course of a minute's time, it was just Konrád and Abram standing face-to-face. There was no other sound, except for the echoing of the gunfire in their ears and the heavy breathing of them both. Neither of them moved as the blood of Abram's parents spilled onto the ground.

"Move into the apartment and take our things," Abram repeated again. "We have never meant you any harm. Our mothers, wouldn't you consider them as friends? If only—?"

The sound of an approaching automobile had drowned out Abram's words. He lifted his voice, repeating his plea. "Take all that we have! Just let me escape with my wife, my children—"

The auto was nearing, driving down the road to the edge of the woods. Konrád had walked the family to this location. He had come to this secluded place for a reason, yet he was certain if the approaching driver looked into the woods he would be seen. And then what? He knew Hitler's opinion of the Jews, yet this he had done of his own accord. Konrád would not sacrifice his future. He could not be seen. But he also had to erase the scourge from his past. With a shaking hand, Konrád had lifted his pistol, pointing it directly at Abram's heart.

Even in the dim light Abram must have realized his own end had come, yet he tried yet again. "What about the treasure? Surely you would want the treasure," Abram asked, jutting out his chin. "I have hidden most of our valuable things and—"

The automobile was nearly upon them. Konrád had only a split second to escape into the woods. The sound of the gunfire surprised even himself. A look of horror filled Abram's face as he crumpled to the ground.

It was only as his legs were propelling him into the woods that Konrád realized what Abram had been saying. Hidden treasure? It made sense. Greedy Jews and opportunist Czechs had robbed his own German countrymen. Abram's family had stripped his family of their home, and that was just the start. Losing their home, their things, had caused both parents to sink into depression. All through his growing-up years, his parents' unemployment, mixed with their increased drinking, had taken its toll. His parents became dark shadows of the vibrant people they'd been before.

Still, why had he pulled that trigger? *How foolish.*

The next day the three bodies were found in the woods without a note about their discovery in the local paper. The new German authority had much more to worry about than three dead Jews, or about Abram's wife and children, who had also disappeared that night.

Once the paperwork was turned in to local authorities, Konrád's family had taken over the Jew-family's home, making it theirs once again. There had been no one to claim the family's fine things, and all their personal items that no one wanted to deal with ended up in the rubbish.

Still, even though his parents had been returned to their rightful place, Konrád couldn't shake the Jew's words out of his mind. He had no doubt the Jewess and her children had escaped to Prague—or the surrounding villages—with hundreds of thousands of other Jewish and Communist refugees.

The lights from the pub glowed just down the street, and new hope buoyed in Konrád's heart. As part of the Gestapo, perhaps he could use government information to find her. And once he had her, he'd be able to seek the treasure that had slipped through his grasp.

All will be made right again. The apartment redeemed what was lost, and the treasure will make up for what was taken.

He strode the final steps to the pub, picturing himself as a knight of old, preparing to conquer for one's own glory and that of the king.

Stepping through the door, the aroma of beer and sausages filled his nostrils, and the voices of his friends consumed the air as they sang in unison to "*Die Fahne Hoch*," the anthem of the Nazi party.

Clear the streets for the brown battalions,
Clear the streets for the storm division!
Millions are looking upon the swastika full of hope,
The day of freedom and of bread dawns!
Millions are looking upon the swastika full of hope,
The day of freedom and of bread dawns!

Konrád's voice rose with the others, joining with them as one as he entered with clenched fists and a new resolve in his heart.

— FOUR —

London, England
Monday, December 12, 1938

Amity turned over the telegram in her hand, almost afraid to open it again and reread her brother's request. Andrew had written a letter every month. He'd stopped by to visit her when he was in London and not traveling throughout Europe. Yet as much as she loved her brother, Amity always felt inferior in his presence. While she'd had no desire to attend college, Andrew had excelled at university in political studies, and at the young age of twenty-three had gotten a job at London's Home Office.

After she'd come to London to live with her brother, she'd lived aimlessly for a time, questioning what she should do with her life. And that's when Andrew had told her about an open position. Not long after, Amity found herself as a tutor for a young woman. Amity liked her job, but she'd always imagined doing more with her life.

Back in Chicago she'd spent her free time volunteering at the Children's Home and Aid Society, helping orphaned children. As much as she enjoyed Celia, Amity missed the children. She'd even written Andrew just last month, asking him if he thought she should return to Chicago. Yet she hadn't mailed it. Why not?

As much as Amity felt she'd be more useful in Chicago, she hated the thought of leaving Celia...and her father, Clark. Even though she worked to keep her relationship with her employer strictly professional, Amity looked forward to every moment she was with him, even ordinary ones.

He thinks of me as an employee and a friend, nothing more, Amity often told herself as she drifted to sleep at night. Yet was that the complete truth? There seemed to be a special connection whenever she met Clark's gaze.

She took the telegram from the envelope, read it again, and then turned it over in her hands. What had Andrew meant by Jewish welfare work? If only he'd telephoned instead of sending this cryptic note.

Amity dressed for dinner in a green velvet skirt and jacket, which seemed fitting for the Christmas season. No one she knew had dressed for dinner in Chicago, but the custom had grown on her. What a wonderful excuse to put on nice clothes, fix one's hair, and prepare for a fine conversation.

Thirty minutes later she was sitting at the long dining room table across from Celia and to Clark's right side. As she turned to look at Celia, Amity was surprised to see the smile on her face. Amity had told Celia about Andrew's telegram, and after Celia urged her not to go because of the danger, she had decided to refuse Andrew's invitation. But something in Celia's gaze told her that Celia had changed her mind.

After the housemaid, Bonnie, served their salad and bread, Amity shared Andrew's telegram with Clark. He was focused on her face, intent on every word, but Amity couldn't quite read the emotions behind his narrow-gazed expression. Was it worry or fear he was feeling? Or was it bothersome to him that she'd be gone? Maybe a bit of both.

But it was Celia who spoke of first. "Czechoslovakia…It does seem like quite the adventure, doesn't it?" She turned to her father. "Just like one of your novels, Daddy. I can just imagine the city being full of spies. I believe Hitler is going to take over all of Czechoslovakia soon. He no doubt already has spies sitting in cafés and strolling over the Charles Bridge as we speak, tagging along behind those who've escaped to Prague for safety. Didn't you say, Amity, that the city is filled with refugees from Germany, Austria, and the Sudetenland?"

"Yes, from what I've read in the paper, trainloads of families left the new German protectorate and fled to the center of the country, where they hope to find safety."

"Until the Germans set new sights on all of Czechoslovakia, that is. What will happen to them now?" Celia commented. It was a question no one could answer.

Clark took a drink from his glass. "And what have you heard from Andrew about the situation?"

Amity shrugged. "His last letter was brief, but it did mention an upcoming journey to Prague. I had no idea that he'd want me to join him. It all really doesn't make any sense."

"Maybe he needs someone to cheer up and inspire the Jewish refugees, especially the women. I was reading just today that Hitler is forcing Aryan men to divorce their wives or lose their jobs—"

"Simply lose their jobs?" Celia huffed. "It may be that in the beginning, but I doubt that's where it will end. I also imagine these men and women are worrying about their lives. Who wouldn't be?"

Clark looked from Celia to Amity and then back again. "I am afraid you are most likely right, and I am impressed. I never thought I would have such a lively political conversation with my little girl."

Celia adjusted her collar on her suit dress. "I am far past being a little girl, Daddy, and you can thank Amity for that. She told me just yesterday that every educated lady should understand the happenings of the world."

Amity cleared her throat and cast a gaze at her young charge. "And what is the rest of that statement?"

Celia offered a sly smile. "Amity says that every educated lady should understand the happenings of the world...and her place in it."

Celia cleared her throat again and tilted up her head. "And as for our place, we must be humble, thinking not more of ourselves than others. We must be kind, always willing to offer a helping hand. We must be cunning, understanding who is worthy of our trust. We also must be truth-bearers, knowing that the greatest truth we can fill our mind and heart with is the Word of God."

The room was silent for a moment. Even Bonnie held the silver tray in her hands instead of setting it down on the buffet, as if not wanting to disturb the moment.

Amity felt Clark's eyes on her, and she took a sip from her cup and then turned to him. She anticipated tenderness in his gaze, and she was not disappointed.

"Did you pen that yourself, Amity? It's quite brilliant."

"If you put it that way, it sounds like I'm a great writer or something." She laughed. "Don't worry, Clark, I have no intention of vying for your job. It's just something I thought about the other morning when I was reading my Bible. The global news can be so pressing. I felt it was important to remind Celia that no matter what storms rage—whether the storms of the heavens or the thunder of men's battles here on the earth—we women have an important place. The important part is not always protecting ourselves and our own interests, but also looking out for the welfare of others."

He reached out his right hand and placed it on her left one, which was resting on the table. "You're an insightful woman, wise beyond your years." He squeezed her hand and released it, but even after letting go she still felt the warmth from his hand.

"I hope that is a compliment," she teased, trying to pretend his touch hadn't completely upended her inside. "Our neighbor, Mrs. Whitmore, is wise too, but I'd rather not find myself a cane."

"It is a compliment, I assure you. So many young people these days have minds filled with folly." He frowned slightly and moved his salad around on his plate with his fork. "And you say God was speaking these things to your heart a few mornings ago?"

"Yes." Amity's voice held a quiver. The tender tone warmed her chest. Yes, there was another sensation too. As they spoke, a deep peace settled over her. It should have been an unfamiliar peace due to the state of the world, but this peace came upon her often when she sat down with her Bible and considered God and all His goodness. It was almost as if He was warming her soul with a touch of His heavenly presence. Yet she'd never felt the holy touch in the middle of an ordinary conversation like this. Goosebumps rose on her arms.

"Yes, over the last month or so as I've sat down with my Bible I've had this impression that God was asking something of me. It's as if there are people out there who need to be cared for." She sighed and broke off a piece of her bread, but the feeling of fullness within her made it hard to think of eating. "At first I thought it was simply the worries of the newspapers that were burdening my soul, but as I've read God's Word I've been more drawn to stories of compassion." She smiled and looked to Celia. "I'm not sure

I'm making any sense, but as I've told Celia, we women mustn't just focus on the world but also on our place in it. We can each help someone in some small way, can't we?"

No one spoke as they finished their salads. Amity hoped Clark didn't notice she could hardly swallow a bite. Next they were served Lancashire hotpot, one of Clark's favorites, but no one seemed much interested in dinner. They talked about other things—about the fresh snow and the upcoming Christmas programs around the city. And then when their food had turned quite cold, Clark put down his fork and pushed back his plate.

"This is the last thing I expected myself to say tonight," Clark said with a heavy sigh. "You see, Mrs. McGovern—who always knows every coming and going of the house—let it spill earlier that you were considering a Czechoslovakian holiday. Between that hour and now I've considered at least a dozen persuasive speeches that would talk you into forgetting that idea, but now I know to give even one of them would be to make my interests of greater concern than God's."

"What do you mean?"

"I'm not sure what your brother has in store for you with this Jewish welfare work, but Andrew has a good head on his shoulders. I am certain he wouldn't ask his sister to come into a situation that is too dangerous. More than that, it seems God has been preparing your heart for a while."

A heavy burden lifted from Amity's shoulders at those words—one she hadn't known she'd been carrying. "Then it is all right if I head off on a holiday? Perhaps two weeks?"

The smile on Clark's face faded slightly, and tenderness flashed in his blue-eyed gaze. "On one condition—that before you dash off you sign a contract for another year's work with my daughter, if not two years. Yes, we could handle two."

Amity clasped her hands together. There was no way to hide her delight. "I'd be honored, absolutely honored." And at that moment there were no worries of what the next two years might bring. There was no thought of war. Even thoughts of Czechoslovakia were in the back of her mind. For now, Amity's mind was settled on the fact that for the next two years she'd have these beautiful people in her life. And for this moment, that was enough.

— FIVE —

Jívová, Czechoslovakia
Saturday, December 17, 1938

Pavla Šimonová peered through the dingy window of the dilapidated shed and watched the older woman—their family's former maid—hang her laundry. Mrs. Smidova had come up with the system to let Pavla know when it was safe to leave the shed and enter the Smidova family home. When she hung her laundry, Pavla was to watch. If the yellow handkerchief was the last thing to be hung, it was safe to go inside. It meant her husband had gone to the hospital for the day for work. It also meant their closest neighbors were at the market shopping.

With quick movements Mrs. Smidova hung a dark-blue dress, a red apron, and finally the yellow handkerchief before she hurried inside. Even though the sun was out, the air was icy cold, and the idea of finding warmth caused Pavla's heart to leap. She turned from the window and kneeled to the pallet set up on the floor. Both children slept, their cheeks bright from the cold air.

She placed a hand on each of their shoulders, shook them slightly, and then pushed their hair back from their faces. "Hurry, children, it's market day. We only have an hour."

Ondřej rose and rubbed his eyes. "*Mami?*"

"Come. We get to go inside. We get to wash up."

"No. It's too cold." He snuggled down and tucked the thin blanket up around him again.

Klára's light-brown eyes fluttered open. "Will there be food, *Maminka*?"

"Oh, I do have breakfast for us. Apples in a barrel, *ja*?" She pointed to the barrel behind them, the one they had been eating from for a few weeks.

"I'm tired of apples," Klára moaned. "Breakfast, lunch, and dinner."

"We must not speak in such a way. There are so many others..." Pavla let her voice trail off. She refused to speak of them—her family, her friends. What had become of them? She feared the worst. What type of persecution would they face? Would they, too, be killed? Pavla worried they all would be eventually if Hitler's storm troopers had their way.

A hollow ache filled her heart, her gut, and her chest at the knowledge that her husband and in-laws had been killed. Why them? It made no sense, yet Mrs. Smidova had sworn it was true. Their bodies had been found by children playing in the forest a week after they'd gone missing. Yet as soon as she saw Abram and her in-laws being led away by that German soldier, she'd made the split-second decision to escape with her children. It had been her son, Ondřej, only eight years old, who had suggested they come to Mrs. Smidova's house and reminded her of the way.

Now, even though she tried to wake him, Ondřej still refused to budge. He flung his arm over his face, as if not wanting to be disturbed. Maybe his dreams had a bit of happiness in them in contrast to the loss and pain around him. Pavla hoped they did.

All she had to offer her son was one minute more of sleep before she fully awakened him to the living hell their lives had become.

With a wide yawn and slowly blinking eyes, Klára sat up and crossed her arms over her chest. "I do not wish to be unthankful, *Mutti*. So many others don't have what we have, but I do not want to eat apples today. And I want my own room. My own bed."

"Oh, but we can't go back, now can we? We are on a great adventure. You have always liked camping, *ano*?" She forced a smile. "Let us try to wake Ondřej, and we will see what's waiting for us inside the house."

Klára's eyes grew large and round, and they filled with tears. "What if there is nothing?" she moaned.

Pavla pointed a finger in the air. "Oh yes, but what if there is something? Let's hope for that."

A slow moan escaped Ondřej's lips, and he winced as he sat up. Then he rubbed his neck. None of them had gotten used to sleeping on old blankets spread on the ground. They missed their beds, their mattresses, their feather pillows and quilts. What luxury they'd had before, and she hadn't even realized it.

"I am tired of camping too," Ondřej pouted. "I want to go home. I want my birthday cake," he mumbled.

Pavla looked at her son in shock. From the moment her husband was taken away and she had escaped with her children, eight-year-old Ondřej had been the strong one. He had not complained. He'd directed the way to the Smidova house from the few times he'd visited with his grandmother. Even during their long days hidden in the shed, he'd told stories to his sister and played with her, entertaining her. He became their one bright light in the dark world. But was he crumbling too?

Pavla grimaced at her sour attitude, but even more than that, sadness filled her that she'd missed the opportunity to bake him a birthday cake, something he'd looked forward to throughout the year. She had put off making his cake for his birthday on the seventh of November because she'd come down with a fever and had been in bed for two days. She'd planned on baking it the next day, but that never happened. The neighbors had come that night, telling them the Germans were breaking the windows of the Jewish businesses in town and looting them, even burning them to the ground.

Later that evening a German solider had come to the door, demanding Abram and his parents come with him. If only she'd known when her husband left that night that it was the last glimpse she'd have of him.

Even though nothing had prepared her for what they'd face on the run, Pavla was thankful she'd left when she did. During their last brief exchange, Mrs. Smidova had told her how everything had changed in Olomouc. The name of the main city square had been changed to Adolf-Hitler-Platz. And at the *Marktplatz*, in front of the *Marienpestsäule*—the plague tower—German soldiers diligently watched everyone who was coming and going.

Pavla had grown up in the small village of Vysoké Mýto, but when she met Abram she had gladly moved to the larger city. Olomouc had many ethnic Germans, but that hadn't bothered Abram. He was one of the friendliest people she knew, and he didn't know a stranger. It was hard to believe he was gone. Why would anyone want to single him and his parents out and kill them?

These were the things that kept her up at night and plagued her now. Abram had always cared for those in his community, and he had always cared for her. Pavla looked down at her wedding ring with a cluster of rubies. That ring was just one evidence of his love.

He had bought her a few other nice pieces of jewelry, all of them left behind. The only thing Pavla wished she had grabbed was the first wedding ring he'd given her. They hadn't had much money at first, and Abram had slipped a simple gold band on her hand the day they had married. On their first anniversary he'd given her the ruby ring, yet the first one always occupied a special place in her heart. She'd kept it in her jewelry box on top of her dresser. Oh, how she wished she would have thought of grabbing that ring. Actually, she wished she'd grabbed all of her jewelry. In desperate times, those jewels could have been used to buy food, shelter, safety. But it was too late now, wasn't it? Those things had no doubt already been taken by others after her disappearance. She rubbed her eyes, refusing to cry. Then she slipped her ring around so the rubies were on the inside and only a thin band showed outwardly.

Pulling herself from her sad thoughts, Pavla clapped her hands together. "We must hurry now, children. Let's go inside. We don't have much time." She smiled again at Ondřej and Klára. "I imagine it's warm. My guess is that there may be warm water for a bath."

With news of a possible bath, both children jumped to their feet.

Once outside, the children walked cautiously by her side. They each grasped one of her hands as they hurried across the garden to the main house. Reaching the back door, she released Ondřej's hand and reached for the knob. It was indeed unlocked.

They stepped into the kitchen, and the aroma of fresh bread caused Pavla's senses to come alive. A small gasp escaped Klára's lips, and the small girl's fingers squeezed around her mother's hand.

Pavla was about to tell her daughter, "*Ne*, not for us," but then her eyes moved to the kitchen table. Three places were set with small, white plates. Next to them sat three teacups. A teapot, still steaming, was on the table. And a small cup of milk, real milk, was next to it. On each plate was a slice of bread and a thin piece of cheese. Pavla's free hand covered her mouth. Tears sprang to her eyes, and she never thought she'd find such joy in simple bread and cheese.

Next to the stove, a tin tub had been filled up. Steam rose from the top of the water, and next to the tub was a new set of clothes for Ondřej and another set for Klára. Pavla could tell the clothes weren't new, but that didn't matter. Her children would finally be able to change out of the clothes that they'd thrown on in haste after leaving their home more than a month ago.

She hadn't known what they were to do or where they were to go until just a few nights ago, when Mrs. Smidova had snuck over to the shed and said she had important news.

"There are rumors," Mrs. Smidova had whispered, her breath floating before her in the cold night air. "I heard from my sister in Velká Ohrada. There is a rumor that Great Britain is prepared to allow several thousand Jewish children to enter the country."

"How can we know if this is true?"

"I wrote back and asked the same thing. Surely if it were true I would have heard something. The papers have not published such news, and if they are on foreign broadcasts, well, who can understand all they are saying. I wish I had better English."

"Do I go to the British Consulate?"

"No, my sister did that, trying to find information for a friend. They told her they did not know the correct procedures. They claim a private agency is in charge."

"Not the British Government?" Pavla had a hard time understanding that since the government controlled so much of their lives.

Now, as she sat beside the tub, which was supplied with a piece of soap on a stool and some fresh towels, Pavla wasn't sure whether to feed her children first or help them into the bath. But they made the decision for her. Klára hurried to the bread and tea while Ondřej moved to the tub.

"I remember when we'd visit Uncle Rudi up in the cabin. He had a tub like this. Uncle Rudi even had a small boat that *Táta* had given him, and I used to play with it. Maybe next time..." Ondřej's voice trailed off as he realized what he was saying. His face fell.

"*Táta?*" Klára stopped eating at the mention of her father. "I want *Táta*." Her lower lip quivered.

Ondřej's eyes grew wide, and he paused the unbuttoning of his shirt. With wide, sad eyes he looked to his mother. "I'm sorry, *Mutti*."

She placed a hand on his shoulder and resumed the unbuttoning for him. "You never should be sorry for mentioning your father. He will always be part of us, and we will see him again, though not on this earth."

Ondřej nodded. Then he removed his clothes and stepped into the bath. He turned his back to her as he did, and Pavla knew he did so to hide his tears.

Oh, my poor, sweet boy. He's trying to be so strong, so brave. Abram would be proud of their son. There was no doubt about that.

After she helped Ondřej wash his back and hair, Pavla moved to the table to eat the food that had been prepared for her. As she settled into the wooden chair, Klára pointed to an envelope on the table. Sure enough, it had her name on it. A gasp escaped from her lips as Pavla opened it. The envelope was filled with Czech *koruna*. Where had Mrs. Smidova come up with so much money? And why was she giving it to her?

With shaking fingers, Pavla pulled the letter from the envelope and began to read.

Dear Pavla,

Months ago Abram approached me, asking for my help. As you know, I worked for his family for over twenty years until it became too difficult to make the commute from the village. I have known Abram since he was Ondřej's age. He was like a son to me. It was with such great joy that he came to see me, and I could see in his face all the worries for his family. With Hitler's declaration that he would unite all areas where ethnic Germans lived, Abram knew that the Sudetenland was in danger of Nazi occupation. No one guessed that France and England would back down so easily, but that is another story for another time.

During our visit, I promised Abram that if you ever had to flee your apartment in Olomouc that I would give you shelter here. I told him that I'd gladly open my home and make a place in our spare room, but he was the one who made me promise not to tell anyone and instead to offer you the back shed. I realize his wisdom now that I've seen so many friends embracing Hitler's views and ways. If I had done things my way it would have put all of you in danger. I am glad you have remained hidden.

Tonight, just after midnight, a man with an oxcart will come around to pick you up. I have made arrangements for you to be taken to Brno and then to a village outside of Prague that is accepting refugees. You may find some of your friends from Olomouc there. I hear there are agencies working with the refugees, helping them find safe passage out of this country and providing them a means to start a new life. I hope these rumors are true. I also must apologize, but I have used some of the money provided by Abram to purchase your transport and stays long the way.

Oh, and you may wonder why I hadn't mentioned the money earlier. It took me a good week after you arrived to remember that Abram had given me an envelope, urging me to hide it in a safe place. I'd nearly forgotten where it was hidden away, but the good Lord must have reminded me just when the time was right. I was pleased to make this discovery of your husband's provision, just as much as I'm sure you are. He always was a bright lad, so insightful about the ways of the world. It made sense that he thought ahead about such matters. It was always that way with him, even as a child, God rest his soul.

Remember the oxcart. Friends will care for you from there, and please burn this letter after you read it. My husband knows not how I'm helping you, and I don't want to bring any challenges to my family. I'm sure you understand.

Love,

Hedvika

Pavla read the letter again to make sure she remembered everything. She was halfway through reading when she realized that Ondřej was wrapped in a towel and reading over her shoulder. At first she pulled the letter away from his eyes but then changed her mind. If anything happened to her, he would need to know about the money and the people who would be helping. A shiver traveled down her spine. It pained her to consider her young son having to care for his younger sister without her help, but in the world these days, that was a possibility.

She held up the letter so Ondřej could finish reading it. Then she patted the envelope, and he smiled again, relief on his face. He offered a slight nod and she rose, took the letter and crumbled it, and then put it into the wood burner. They couldn't bring any harm to Mrs. Smidova after all she'd done for them.

After Klára's bath, Pavla took hers and then noticed a simple dress hanging in the hall. Without a doubt she knew it was intended for her. The style was not current, but the dress was clean. Pavla slipped it on. It must have been Mrs. Smidova's when she was younger, and Pavla was thankful for it.

Taking note of the time, she quickly washed their dirty clothes in the tub with plans to hang them to dry inside the shed. Then she quickly dumped the tub outside in the bare shrubs next to the house and returned it to the kitchen. Next, she cleaned up the rest of the mess, hoping there would be no sign of their presence.

Before she left, Pavla wished she could write a note and thank Mrs. Smidova, but in the end she knew it could do more harm than good.

Instead, she took her children's hands and slipped back the way they had come. They would be cold again through the night, of that she had no doubt. But at least inside they carried a bit of warmth. Abram had provided for them and made sure they would receive help. Just knowing that warmed her soul. The only question was what would happen when she got to the camp with the other refugees. What would they face then? Was there anyone to offer help?

Once back inside the shed, Pavla folded the envelope and placed it in her dress pocket, keeping it close. At least she had something to cling to, and then she remembered how Abram had turned to God during every difficult time. Thinking of him made her wish to do the same.

As the children played quietly in the sunlight that streamed into the shed, Pavla considered a portion of Scripture she remembered learning as a child. "Cast thy burden upon the LORD, and he shall sustain thee." If ever there was a time she needed the protection of *Ha-Elohim*, it was now. And for the first time since she'd escaped with her children, she released her grip slightly and dared to cast her cares upon the Lord, if only for a moment.

— SIX —

Prague, Czechoslovakia
Saturday, December 17, 1938

A cold breeze rose off the Vltava River and danced around the statues of the saints lining the Charles Bridge. Only a sliver of the sun's rays could be seen over the red tiled roofs spread to the west, and Amity Mitchell hoped her brother would arrive soon. She didn't like the thought of being a stranger in a land in which she didn't know one word of their native tongue, especially with darkness descending. There had been a note at the hotel that Andrew had some business to attend to, but he encouraged her to walk to the bridge and enjoy the view of the medieval town, with the view of Prague Castle, as it faded into the night.

Amity glanced across the stone Gothic bridge again and then let out a low sigh, wrapping her arms around her. A tower had been erected on each end of the bridge, and dozens of statues stood like sentries along the stone sidewalls. Couples, students, and workers getting off for the day crossed the bridge in clusters. No one seemed to notice her.

In London, she had thought visiting the bridge at sunset

would be fun and adventurous. After all, Andrew had sent a postcard of the ancient landmark graced with the beautiful Catholic saints. Yet standing here alone and sensing the tension that filled the city was neither fun nor adventurous. She just hoped that her nearness to these silent saints provided some type of protection.

Amity tightened her scarf around her neck and approached the closest statue, *Saint John of Nepomuk*. She noticed the plaque on this one shone, reflecting the fading light. And as she watched, a man and woman strolled by. Each person mindlessly touched the worn spot as they passed, as if doing so would bring good luck.

Though raised in church, with a strong Christian faith, Amity didn't recognize the name on the statue, nor did she know the story behind his sainthood. Yet surely he had done something magnificent to achieve such honor. Something worthy of recognition. But to her, the statue remained merely another stone piece of artwork, bringing a moment's distraction to a weary and anxious traveler.

Beyond the dark, silent statues, Old Town sparkled with what seemed like thousands of tiny lights. With Christmas around the corner, greenery and colorful decorations caused the stones of the city to glow. Yet the light was cold, haunting.

From the moment the airplane touched down, the cold was hard to miss. It was more than the chill of the air, of course. Much more. All of Czechoslovakia seemed to be depressed, restless. Even in the midst of the beauty, Amity sensed fear. Almost a foreboding of tragedy, as if the ancient streets and buildings stirred with a memory of what war looked like, felt like, on these very streets.

Footfalls sounded behind her. Amity cocked her head to listen closer. A smile filled her face as she recognized them as belonging to her older brother, Andrew. The footsteps were slow, sure, and unassuming. Everything Amity was not.

With a squeal of delight she turned around and flung her arms open wide, laughing at her brother's surprise.

"How do you do that? Even before you could walk, I've found it impossible to surprise you."

"Obviously, Andrew, you're mistaken. I'm an Illinois girl standing on an ancient bridge in Czechoslovakia, with little idea of why I have come."

She placed a fist on her hip. "So, what's the urgency? Have you met a girl and need a best sister to stand by your side as you wed?" She ignored for now the fact that he'd mentioned Jewish refugees. For the moment Amity wanted to pretend they were just a brother and sister meeting on holiday.

"I wish that were the case. It's nothing like that. No good news, I'm afraid. And we have plenty of time to discuss the reason you've come once we return to the hotel." He linked his arm through hers and swept his other hand toward the city before them. "First, what do you think?"

Amity stroked her brother's cheek where a trim beard now grew. "Maybe not a marriage, but I *do* believe you have a certain someone special in your life. I've never seen you so…so put together."

"No, I do not." He seemed uncomfortable with her topic of choice. "Maybe I've just learned to dress myself. Now, seriously…" Andrew's hand lifted toward a large white castle sitting on a distant hill. "Isn't it magical?"

"Reminds me of all those stories you used to read to me. All the tales of knights and kings and queens. Princesses being saved from horrible dragons. England has beautiful castles, but this place—it seems to breathe history." Another cold wind blew, and Amity pulled her coat collar tighter under her chin.

"Yes, and it seems we're part of history in the making, even now."

"You mean with the Germans?"

"Yes...but, sister, you cannot speak so feely. You never know who could be listening."

Amity glanced around her, but only silent statues stood within hearing distance. Still, she knew from the look on Andrew's face not to argue.

"Come, let's go back to our hotel." He motioned her to follow. "We can talk there."

Amity tucked her hand into the crook of his arm again and matched his pace. The night was silent as they strolled along.

"Prague is still one of the most beautiful capitals of Europe. I've come here often for work, and nothing has changed. The museum, the opera, the restaurants and theaters, and my favorite part of the city—Old Town Square with Saint Nicholas Church and Old Town Hall with its astronomical clock—they are all as they were before, yet everyone here is holding their breath. They know—we all know—that the whole country will soon be in Hitler's grasp. Maybe the whole continent will. If only our prime minister would understand that. If only he would get his head out of the sand."

"Our prime minister is trying to stop bloodshed." She said the words she'd read in the paper and heard repeated again and again on the radio.

"Whose bloodshed? Is English blood better than any other? Give Hitler an inch, and he'll take a mile. Give him the Sudetenland, and soon all of this country will be under his control. There is no bargaining with a madman. And then...well, we'll discuss that in the morning. You must be tired after your trip."

"It must be important...what you have to tell me."

"More important than you know."

Within thirty minutes they had made their way to Wenceslas Square and the Hotel Evropa. They gathered her luggage, which was being held at the bell counter, and five minutes later Andrew opened the door to a large room with two beds and a private bath.

"Just like at home, don't you think?" Andrew turned the knob for the light and scanned the room. Louis XIV furniture had been arranged on lush green carpet, making it appear more like a museum than a hotel room.

And even though Amity had grown accustomed to English luxury, it was nothing as ornate as this. Clark had much simpler taste. She couldn't help but chuckle.

"Home—like this? In your fantasies, maybe. I think our first floor back in Chicago could fit into this room. But it is good being with you again. I get a sense of home when I'm with you."

Amity offered her brother a quick hug and then removed her gloves and slowly unbuttoned her jacket. She felt weary from travel, and nothing sounded better than a hot bath and a snug bed. But before that she had to know why her brother had brought her all this way.

With a heavy sigh she plopped onto the bed. "Now, spill it. What's so urgent? I know Hitler's up to no good. I've been following his progress in the London papers."

Andrew removed his jacket and hung it on the ornate coat rack. His hair was disheveled, but he gave it no mind. He ran his fingers through his hair again, brushing it back from his face, and sat down in a leather armchair. But instead of allowing himself to settle back into it, he leaned forward and unbuttoned his starched, white cuffs, letting out a low sigh. "How much are you aware of what's happening in Germany?"

"How much? It seems that's all the world is talking about these days. Everywhere I go I sense apprehension over news reports, especially about the strength of the Nazis and the effect their propaganda is having on the German people."

"And you're aware of what's happening to the Jews?"

"Families divided and Jews arrested and beaten by the SS…Hitler's storm troopers…Yes, of course. Some people don't believe the reports, but why would anyone make up such lies? The thing I don't understand is why Hitler's threats are shrugged off by Britain. They've already 'incorporated' Austria into the German Reich. Followed by the Sudetenland. Who's next?"

Instead of answering, Andrew pointed to the window where a sliver of moon could be seen hanging over the city.

"The rest of Czechoslovakia, yes. That's what I was afraid of. Isn't this place considered a city of refuge for those who've escaped Germany and Austria—those being hunted by the Nazis?"

"I'm proud of you, sister. You're much more aware of what's going on than I thought you'd be. Sometimes I still think of you as the sixteen-year-old kid I left back in Chicago."

"I am a tutor now, and current events *is* an important topic. I'm worried about all the Jews who hoped to stay beyond Hitler's reach. What will happen to them if he takes over the rest of this country?"

"Oh, it's not only the Jews who have the problem. It extends far beyond that. Whether Czech, Austrian, or German, this country, this city, is filled with enemies of the Reich—social democrats, Communists, scientists, prominent literary figures and other intellectuals—although you are correct that there are many Jews too."

Amity kicked off her shoes, wiggling her toes, glad to be able to stretch them after a long trip. "So what's going to happen to them?"

"We're not going to wait to find out. Currently, with the exception of a fortunate few with personal contacts, the refugees are housed in makeshift camps outside the city where they exist in appalling conditions, without any means of support."

"Is this why you've asked me to come? To help these people?" Tension grew in the pit of her stomach. Both she and her brother had been raised to give and care for those less fortunate. Living in Chicago, they'd witnessed firsthand the influx of people who'd come to the city seeking jobs and a new way of life, especially Negroes from the segregated South. Whole families uprooted from Southern plantations had moved north, attempting to make a new life in the ever-growing city. More than once, Amity had slept nestled between strangers her own age—girls from other families who lived with them for a time until their families could get on their feet.

Andrew sighed. He shook his head as if reading her thoughts. "This is nothing like we faced growing up. It's worse, Ami. Far worse. Especially for the little ones."

"Is there no one helping?"

"Yes, but not enough. Kindertransports are already taking place, rescuing children from Austria and Germany and placing them with relatives or foster parents. But so far there is little help here." He chewed his inner lip, a habit he always had when he had to ask something hard from her. Then he continued.

"I came to get a grasp on the situation. I tried talking with some of the parents, but it's been overwhelming. We've set up an office, and we have more questions than answers: 'How long will it take before my children can go?' 'When can I follow my child?'"

Andrew sighed. "Even harder are the answers. There are so many, it will be impossible to get them all out. There are mothers with children who are too young to be parted. Some children became separated from their parents and are now drifting with tens of thousands of refugees. Like I said, there are children's agencies that were getting hundreds of children out of Germany and Austria, but the same is not true for Czechoslovakia. I can't help wondering what will happen to the threatened children here."

Without having to ask again, Amity could see on her brother's face that this indeed was why she'd been asked to come. The Jewish refugees he'd sent for her to help were children.

Andrew stroked his beard. "Tomorrow I will take you to a sight you won't believe. There are thousands of refugees who've fled the Sudetenland into Czechoslovakia ahead of Hitler's army. My job with the Home Office is to work with the British Committee for Refugees. Finding a way to get the little ones out, Ami, is why I've asked you to come."

— SEVEN —

Jívová, Czechoslovakia
Saturday, December 17, 1938

Pavla shivered as she pulled her dingy, cream-colored sweater off her shoulders and placed it over her son and daughter. She wasn't sure how much the thin sweater would help, but she had to try. She was thankful for the clean dress from Mrs. Smidova, but what she wouldn't give for the blankets and coats she'd left back at their apartment in Olomouc. Icy fingers of cold air pushed their way through the decaying wood, as if seeking to pull all warmth from her skin and all hope from her soul. She rubbed her arms and sat next to her sleeping children, attempting to remember happier times.

Years ago, they'd purchased the sweater from one of the finest women's clothing shops in Malá Strana. Abram's parents had watched the children for the weekend, and he'd taken her on a short holiday to Prague. She'd enjoyed the two-hour train ride with her husband, reminiscent of the times they had together before they had children. They'd visited the Prague National Museum, which they'd done on one of their first dates, and then Abram had taken her shopping for her birthday, spoiling her as always.

He was an important business owner back then, and he liked to show her off at private parties and community events. She enjoyed being by his side, but the busyness of life often took away the time they had to just enjoy being together. Had that really been their life—filled with fine dinners and theater tickets? It seemed like a dream. Especially when now the things she cared for most were finding food for her children and keeping them warm.

A sad smile touched the corners of her lips as she adjusted the sweater over her daughter's thin frame. Last she'd heard from Mrs. Smidova, a German family had moved into their apartment. What had that family done with all their things? If she'd had time, what would she have packed? Photographs, personal mementos, some of their finer clothes…and once again she thought it careless of her not to have grabbed what jewelry she had as well. Of course, other than the jewelry, none of that would have helped them now. If anything, those things would have just been a burden to carry along.

Her focus now was on saving Klára and Ondřej. Abram, the love of her life and her protector, was no more. The tears didn't come as she thought of him. She'd cried herself to sleep every night since they'd run away. There were no more tears to cry now.

Pavla lowered her weary body onto the thin mattress that Mrs. Smidova had put into the shed and curled herself against Ondřej's back, wrapping her arms around both her children. She released a heavy sigh and closed her eyes. At this moment they had a place to rest, hidden from the elements. Tonight her children had gone to sleep without growling stomachs. Tonight she had her two children with her. The same could not be said of so many other Jewish families whose stories she'd heard about. And just a few hours from now, she and her children would be taken by oxcart to a new place. She wasn't sure what would happen then, but she hoped what Mrs. Smidova said was true, that once they reached the refugee camps there would be people, organizations, to help them and give them provisions for a new life. Yet even as Pavla longed for a new life, her heart ached for her old one.

Pavla closed her eyes and tried to remember her husband's face. He had high cheekbones and a handsome nose. His mouth was large, especially when he broke into a smile. His hair had been light like his mother's, which was probably one of the reasons for Klára's light coloring.

Abram's form had always been powerful and commanding. She remembered the first day she'd seen him dressed as a Talmud student. Even under his cloak and cap, he looked more like a warrior than a pious student. His narrow face, shadowed by a beard, held a hint of a smile.

Under arched eyebrows shone intelligent blue eyes that had followed her all through the day at her cousin's wedding. It was less than two years later when they had their own wedding. She closed her eyes and could almost imagine Abram entwining his long, strong fingers through her raven hair. It was hard to believe her husband was gone.

The happenings of that night remained clouded in her mind, and she knew nothing about what had happened to her husband and in-laws before they were killed. They had received word earlier in the evening from their neighbors that the Jewish buildings in town were being broken into and looted. Pavla went to put her children to bed while Abram, his father, Omer, and his mother, Rebekah, were discussing whether it was wise to go out and check on the state of their business. Abram had come upstairs to tell her that the synagogue was burning. Not long after that, someone had knocked on the door, but she could not hear the conversation. She had walked downstairs to see who had come, and had watched in horror as a German soldier ordered Abram and his parents to leave the house with him.

Pavla had never lived alone before. She'd never had to care for her own needs or those of her children. She'd never had to figure out where to find food or shelter. She'd moved from her parents' house to Abram's, but now whatever happened to her children was all up to her...or was it?

All her life Pavla had heard about *Elohim*. She'd always trusted that what her family told her about the one true God was true. He had always been a part of her life and community. Just like the sun and the moon, the clouds and the rain, He was always there.

But after she had lost everything, it was hard to think of *Elohim*. If He was present and saw all that happened, He must have allowed it. How could a loving God allow such things to happen? Weren't the Jews His special people? Why were they being persecuted in such a way? None of it made sense.

Still, the emptiness deep inside wouldn't go away, and Pavla could only hold *Elohim* back for so long. Her arms were getting weary from holding Him at bay. In a strange way she longed for the comfort He provided even though she didn't understand His ways. And as her eyes fluttered closed, she wondered again if she'd done something to make Him angry—if she'd believed in something that would cause a curse upon her family—but she couldn't think about that now. Instead, she pushed aside her questions and simply sought His presence. If there was ever a time she needed to feel God's closeness, it was now. A passage of Scripture that Abram had been helping Ondřej memorize over the past couple of months came to her mind.

Though I walk through the valley of the shadow of death,
I will not fear the crafty wiliness of the evil-doer;

For thou art with me! Thou art in all my ways;
The firm staff of faith is my confidence!

Ondřej had memorized more verses than that, but she couldn't remember them all now. Instead, she let those words play in her mind over and over.

I will not fear. I will not fear. O Lord, help me not to fear.

As the hour grew close to midnight, she woke her children and had them gather their things for the journey ahead. Even though Pavla was cold, hungry, and weary, her thoughts of *Elohim* had given her new strength. She was not alone. God was at her side. No matter what lay ahead, He would be with her, with her children. Even when Abram couldn't, God could—and would.

— EIGHT —

Prague, Czechoslovakia
Sunday, December 18, 1938

The next morning Andrew and Amity had a quick breakfast in the lobby of the Hotel Evropa, and then he took her to a small building a few blocks from Wenceslas Square, where he'd set up an office to help process refugees. She had awakened this Sunday morning to the sound of hundreds of church bells all over the city, and as they set off on their short walk, the streets were nearly empty. Only the most faithful had ventured out to attend Mass.

If she had been back in London, she would be attending church with Clark and Celia, but today she was worshipping and serving the Lord in a different way.

People were already gathered at the building even though it was still early in the morning. The crowd watched silently as they approached. The people looked tired, weary, and cold.

Amity's heart broke as she eyed the clusters of families. Her gaze turned to the children. They should be laughing and playing. Instead, they stood silently beside their mothers, their faces downcast.

Andrew unlocked the door. He motioned for Amity to go through, and then the crowd spilled inside, filling every inch of the lobby space. Still, not everyone could get in the door.

Even with these challenging circumstances, Amity was impressed to see how the refugees cared for each other. No one pushed to the front. No one demanded attention first.

How tired they must be trying to find help day after day, searching for hope.

"We'll be with you in a moment," Andrew called out with a smile, and then he led Amity to a back office where there were two metal desks, two chairs, and a line of file cabinets. Brass hooks hung on the paneled wall for coats and umbrellas. In the far corner was a sink and a small wood-burning stove. A neat pile of wood was stacked next to it. A tall window looked out upon the street. To the side was a small toilet room. All the necessities of life.

Already tears filled her eyes at the thought of all those families being trapped in this city, desperate to escape. Andrew pointed to the chair behind one of the desks. She quickly sat, suddenly feeling the weight of the world upon her shoulders. Amity didn't know what question to ask first, but they all came tumbling out. "Where do they all come from? Are all of these families trying to get out of the country, hoping to get to England?"

Andrew nodded his affirmation. "'Fraid so. They're all trying to get out. And where have they come from? Everywhere the Nazis have gained control."

Amity unbuttoned her coat with trembling fingers. "And where are all the men? I only saw a few."

"It's a hard answer." He sighed. "Some are dead, considered enemies of the state and targeted by the Nazis. Others are in camps or imprisoned. For the lucky families, the men have been sent ahead."

She furrowed her brow. "They sent the men ahead without their families?"

"Yes, usually because they were labeled political enemies, like well-known Communists from Austria or the Sudetenland. There were organizations prepared to get these targets out quickly. The only problem was, they seemed to forget they were leaving families behind."

Even though her stomach still quivered at the enormity of the problem, Amity rose to her feet, ready to help in any way. Ready to do something, anything to help those poor people.

She stood and took a step toward her brother and grasped Andrew's arm, holding it tight. She wanted to thank him for asking her to come, but she knew if she released the words, sobs would accompany them. She had no idea what her brother needed her to do—how she could possibly help the children—but her heart ached to do something.

Andrew must have seen the emotion that transformed her face, for he wrapped a brotherly arm around her shoulders. "Before you say anything, I need you to listen to me. Even though you will see so many needs, you need to forget those for now."

She nodded. "That will be hard to do, but I'll try."

"What I need you to do is to make a list."

"A list?"

"Yes, a list. Getting a child's name on a list is the most important way you can help a refugee. Everyone has to be on a list in order to be considered for travel documents. It's the only way for them to leave the country. Then we will submit our list to London, along with a file we will create for each child. These files will include information about their families, the types of students they are, and any other information a family might need who is willing to care for the child." Andrew pointed to a camera on the desk. "We will take photos of each one and include them in the files. We will then set out to find sponsors for the children. The list will show us which children need to have sponsors first."

"What happens then?"

"This is the hard part. Our list is put into a pile with the other lists provided by various organizations around this city. We have no control over what list they will chose to work from. Then, looking at the names and files, people in an office in London will make these life-and-death decisions. Bureaucrats with full schedules and more papers to process than they know what to do with will decide who should stay and who should go. It will be critical that all the paperwork is filled out perfectly. They've never seen what you'll see, and because of that it's easy to reject an application for the smallest infraction."

He swept his arm toward the door. "All those lives will be forever impacted by government men sitting behind desks with rubber stamps, whether we like it or not. It's your job to gather the names of the children, prepare their files, and take their photos. These people have been overlooked by other organizations. If we don't get their names on a list to submit—and make sure their paperwork is done—they won't have a chance."

"Wait—only the children? Not their mothers?"

"That's right. I have a friend, Dorothy, who is working on transports for mothers and children. She is in an office not far from here, but there are only so many sponsors. There is only a limited amount of money available. It is easier to find foster families for children." Andrew ran his fingers through his dark hair again until it stood on end. Then he shook his head, as if not wanting to have to explain the truth of what would happen to those left behind.

"Many of these mothers do not know that they will have to

send their children away without them, and we have no way of knowing if we will ever be able to provide a way for the mothers to join them. That will be one of the hardest parts of your job, explaining that reality to these women, who have already lost so much."

He paused, and Amity had a feeling he was reluctant to tell her whatever was coming next. "I'm going back to London. I'm going to take as many files as I can carry and find good people who will open their homes to these little ones. I'm heading back in just a few days and—"

"Wait!" Amity held up her hand, halting his words. "A few days? You're leaving me here to do all this on my own?"

He lowered his gaze and fixed his eyes on hers. "I didn't want to tell you when I sent the invitation. I was afraid you wouldn't come if you knew the truth. The best way I can help these children is by finding homes for them in England. And I need you—someone I trust with my whole heart—to take care of them here."

"And not getting their name on the list?"

Andrew moved to the window. Even though it was a beautiful view of red tile roofs and medieval spires, he focused instead on the line of people. "They believe they're as good as dead."

Amity let her eyes flutter closed, the severity of the situation overwhelming her. "Do you agree with that?"

"Unfortunately, yes." He smoothed down his hair the best he could, but it did little good. He usually looked so put together, but today he looked like a mess. This whole situation was clearly eating him up inside, as if all those little ones belonged to him, as if they were his personal responsibility.

I have to help them. I have to help Andrew's children. But how would she do it? It was so much to handle with him gone.

Suddenly she felt ill. The toast and jam and lunch meats she had for breakfast felt like bricks in her stomach. She opened her eyes and moved to the desk, taking a seat. Her stomach ached, but her chest hurt even more as the weight of what Andrew was asking her to do settled over her.

She pressed a hand to her forehead and looked at him. "But if I'm the one putting all the names on the list, then I'm making the choice between life and death. How would I ever choose?"

"You can't think of it that way. You're not the one choosing death, Hitler is. Instead, God has chosen you to save those who you can. To give the choice of life."

The thankfulness she had felt a moment ago for being here, for having the opportunity to help, dropped like an invisible glass ball from her hands, shattering at her feet. Suddenly she wished to be taken back to a week prior when she knew little to nothing of Czech refugees. Life was so much easier as a tutor, when her biggest problem was getting Celia to focus on her lessons. She would gladly hear Mrs. McGovern fret about the cost of fresh flowers from morning to evening if she no longer had the knowledge of the refugee children and their need to escape before Hitler's men descended on them. Because now that she knew, she had to answer to her conscience, and more importantly, to God. If she walked away, she'd never be able to forget what she'd learned.

"It's too much. It's just too much," she mumbled.

"You will have an assistant named Madeline. She's out at one of the villages today, but you will meet her tomorrow. There are other volunteers who stop in to help every now and then. Don't be surprised by this—they do what they can when they can. I also have a friend from Brno, Marek, who might come to help, although I've yet to confirm that. I will try to give him a call today."

Andrew spoke in a low voice. He focused on her face as if willing her to remember his every word. "The women and children outside these office doors are the ones who have made it into Prague. But there are so many more. Seas of people." He pointed to a map behind him mounted on the wall. "Camps dot all parts of the compass around Prague. These pins mark the areas where they've been set up. I have been to each one at least once, and they seem to get worse and worse the farther they are from the city."

"Do you have any idea the number or people, the number of children? What are we talking about?"

"There is no way to get an accurate number, but we have a good guess. In the villages around Prague there are some 200,000 despairing and destitute people. We have no idea how many of them are children."

"So many. All from the Sudetenland and other areas the Germans have occupied?"

"Yes, and that's not including an equal number who were sent back to the occupied territory, driven back onto the trains at the point of the bayonet by their own countrymen." He lowered his head and shook it. "I've heard whole families are being sent away to camps, or they are being persecuted in their own towns. There is nothing we can do for those people, but we can't leave those who are here to their fate."

"Where are these people staying? Surely there wasn't enough extra housing for all of them."

"Not even close. Those in the villages are staying in old schools, abandoned buildings, churches. Most are unheated. There are broken windows, and blankets are scarce...Well, you get the picture."

"What about food?" Amity placed a hand over her stomach again, feeling guilty for having indulged in this morning's breakfast when others had so little.

"Food is being provided by different relief agencies, but it's rationed. There's never really enough to go around." He turned back from the window, despair evident on his face. He passed his hands slowly over his forehead and then rubbed his eyes, as if trying to push back all his worries. "Did you bring any money?"

Amity nodded. "Nearly five hundred pounds. I figured you'd need it. My savings, all of it, but it seems so inadequate now."

"It'll be a start. I need to pay another few months of rent for this space. It isn't much, but the hotel isn't cheap. The people need provisions too. We'll need money for the train fares and food for the trip to England. We'll quickly have to find more benefactors." He offered a half smile. "I've already used up what money I had, and I've been calling around to friends."

She sighed. "I can only imagine how much they enjoy those calls."

"People are catching on, asking friends to help too. Some are willing to give money to help with supplies and things, yet even if they can afford it, many are not interested in sponsoring a child. It's just too much responsibility, they say. They don't like the idea of taking a child they've never met before into their home—and they don't know much of their background. I'm hoping I can change a few minds by showing them some photographs."

The hairs on the back of Amity's neck stood up. "It's not as if the children or their parents have asked for this. They are helpless victims."

Andrew shrugged. "They worry these children will bring problems into their homes."

Amity stood up and removed her coat and hung it on one of the hooks as a new fervor surged through her. The stove was crackling, radiating heat. If so many others would not do something, she would, even if it made her uncomfortable. Even if she had to do it alone.

"And how much does it cost to sponsor a child?" she asked, wondering if perhaps the cost was the most prohibitive part.

"Fifty pounds, which is a lot, considering most families make only ten times that a year. And that is just to file the paperwork. The families must also be able to support the children until they are eighteen."

"If that is the case, what is the fifty pounds for?"

"A prepayment for the child's return to their home country someday. When it is safe, of course."

Amity nodded. *Will that ever be the case for any of these children? Only if a miracle happens.*

"And you really are going to put me in charge of making this list? Can't I take a simpler role? What about doing the kind of work I did in Chicago, handing out blankets and bowls of soup?" That she knew she could do.

Andrew approached her and placed a hand on her shoulder. "That would help them for a moment, but it would do nothing to help with what they need most—an escape."

She touched the top button of her blouse as the severity of the word struck her. Then she moved her fingers to her throat, trying to breathe, overwhelmed with the responsibility she was about to take on. She was thankful now that she hadn't known what she was going to be asked to do before she'd come. She probably never would have had enough courage to travel to Prague. But now that she was here, she couldn't walk away. "Where do we start? What do I do first?"

"Today you can get settled. Tomorrow we'll visit some of the camps. I need to head back to London in less than a week, but before I go I'm going to take you to meet my friends at the British legation. Dress nicely when we go there. It's at Thun Palace, and you'll be meeting several officials."

"You should have warned me. I would have packed differently."

"I'm sure you'll do fine. You always manage to turn heads no matter what you're wearing. I think you'll become a special friend to Mr. Gibson, the passport control officer. Your list will make his job easier too. They, too, want to see as many children as possible get out of Hitler's grip alive."

Nine

Prague, Czechoslovakia
Sunday, December 18, 1938

Konrád sat at the window of the small apartment overlooking the Vltava River. A muffled noise sounded from behind him. "Please, Emil, you do not need to whine like a puppy. I told you we will talk as soon as I finish my cigarette."

He lifted the cigarette to his lips and took a long drag. The tobacco was strong, dark. He knew being in Prague would have its benefits. This was one of them. There was no rationing as of yet. Lots of luxuries to enjoy.

Konrád sat in a rickety wooden chair, his leg crossed over his knee, and stared out at the automobiles that wove through the narrow cobblestone streets and stone bridges. He'd just arrived in Prague and had found an apartment. His plan was coming together perfectly.

Finding this enemy of the German state now bound before him had been the hardest part. Now that he'd located him, using Emil as a mole to find the others would be the easy part.

He pulled the list from his pocket and read it again. There were twenty names, and that was just the beginning. There seemed to be an endless number of men, and some women, considered important enemies of the German state. They hid around this city like cockroaches, scurrying to stay out of view, but Konrád would not mind tracking them into dark corners. First, though, he had the matter of hidden treasure to deal with. He had enough time and resources to benefit both himself and his superiors.

Konrád had been given a healthy bank account, but he'd rather inflict injury than pay for information. Fear worked better than bribes any day.

He finished the cigarette and then flicked it into the ashtray, letting it smolder. Next to the ashtray sat his pistol. From the terror on Emil's face, Konrád doubted he'd have to get rough with the man. Threats of him being hunted down if he tried to leave the country would keep Emil in Prague. And a promise of receiving an exit document in a few months' time would ensure that Emil didn't stray far from his side.

Konrád tapped his fingers on the windowsill in a steady rapping. "So, from what I've learned, your sister and nephew have already made it to London. How very fortunate. You were one of the few who projected clearly into the future, sensing the danger to come. Do what I ask, and I will release you to join them." He turned, glancing over his shoulder. "I will free you from your ropes soon, but if you run it will be impossible to cross the border. The only way you'll be able to leave and join your family is to provide me with the information I need."

The man's eyes widened, and Konrád knew he had his attention.

"You may be wondering what type of information I need. There are some people I need to find. You may know some of them personally. After all, you all worked so hard together, speaking out against the Nazi party, building a resistance network, smuggling men and goods out of the country, and pleading with outside help to support your cause."

The man looked down and finally relaxed against the ropes that held him tight, as if accepting defeat.

"Ah, you did not know we were watching so closely, did you? I'm also sure you didn't realize one of our own had infiltrated your group. And just to think, you considered them all friends, compatriots, didn't you?"

Konrád tapped his chin and then rose and moved toward the man. "And maybe the traitor is even the one who found a place for your sister and nephew. I believe they are now in North Highlands, yes?"

Tears filled the man's eyes, and a low moan escaped.

What a weakling. People shouldn't be so trusting.

With one smooth movement Konrád yanked the rag out of the man's mouth. The man coughed and gagged, and then his head dropped to his chest. His breathing was hard and ragged. Konrád smiled, knowing the ache in the man's heart overwhelmed the pain of his bound hands and feet.

"Please do nothing to harm my family. Take my life. Take it now. Just leave them be."

Konrád moved back to the table by the window and used the smoldering stub of the cigarette to light another.

"If only it was that easy." He turned back around, cigarette in hand, and tried to make his voice gentle, believable. "I need you to get a little information from some refugees who are trying to get out of the country."

A trembling started in the man's limbs, one he couldn't hide. "I—I could never turn in anyone. I would never be disloyal to my friends." The man jutted out his chin and feigned defiance.

"Friends or family, you decide. But first I have another request." He offered a half smile. "There is a particular refugee I wish for you to find. Not for the German state—they have no need of this person—but for myself."

The man lifted his gaze to meet Konrád's, the smallest glimmer of hope lighted in his eyes. "You mean I will not have to turn in any of my friends?"

"No, not now. Not yet."

"What do you want with this person? You won't hurt him, right?" Emil asked.

Konrád knew what his captive wanted to hear. He knew what this weakling *needed* to believe if he was to comply with this request and keep his conscience clear. And Konrád knew better than to tell Emil that it was a woman he sought. Not yet. First he would make sure Emil was working for the organization the woman would most likely come to for help.

Konrád flicked his cigarette into the ashtray and watched as the blue-gray smoke rose and twisted in the air. "You are correct. I have no reason to hurt this person. I only want to talk. This person has something that I want, that I need." He smiled.

Emil's shoulders relaxed, and he no longer strained against his ropes.

Konrád leaned down and reached his hand into his boot, pulling out a small jackknife. He approached Emil and touched the knife against his throat. Emil winced, and Konrád pressed until the smallest trickle of blood flowed down the man's neck.

"You will wait for my instructions, and you will do as I tell you. Are we clear?"

Emil nodded slowly without saying a word.

"Good. Now that we have an agreement, you must get some rest." Konrád pulled a white handkerchief from his pocket and wiped the blood from his knife before stuffing the cloth back into his pocket. "Your work starts tomorrow."

Konrád kneeled before his new associate and slowly cut the ropes that bound the man's ankles. He waited, almost expecting the man to try a quick kick to his groin and attempt to run, but instead Emil sat patiently and waited for Konrád to release his wrists.

It was then Konrád knew he had this man just where he wanted him. His fear over bringing harm to his sister and nephew would make him like a Czech marionette on strings, willing to do Konrád's bidding, even when his conviction urged him otherwise.

He smiled, thinking about all those refugees who would believe they'd found a friend in Emil. When would they realize they had nowhere to run? Perhaps for some, not until they marched into the death camps. Yet knowing the Jews, even then they'd cling to false hope in their God. A God who would fail them in the end—at least as long as Konrád had something to say about it.

TEN

London, England
Monday, December 19, 1938

Clark paced in his bedroom. The fire roared in his fireplace as his thoughts roared in his mind. He couldn't just sit here and worry and wonder what was happening with Amity. He had to know why Andrew had requested she join him in Prague. He had to know she was safe. All this worrying and wondering was about to drive him mad. He either had to figure out how to connect with someone who knew what was happening in Prague, or he had to go there himself. Maybe both.

Why did I let her go? Believing that God was directing her to do something grand and meaningful had been noble at the time, but the fact was that the woman he cared for very much was in a foreign country that was the center of Hitler's lust for more land and more control in Europe. The German chancellor was determined to become the high king of the former Austro-Hungarian empire, and all of Czechoslovakia was in his sights, with Prague as the jeweled crown to top off his conquest—at least until his bloodlust got the better of him once again.

Clark paced a few more times and tried to figure out how to discover what was happening in Prague without Amity feeling as if he were checking on her—which was exactly what he wanted to do. Clark considered what he would do if he were penning a novel and needed insider information for his research.

He paused and scratched his head. *If I were to set a novel in Prague and wanted to know the heartbeat of the city without going there, who would I talk to?*

In his work as a novelist during the past twelve years, he'd met with all types of people to get behind-the-scenes information. Fans of his fiction praised the true-to-life details, and newspaper reporters often tried to trick him into spilling his sources. A few times the police even came to him, asking him for leads about crime circles in the city. Clark always claimed he simply had a smacking good imagination. After all, if he were to give away even a hint of where he got his information, he'd never be trusted again.

Clark had met with numerous contacts over the years, but today one face came to mind. Antonín Valtr was a Brit who'd lived the first twenty years of his life in Prague, which was then a part of the Austro-Hungarian Empire. A dealer of medieval books and art, Antonín traveled to Prague often, and Clark had no doubt Antonín still had important connections within the inner workings there. There was only one way to find out.

He paused and stared at the beamed ceiling and then smiled, knowing it was time to pay a visit to his old friend. He moved to the tall bookcase and reached up to the second shelf from the top, pulling out a copy of *Great Expectations* by Charles Dickens. What once was a first-edition copy was now only a great ruse.

Clark carefully opened it up, remembering the first time he'd been given this gift. He'd just finished the final draft of *The Hidden Staircase to Splendor*, and Antonín had been his informer on the details of illegal art trade. It wasn't until Clark had gotten home that he'd opened the brown paper wrapping to see that the center of the book had been hollowed out, and his friend Antonín had left him a note inside.

"For the past twenty years this book held my pistol at my bedside table. Now that I've retired I'm leaving it to you. Don't be a stranger. I like being a hero in your books."

On the other side of the paper was an address. Clark knew the part of town. It was new construction of small family homes—the last place you'd expect to find a former art dealer, yet the perfect place to hide if you never wanted to be found again.

Clark hadn't talked with Antonín for more than three years. Everything had stopped—his work, his interest—when Gwen became sick. He slipped the paper into his pocket and then placed the book back onto the shelf, hoping his old friend didn't mind a drop-in visitor. Clark had no idea if Antonín still had his finger on the undercurrents of what was happening in Prague, but he hoped he did.

With quickened steps, Clark dressed for the inclement weather and then hurried down to the kitchen. That was one room he and Celia rarely entered, yet Clark knew that was exactly where the staff would be gathered on a day like today when the snow kept them inside. With purposeful strides he approached the door. He could hear talking and laughter. As he pushed the door open, all the conversation stopped, and six heads turned his direction.

"Sir, can I help you? Is there a problem?" The words were out of Mrs. McGovern's mouth first. But it was his driver, Godfry, who jumped to his feet, standing at attention.

"No problem, Mrs. McGovern, but I thought I'd like to go for a drive." He turned to Godfrey. "Can you get me the keys? I shan't be gone long."

"You want to drive, sir?"

"Yes, I do."

"But you haven't driven alone—"

"In three years, I know. But that doesn't mean I don't know how to drive." Clark forced a smile, knowing that all eyes were on him. "Christmas is in a few days, isn't it? I have a few errands to run, if you know what I mean." As soon as the words were out of his mouth, Clark chided himself for being deceitful. After his visit, he'd have to stop by some local shops.

"Oh, yes, sir. I'll get the keys. The auto is already fueled up and ready."

"I appreciate that."

Godfry's face reddened as it always did when he felt nervous or embarrassed. "Are you certain you don't want me to drive you, sir?"

"I am certain, Godfry, although I appreciate the offer. Even a man in mourning has to remember there's a life out there worth living." The words had slipped out, but even as he said them Clark realized how true they were. He had brought life into his home when he'd hired Amity, and now that she was gone, he was starting to notice how much they still hid themselves from the real, pulsating life outside these walls.

Mrs. McGovern rose to her feet too. She shuffled toward the kitchen pantry in a flurry as if she someone had just stoked a fire under her. "Would you like me to pack a lunch for you, sir?"

"Dear lady, we just finished breakfast. I'm full and I know a secret. If I do get hungry, there are things called restaurants."

Laughter spilled from the lips of the maids and gardeners who still sat around the table.

Her brows folded. "So will you be eaten' out then, sir?"

"I may or may not." Clark turned to the door to follow Godfry to the garage. "It will be a surprise for both of us, now, won't it?"

"And Celia, sir?" Mrs. McGovern shuffled after him. "She's been lost in a book all morning, reading that new novel about the rampages of Attila the Hun, of all things."

He smiled, thankful that even though his daughter was officially on holiday, she still found pleasure in reading and learning. Amity would be proud.

"You can tell her that I've gone out. Surely this close to Christmas she won't ask too many questions."

Mrs. McGovern tipped up one eyebrow as if to say, *And how much do you really know your daughter, sir?*

Clark paid her no mind and hurried out into the cold of the morning. *That will give them something to talk about anyway.* He chuckled to himself—their employer coming out of his hibernation in the dead of winter, of all things.

No more than thirty minutes later, Clark was parking in front of a good-sized cottage. He eyed it curiously, checking the address to ensure he had the right place. "A chocolate box thatch with a front garden. Goodness, Antonín, you are enjoying the simple life, aren't you?" He turned off the car and slipped the key into his jacket pocket, telling himself that he was doing Amity a favor by keeping an eye on her.

Clark hadn't even raised his hand to knock at the door when it swung open, and he found himself being welcomed in by his old friend. As Clark stepped into the doorway, the warmth of the room hit him first. Next, the tasteful decorations of the large reception room grabbed his notice. At least a dozen pieces of fine art hung on the walls, and the furniture was tastefully modern. Just like the pistol hidden inside the first-edition copy of a Dickens novel, Antonín knew how to protect himself from curious gazes.

"Clark Cartwright, old friend, it is a good thing to see that you're still breathing." Antonín pointed to Clark's coat, and he happily passed it over.

Antonín hung the coat on a black iron rack and then turned back to Clark. "Just not more than a month ago I was meeting with a contact in Milan who claimed that a character in one of your novels was strangely similar to myself. I was flattered, of course, but disappointingly couldn't reveal our connection. What took you so long to look me up? Would you like a drink? Come, warm yourself by the fire." The man's arm swept the room, and he pointed to one of the cushioned, shell-back chairs positioned close to the stone fireplace. A small fire danced and crackled in the hearth.

"No drink please, and I wish I could say I've come to again receive inspiration for one of my novels. Valentýn Oto is one of my most popular characters, and I've even received letters from women wanting to know his current marital status." Clark chuckled as he sat, his body relaxing into the gold cushioned chair that was surprisingly comfortable despite the art deco style. "But the truth is, I've come on a personal matter."

"Please, by all means, forward their requests. I haven't been on a good date in ages." He steepled his fingers and placed them to his lips. "But let me guess, this personal matter has something to do with a *friend* in Germany, Austria, or the Sudetenland perhaps?"

"Close, Prague. My daughter's tutor just traveled there. Her brother works for the British Home Office and asked her to come assist with the Jewish refugee situation."

Antonín nodded. "A situation I know well. For the last few years, as Hitler's hatred of the Jewish people has been displayed in his speeches and treatment of the Jews, I've been busier than ever. The mounting war has caused the art market to go mad. Leave it to a crazy German dictator to pull me out of retirement."

"Let me guess...foreseeing the future, wealthy Jews have been trying to get their art out of the country?"

"Yes, it started as that, although ever since the annexation of the Sudetenland in October, most of the calls I have been receiving from former clients has been about getting *themselves* out. They're desperate. Whole families pushed out of their homes and forced to live in refugee camps."

He shrugged. "Thankfully I have a nephew there who has been a tremendous help to me. He has always had a great concern for social causes. He has a British passport because he was born here, but he was raised in the Sudetenland. I have helped as I can with those fleeing. They are my countrymen, after all. Jewish or not, they are Czech citizens. I have worked with different art dealers, and we have been able to sponsor some of the artists to come here for work. The only problem is that in most of these cases the men have had to come alone, leaving their families behind." Antonín clucked his tongue. "Quite a heartbreaking situation. The refugees who have made it to London have been working with the Home Office, trying to get their families out, but it's a sticky mess."

"Do you think that's why Amity's brother has requested her—to help with the women and children?"

"That would be my guess, but if it were my friend, I would tell her to be careful. Those who want to leave are desperate and will use any deception to find a way to make it on the lists the Home Office is compiling. My guess is that this friend is quite beautiful?" Antonín's lips curled up in a knowing smile. "It is convenient. Too convenient to be used as a literary device in a novel."

"True, but just convenient enough for me to know that maybe God is still listening to the prayers of this old boy. I'd like to think that's the case."

Eleven

Brno, Czechoslovakia
Sunday, December 18, 1938

They had traveled by oxcart throughout the night and all through the next day. The farmer transporting them looked to be Pavla's age—in his late twenties. He had small Klára on the bench next to him, wrapped up in a large woven blanket. Pavla and Ondřej sat in the back, and whenever they approached a checkpoint, the farmer would pull off Klára's hat, revealing her light hair that fluttered in the cold breeze.

Then, with a smile, the farmer would show the German guards his papers and tell him that he, his wife, and their children were traveling to visit his mother in Brno for Christmas. Pavla hadn't asked to see the papers. She didn't know whether he indeed had children of similar ages as her children or if they were forged. It didn't matter, really, as long as the papers led her to safety. Thankfully, Pavla's children didn't look particularity Jewish, and it was easy to conceal the fact that she was too, with her raven hair hidden under a scarf.

Then, as soon as they passed the checkpoint and were out of view, she'd pull Klára off the bench and into her lap, wrapping her arms tight around her.

"I'm cold, *Mutti,*" her daughter said, snuggling as tight as she could into Pavla's lap.

"I know, *beruška*, my little bug. We will be there before long." As the oxen trudged on, Klára stopped asking how much longer they had to go. Instead, she slept limply in Pavla's arms. Pavla sent up a prayer, thanking God for her daughter's deep sleep, and she didn't think more of it until they arrived at the safe house in Brno.

As the moon rose high on the second night of their journey, the jostling of the wagon stopped. Pavla sat up, with Klára still on her lap, and realized she must have fallen asleep. Pavla opened her eyes wider, seeing that they were parked behind a small cottage.

The farmer lifted Klára from the back of the wagon and then paused, looking at Pavla with alarm.

"She is burning with fever. Why didn't you tell me sooner?"

Pavla scooted to the end of the wagon. "She is?"

She touched Klára's cheek. She indeed was terribly hot. Pavla gasped. "A doctor. We must find a doctor!" Her words echoed off the bare trees in what appeared to be an orchard.

"Shh," the farmer scowled. "Please do not be so loud. You will alert the neighbors. We don't want anyone to know you're here."

The smile he'd had all through their journey was gone. A scowl now replaced it. Had it just been an act? He picked up Klára and hurried inside. Pavla longed to follow him, to check on her daughter, but first she had to wake her son. With urgency she leaned close to Ondřej's ear. "We are here. We are safe. We have to get inside."

He lay still, unmoving. She touched his face. Unlike Klára's, which radiated heat, his was icy cold. She sucked in a breath, wondering when was the last time she remembered him stirring.

"Ondřej!" She grabbed his arms and shook him. "Ondřej, wake up, wake up!"

She thought she saw the slightest flutter of his eyes, and suddenly a hand clamped around her mouth. With a force she wasn't use to, the farmer dragged her off the back of the wagon bed. She stretched her arms toward her son but refused to cry out. The man's hold was strong, and she was certain he'd hurt her if she made any more noise.

He dragged her up the steps into his house. She tried to gain her footing, but it was no use. With a few more steps, the man opened the door of the cottage and pushed her inside, following her in. Pavla reached for a kitchen chair, trying to get her balance, but instead she fell and hit it with her chin. She bit her tongue as she hit and tasted blood. The feeling of warm liquid dripped down her neck from a gash in her chin.

"Radek, please!" A young woman with a halo of brown curls rushed forward, shouting. She turned from where she was slicing bread and gasped at her husband, who hovered over Pavla. "What are you doing?"

He paused on the top step and turned to her. "Stupid Jew!" It was more of a growl than a shout. "Does she want to alert all the neighbors to us?"

"We already told them we were having guests for the holidays. I don't think they could have heard her. Please sit down."

He waved a hand to the doorway. "There is yet another one out there, half dead." Radek cursed under his breath. When he turned back around, Pavla noticed his hands were shaking. He paused, glancing back over his shoulder. "Do you know, Emílie, that every time they stopped us, they took down our names. I was not told that would happen. The Germans have our names now."

"How long do you think it would have taken for the Germans to get our names? And my grandmother is Jewish—did you forget?" Emílie pointed to the doorway. "Go get that child out of the wagon." Her face softened as she looked from Klára, who was resting on the sofa, to Pavla, who had brought herself up to a sitting position. "Look what you've done. Who should I help first?"

Pavla pulled a handkerchief from her sweater pocket and dabbed her chin. "My daughter—please, help my daughter." Her mouth tasted like iron from the blood, but she gave it no mind as she rushed to Klára's side. "I am so sorry I was yelling. I had been sleeping. Then Klára was so very hot, and Ondřej…for a moment I thought he was dead. His skin was like ice."

She heard movement, and she turned to see Ondřej staggering along at the man's side. He paused as his eyes fixed on his mother. He pointed to the bloody handkerchief. "Did that man do this to you?" he spat.

"I fell, that is all." She rose and moved to her son. She touched her hand to his cheek, still alarmed by how cold he was. "Please come stand by their fire."

His crossed his arms over his chest. "I don't want to go near *their* fire."

She put her arm around him and scooted him closer to the fire. "They are helping us. I should not have cried out like I did."

The farmer placed Pavla's small carpetbag at her feet without a word, and then he turned and stomped toward the door. "I'm going to take care of the animals. I will eat when I get back."

Ondřej watched the farmer leave and then kneeled, lifting his hands to the fire—the draw of the heat too much of a lure.

Seeing that her son was getting the warmth he needed, Pavla moved to the sofa and kneeled by her daughter. With quivering fingers, she brushed her daughter's hair back from her face. "Is there a doctor we can call? I do not have any medicine. I have a few crowns, though, to pay—"

"No, we do not want to get the doctor. He is one of the leaders of the Nazi supporters in our town. He is the last one who needs to know we are hiding Jews in our house."

Pavla shrank back. She wasn't sure what these people thought of her and her children. Had they changed their minds about keeping them?

Around Olomouc, she and Abram had been business owners and important citizens. They had been friends with many people from all types of backgrounds, but now she realized for the first time how different she was in other people's eyes.

Emílie's eyes softened as she looked at Klára. "We must undress her and get her into a cold bath."

"A cold bath? No." Pavla wrapped her arms around her daughter. "I can't do that."

"We have to get her temperature down. A fever this high can cause seizures. Or worse, we could lose her."

Tears filled Pavla's eyes as she unbuttoned her daughter's dress. Klára was limp as Pavla pulled the dress over her head. She left on her undershirt and panties. The white of the underclothes was a sharp contrast to the pink of her fevered skin.

With quickened movements, Emílie retrieved a tin tub from the porch and filled it from water from the sink. It was nearly full when the door opened again and Radek entered.

His eyebrows were folded down in a scowl. "Where is my dinner? I told you I'd be right in."

Emílie turned off the water and swept her hand to the counter. "I cut some bread, and there's cheese in the cupboard. It's the best I can do." Emílie lowered her voice. "The little one has a fever, just as our Bernard did."

Radek looked down at the small girl as Pavla lowered her into the water. Sadness filled his face. Pavla wasn't sure how long ago it had been since they'd lost their son, but Klára's fever had spiked their emotions. Klára cried out as she sank into the water, and Pavla took that as a good sign.

With tenderness that Pavla hadn't expected, Radek approached her. "I'm sorry I knocked you down. When I felt the fever and heard your cries, I felt an anger I didn't expect. Anger that death had robbed us of our son not even a year ago yet. Please forgive me."

"Of course. I am so sorry. I hope the neighbors..."

"Worry not about the neighbors. Like my wife said, they most likely didn't hear a thing. Even my daughter slept right through it. One girl left," he explained.

Now warm from the fire, Ondřej moved over to stand by her side. "Will she be all right, *Mutti*? Klára will not die like *Táta*, will she?"

"We must pray, Ondřej. Pray to God that isn't the case."

Without hesitation, Ondřej dropped to his knees and gripped the side of the tub. "May the Holy Blessed One overflow with compassion upon Klára, to restore her, to heal her, to strengthen her, to enliven her. The One will send her, speedily, a complete healing—healing of the soul and healing of the body—along with all the ill, among the people of Israel and all humankind, soon, speedily, without delay, and let us all say: Amen!"

Tears filled Pavla's eyes and a soft cry came from Emílie's lips as she clung to her husband's side.

"Was that a Jewish prayer?" Radek asked.

"Yes." Pavla nodded, and then she turned her attention again to Klára. The young girl's light hair floated on the top of the water. "Even though we were not always faithful to attend the synagogue, my husband taught my son some Scriptures and some prayers."

"It was just beautiful." Emílie sniffled as she pressed her check against Radek's shirt. "If only the Lord would answer. He did not for us, and I have not prayed since, but at this moment I will pray for your daughter."

They stood in a half circle around the tub, praying quietly in their hearts. Just a few minutes had passed when Klára opened her eyes. "*Maminka...*" Her chin quivered. "Can I get out now?"

"Oh, sweet child!" Pavla touched her face and noted that her fever had indeed gone down. She looked to Emílie, who nodded her agreement that it was all right to get the girl from the tub.

Emílie wrapped a towel around Klára's shivering form as Pavla lifted her from the water.

Klára place a hand to her ear. "My ear hurts...Oh, *Maminka...*"

Emílie finished wrapping the towel around the girl and then moved to the cupboard. "I have some garlic oil. Let's put her to bed, and I'll warm some and drop it in her ear with a dropper. It works with all my children, and I have some homemade elderberry syrup too. It's good for fever, but I know now that the quickest way to drop a fever is a cool bath."

Less than ten minutes later, Pavla was nestled into a warm bed with Klára on one side and Ondřej on the other. It was the first time she'd slept in a bed since the night before they escaped, and Pavla couldn't remember feeling something so wonderful. And for the first time in weeks, Pavla didn't cry herself to sleep, knowing there were those out there who wanted to kill them just as they had killed her husband. Instead, she would fall asleep knowing there were still good people in the world who opened their homes and their hearts to strangers.

Pavla let her eyes flutter closed. They had stumbled into this house with everything seemingly wrong, but by the end of the night all was well, mostly due to the urgency of a young boy's prayer.

TWELVE

Prague, Czechoslovakia
Wednesday, December 21, 1938

The taxi made slow progress in the dense morning traffic—a merging of modern vehicles and ancient farm carts, history and modern travel attempting unity with little success.

The air was gray, perhaps from the cloud of exhaust fumes puffing from the vehicles in motion, or maybe from the foggy cloud cover that had arrived with the first rays of dawn. As the taxi moved along, the ancient city gave way to tumbled-down flats, and beyond that, small country homes.

Amity saw the first camp from a distance, and she straightened in the automobile's leather seat. It was a municipal building that had been transformed into a temporary shelter. And from the long line of people already extending from the front door, she could see the space had reached its capacity, with still more people seeking help.

She and Andrew had spent the past few days together talking with the refugees who were lined up by the Prague office and making important visits to various officials at the British Embassy in Prague. Thun Palace had been opulent inside and perfectly orderly, as she expected. Amity especially appreciated meeting Mr. Gibson, the passport control officer, who thanked her for her volunteer efforts.

"It's not every day a beautiful young woman comes to a country such as this, especially to speak up for the defenseless," Mr. Gibson had told her. "Please, you have to do me the honor of taking you to dinner sometime. I'd like to get to know such a smashing young woman better."

Amity had brushed off the invitation by launching into a dialogue about the poor and wretched children, speaking with passion until Mr. Gibson had turned glassy-eyed and had excused himself for another reception he had to attend.

Amity's stomach felt like a jumble of nerves as they entered the front doors of the municipal office. Inside the building, she scanned the room. Her chest filled with a dull ache at the sight of children whose parents had no choice but to leave them behind.

The first open foyer had been set up with two long rows of cots. Every bed was full, and blankets lined the floor. Children clustered on them in groups. Some slept. A few stared at the ceiling in silence. One about Celia's age sat in front of the window and read a book with intensity, as if hoping to be carried away to any other time and place.

Amity turned to Andrew, and the sadness in his gaze reflected in her soul. "So many," she mouthed.

Andrew only nodded.

A young girl, no more than three or four, lying on a cot nearest to the door, awoke. Her wide-eyed gaze told Amity that the nightmare had come to her not in her sleep but upon her waking.

Amity finally understood even deeper the implications of the Nazis' plans for the Jews as she peered into the eyes of a tearful child. The girl clung to a housecoat with a pattern of yellow faded flowers—maybe a housecoat that had belonged to her mother.

The youngster cried out in Czech—a language Ami couldn't understand—and stretched her arms toward the door. Compassion filled Ami's chest, and before she could stop herself, she sunk to the floor and scooped the young child into her arms.

"Her parents?" Amity looked up to Andrew. "Where are they?"

"They left on yesterday's transport—to England. They would go only if I promised I'd find a way for their daughter to join them. We'll care for her here until we figure something out. Before we leave today, we'll prepare a file for her and add her to our list."

Amity tucked the girl's head tight under her chin and rocked the child back and forth. The girl's cries subsided, and she snuggled her forehead against Amity's neck. Still, even in her silence, the girl's frame trembled with each breath, and Amity wished she knew the words to comfort her soul. But what comforting words could she give? She didn't have a clue how to help all these children, not even this one.

Peering over the girl's mussed hair, Amity met her brother's gaze.

"Madeline should be here soon to help us with the paperwork. You'll be talking to those who come here and traveling to the refugee camps, discovering the most desperate cases and documenting them. It's so frustrating, though, because even after all this work, I have no idea whether our children are going to be chosen from all the lists they are given. And sometimes I think the Home Office gets so tired of the pressure of trying to decide which list to work from that they push the whole mess to the side."

"No matter the fights there, I'll do my best to help here." Amity brushed a dark curl back from the girl's face, stroking her cheek. She hoped the girl would sit well for her photograph. She couldn't imagine a sponsor seeing a photo of a little one like this and not wanting to help. "It's an easy job, isn't it, preparing files? It's a job I can do?"

Andrew smiled as a young boy approached. The boy apparently hadn't bathed in weeks. Yet when the boy stretched his arms out to Andrew, her older brother did not hesitate to sweep the child into his arms.

"I know you can." Andrew patted the boy's head. "I don't need someone to worry about their food and clothes. We have agencies set up to do that. I just need someone to listen, to collect their stories, and to make sure all the paperwork is done correctly. We need to know which ones have plenty of money to ensure their child's safety and which ones can't afford their next meal. And I need you to help reassure those who can't bear the thought of parting with their little ones that we'll do our best to care for them. You have an honest face. They'll trust you, Amity."

"Yes, but if my heart aches for this one, how can I handle the grief of them all?" She stroked the young girl's back in big circles until the trembling stilled.

Andrew fixed his gaze on her. "The Lord will sustain you. He will not leave you now. And I have more help for you too—a translator named Emil. A good man...you'll like him."

Andrew lifted to his toes and whistled. A man across the room turned, waved to Andrew, and smiled. And that was the thing Amity noticed first. In a room of tears, his smile lit her aching heart.

Amity knew from the first five minutes of knowing Emil that he did nothing halfheartedly or half paced. He looked to be her age. He was just a few inches taller than her with a thin frame and broad shoulders. His clothes hung on him, no doubt because like so many in the city he had trouble finding food. Emil's light-brown, curly hair appeared soft as lamb's wool, and his large blue eyes seemed to trap her in their gaze.

He was handsome, but in a boyish way—not like Clark, who was more mature and proper. If Clark had been here, he would have systematically introduced himself to each family, sitting down with them to discuss their needs. Emil seemed to work in a different way. His eyes scanned the crowd until he was drawn to the one person—one child—whom no one seemed to notice. It was as if he were the defender of the underdog, a voice for those easy to overlook.

Within an hour, Emil had given Amity a tour of the entire building. The room she'd first entered was simply one of many that housed displaced children. At least a dozen others were just as full, the circumstances just as heartbreaking.

When they finished their tour, Emil explained more about the situation of those leaving the Sudetenland. He knew from experience because he, too, had escaped with his life just a month prior. "There are so many of us who are waiting to see if we can get travel documents to England."

Emil gazed off in the distance as if a pained memory filled his thoughts. "Some of my family was able to get out. I am thankful for that." He sighed. "But I have two brothers who were already taken to the camps. They were arrested as soon as the Germans swept into town."

Emil nodded once slowly, emotion filling his gaze. "I hope my family members who left are safe. My youngest nephew is Jan, which is like your John. Honza is his nickname—I believe that is that right word."

"Yes, 'nickname' is the right word. I'm impressed. Your English is very good."

"I lived in Yorkshire a few years as a boy. My grandparents immigrated there, and my mother believed it was important for me to learn a second language—the world is changing so. My grandfather was a Communist leader, and my father after him. I was always more concerned with my studies than politics, but that did not keep my name off the wanted list, did it?"

"Wanted list?"

Emil sighed. "I should not worry you about such things, but that is why so many of us had to leave our homes in the Sudetenland. There has been a growing Nazi party in Czechoslovakia, especially over recent years. Many people have been horrified that part of our country was turned over to Nazi control so easily, but other people rejoice."

"And they targeted you because..."

"Because they know who we are. They know who has been disagreeing with them, who was happy not to be under German control. These are our former schoolmates and neighbors. And as soon as the Germans stepped into the country, they were already turning over lists."

So many lists...some for life, some for death.

Amity rubbed her brow and tried to imagine the people she'd known her whole life turning her in. It was bad enough that these refugees had to run from the Germans, who considered them enemies. But it was even worse that former neighbors pointed them out, making sure they were not overlooked in the scourge.

Emil's face drained of color, but he still tried to force a smile.

"What's wrong?" she asked.

"If you really want to know the truth, those who have come here from the Sudetenland are not safe yet. There are eyes everywhere."

Butterflies danced in Amity's stomach, not of joy, but of dread. A strange sensation came over her, and she knew what Emil said was true.

"You know, every time I am walking with Andrew, I have a curious feeling that we are being followed. And now that I think of it, even when I was standing on the Charles Bridge waiting for him, I felt as if I was being watched."

"Of course you are being watched. All of us are. After all, we are trying to evacuate people who the Nazis are looking for. Prague itself is teeming with Nazi agents."

A shiver ran down her spine. Amity sat hard in the wooden chair in a back room they were using as a makeshift office. She could dwell on what Emil was saying, but she knew it wouldn't change a thing. "I suppose there is nothing I can do about them watching us. But I will say that I am thankful you are here. I am thankful you are translating for me, even when your own future is in question."

Emil looked down at his shoes. They were fine leather, and she was sure he'd once kept them in pristine condition, but now they looked scuffed and worn.

He shrugged. "What else can I do? Just sit around and worry about my fate? If I can help people get out, then I will know that my own waiting is for a purpose. Also..." He winked. "If the Nazis are watching my every move, I'd like to give them something interesting to take notes about."

Unexpected laughter spilled from Amity's lips. "That's so very noble of you." Amity touched his sleeve and then grew more serious. "I will pray for you. I will pray that you will be able to escape all this too."

Emotion flashed across Emil's face. Sadness? Regret? And

maybe a hint of fear. Amity guessed there was much to be afraid of in times like these.

Emil moved toward the window, glancing at the line outside. "Thousands of children need our help. How many will we actually be able to get out?"

Amity noticed for the first time that Emil had an athletic sway to his walk. Had he played sports in school? He looked like someone who would be a team captain. Yet even he seemed to be weary from all that was happening. If someone like him struggled to stay strong, how would the weak ones survive for long?

"I will speak to the families and then translate their information," Emil continued. "These people are desperate. They are willing to do anything to ensure their children are safe." He turned to her, eyes fixed and brows furrowed. "But we must make them aware that we do this because we care, not because we wish to receive anything from our efforts."

"No, of course not. I—I've only come to help." She touched her collar and looked away. "How horrible to think one would try to make a profit of this."

He turned back toward her. The worries of a moment before were gone, and now a soft smile filled his face. "Come, let us go find Madeline. She will be most helpful."

"I have been waiting to meet her. She's another volunteer, I suppose?"

"Yes. She has lived in Prague her whole life. When it comes to situations like these, not only what you know but who you know makes all the difference."

— Thirteen —

Madeline was exactly what Amity expected—a middle-aged Czech woman with shoulder-length silver hair, a round, thoughtful face, and a no-nonsense style with a simple blue dress and black sweater. Next to her was a man who looked to be in his late thirties. Amity guessed he was Madeline's assistant by the way he watched her every move and hung on her every word. His brown hair was gray at the temples, and he held a pile of folders—no doubt filled with files and photos—tight against his chest. He stepped to the side, leaning against the brick wall and watching everything that was happening, but Amity guessed he didn't speak English. Madeline, though, stepped forward, eager to welcome Amity to their work.

Madeline took Amity's hand and held it with a soft squeeze. "I am glad you come. Your brother is good man," she said in broken English. "I am teacher. I saw so much needs, but who listens to me?" Madeline pointed to the man next to her. "This is Marek. He has been helping our cause too."

Emil asked Madeline a few questions in Czech, and Amity could tell that the woman was eager to share all she knew.

"They start by collecting information about the families," Emil said, explaining what he'd learned. "But the problem comes when she attempts to combine her efforts with the other service organizations. There are five in the city, wishing to provide help for their own. Jewish, Catholic, Communist, Austrian, and German." Emil seemed agitated, as if he was ready to get to work and not just talk about it. "No one has found a way to resolve this. These organizations are battling with each other—each wanting their people to leave first. Yet it is costing the people time, and time is not something we have. I have no doubt that Hitler is already making plans to take over all of Czechoslovakia as we speak."

"Well, of course, there is only one way. We must get them to work together," Amity insisted.

"Easier said than done." Madeline moved to the desk and pulled a stack of files from the top drawer, setting them on the desktop with a flourish.

"Surely we can think of something."

"Yes." Emil smiled. "Surely *you* will. That is why you have come. Andrew was telling me stories at breakfast. Is it true that as a child you used to give away all your clothes until you had to rob items from Andrew's closet to dress yourself?"

Ami felt heat rising to her cheeks. "Andrew told you that? Well, truth be told, I always was more comfortable in slacks than skirts. Perhaps that was a good excuse to give my dresses away."

Emil nodded, but she could tell from the expression on his face he didn't buy it. "You say so? I think, perhaps Andrew has a little sister with a heart as big as his...maybe bigger." Unexpectedly, Emil walked forward. Taking her hand in his, he gave it a gentle squeeze.

Amity nodded and offered a slight shrug. "I believe you also have a caring heart, Emil. You just don't want the world to find out."

Emil stepped to the door. "The world I am okay with knowing, but please, Amity, be easy with me, especially if I happen to shed a tear or two."

The first woman entered with two young boys in tow. Between them, the boys carried one suitcase. Missing a handle, their small hands gripped the corners of the case. A large green number was painted on the outside. Though the suitcase was battered and rusty, the boys carried it between them with as much honor as the Jewish priests carrying the Ark of the Covenant.

The woman's piercing gaze looked to Emil first and then settled on Amity. Amazingly, she spoke nearly perfect English. "I met Jewish refugee from Poland. He told me something. 'Go! Go to America! Escape! Go to Israel! Go to Palestine!' I told him it was impossible. My father was born here, my grandfather. I have never wanted to raise my sons anyplace else. Impossible." The women opened her hands to Amity as if offering all she had. "But now, ma'am, I know no other way."

Emil hurriedly spoke to the woman in Czech. The woman listened and then glanced to the boys, nodded, and wrote down something on a piece of paper and handed it to him.

The woman turned to Amity. "Ma'am, I—" she started.

Emil interrupted, "She has the needed funds to care for her boys for now. I told her that we will get word to her when it is time for the trip."

The woman glanced at Emil. "The trip?" From the look on her face, she was wondering if he'd just used the wrong word. Then she realized what he was saying—or rather not saying in front of her children.

"Of course, there are no promises," Amity said. "We need more information about this woman's situation and her needs."

"Yes, of course. I'm getting ahead of myself." He motioned to the chair, indicating the woman should take a seat. Then, for the next thirty minutes she related a story that made the hair on the back of Amity's neck stand on end. The woman's husband was not only a Jew from Germany but also an intellectual. He'd sent his family away but was not able to save his own life. Prague was just one of their many stops on the run for their lives.

Before the woman and her children left, Amity rose and embraced the woman. She felt the woman's shoulders sag under her touch as if she was no longer able to carry the weight of the world.

"Take your sons home, and we'll come for them as soon as we find a way."

As the woman prepared to walk away and the boys also stood, suitcase in hand, Amity wanted to add, *Enjoy every moment you have*. But she knew her words were not necessary.

The family was leaving when Madeline's assistant entered the room. He turned to the woman, said something in Czech, and then led her away.

Amity watched and then turned to Emil for an explanation. "He told her his name is Marek, and he's helping Madeline. Lunch is being served in the courtyard. Since Christmas is in a few days, they have brought milk for the children."

She placed her fingertips to her lips. Who knew that milk would be such a luxury. Back in London, Mrs. McGovern served milk at every meal and cream with their tea. Here things were so different. Again Amity wished she could do more.

Emil must have sensed her troubled thoughts, for he took her hand in his. "It might be worrying you that Andrew is heading home soon—and that there is so much to do and so many needs—but I want you to know I will work with you as long as I can."

"What about your own travel documents? Do you have any hopes of receiving them soon?"

He offered a sad smile. "I have hope, but it's as thin as a thread of a spider's web. There are so many in my situation." He shrugged. "Maybe if by some miracle..."

She placed her free hand on top of his and squeezed. "We should talk to Andrew then. We should make sure."

Emil looked to her with troubled eyes and shook his head. "I do not wish to worry you on this matter. We already discussed it this morning, and Andrew has promised to do all that he can, but there is only so much one man can accomplish...or in your case, there is only so much one woman can." He released a heavy sigh. "We have to remember this. There are nations who are in conflict. There are government offices with their own agendas. So much is out of our hands, Ami."

She looked at him, startled, and he pulled his hand back and placed it on his chest. "What is it? You seemed shocked by something I said. Surely none of this is news to you."

"Oh, it's not that." Her hands were still warm from his touch, and she placed them on her lap. "It's just that you used my nickname, Ami. Only a few people call me that."

Heat rose to his cheeks, and he glanced away. "I am sorry I treated you so familiar. I heard your brother use that name. I am sorry for the mistake."

"Actually, no, it's fine." Her words rushed in. "I can tell we are going to be fast friends, Emil. You may call me Ami. In fact, I will be honored if you do."

FOURTEEN

Konrád offered Emil a chunk of bread, and the man ate it hungrily. He looked away, eyes to the ground as he ate. Konrád waited until he was finished eating to ask him about the day.

"So, you've set yourself up in a volunteer position, have you?"

"Yes, just as requested. It was easy enough. The lines of immigrants are long, and they need help," he blabbered on. "This is a long way from Olomouc. I was hardly interviewed and wasn't asked for references, so eager were they for another set of hands for the work. They seemed to believe me when I said I was worried about my countrymen and wanted to help."

"Why wouldn't they believe you? You don't look threatening." Konrád leaned forward and narrowed is gaze. "Have you discovered anyone of interest?"

"Not really. They are simple peasant women with their children. Jews mostly, some Communists whose husbands have already fled to England."

"Anything else?"

Emil shrugged. "I do not know what to look for. Are you going to tell me? There were so many children at this place. Surely you are not looking for a child. There were some women too. They all looked so desperate..."

His voice trailed off, and disgust caused Konrád to snarl. The weak helping the weaker. It was loathsome to watch. Soon the German nation would be rid of all of them, and then the world would see what a truly pure nation could accomplish at the height of its power.

Konrád pulled out the list from his pocket and started to read. Five names. A few of the names were from the town Emil was from, and familiarity flashed in his eyes.

Emil lifted up his hand as if to ask a question. "Aren't you concerned that if you tell me those names, I will warn them they are being hunted?"

Konrád sneered. "No, that is not a problem. These are the ones who've already been found and are in our hands."

Fear filled Emil's eyes. "Already?"

"So many are waiting until the Nazis take over the country completely, but we are not interested in waiting. Especially with so many refugees coming in. No one knows who is walking these streets, do they?"

Hate shot out of Emil's gaze. "No, I suppose not," he spat, for the first time showing a bit of the fire he had stored up inside.

Seeing that actually pleased Konrád. He'd always wanted a worthy opponent.

Emil stared out the window at the city streets below. "Why do you have me working with the refugees? There are very few men around there. Most of the ones you seek have probably already crossed the border or are in hiding."

"I do believe you're right. And that is why I am not asking you to find a man, but a woman...with children."

Emil's head flipped around quickly. His eyes widened. "A woman? Why ever would you need me to find a woman?"

"I already told you. She has information about the location of something very valuable to me."

Konrád had Emil's complete attention now. Not wanting to disappoint him, Konrád offered a sly smile and rose. He moved to the dresser and opened the top drawer. There, tucked under his things, was a large envelope. He pulled it out, walked to the table next to Emil, and sat.

Konrád took a large family photo from the envelope first. It showed four smiling faces: a handsome young father, his beautiful wife, and their two children. The man stood beside his wife, who was seated in a white, high-backed chair. The man wore a white shirt and a black, double-breasted suit coat. His wife's dark hair was pinned up in an attractive style, and her dress could have come from one of the finest shops in Prague.

Hot anger surged through Konrád's veins when he realized his mother had never worn such fine things until recently. Now that had changed, of course, since this woman's wardrobe was now his mother's.

"The woman's name is Pavla Šimonová. She has two children, Ondřej and Klára. I went looking for them the day after *Kristallnacht*, but they were already gone. It looks like they left in a hurry, but I noticed they left all kinds of information behind." He sighed. "Unfortunately, this woman was an only child. Her parents have both passed away. I couldn't find much communication with other family members—it seems she embraced her husband's family completely—and so my guess is that she didn't run toward her former family home. Of course, that would have done no good anyway, since it is also part of the new German annex of the Sudetenland."

In the photo, a boy stood in front the man, shoulders back, smile wide. He looked to be five or six years old and had black curls. His smile showed he was missing one of his front teeth.

The youngest child, a girl, sat on her mother's lap. Her hair was lighter, nearly blonde, and her eyes looked light too. If Konrád had to guess, he'd say they were blue or hazel. She was a pretty little thing and could pass for Aryan if need be. He might not have left so quickly with the girl's father and grandparents if he had known she was inside.

Konrád had heard many German families were requesting Aryan-looking children to be sent to them from the new frontier, and he knew that one of Hitler's goals was to Germanize as many children as possible. Children were Germany's future, and his new fatherland would need many able men and women to support their future conquests and build a solid foundation for the projected thousand-year Reich.

The girl would have been a pretty prize to send to some high-ranking Nazi official. He would consider that later, after he had found the family. He'd do anything to move up the ranks of the Gestapo. And he'd use anyone to get him there.

"That is their daughter?" Emil asked, pointing, as if also surprised by the child's fine features and light coloring.

"It is, or at least I think it is. Of course, such a beautiful woman..." Konrád didn't finish the thought, but he knew many of his friends would have no problem sleeping with such an attractive woman, Jewish or not.

He looked at the date written on the back of the photo. "This is a couple of years old, so the children would be older now."

"Do you know if they've come to Prague?" Email asked.

"I know they are refugees. They are running. This seems like the obvious place to go."

"And your guess is they will want to get out of the country."

Konrád nodded and then slid a few more photos of the happy, smiling faces out of the envelope.

Konrád watched as Emil picked up the photos, studying them one at a time. In a smaller photo of the boy and girl, they were older. Konrád thought the boy looked more Jewish in his features, but the girl appeared only more beautiful.

"I will have no problem remembering those faces, but what will you do with them after you find them?"

"Ah..." Konrád chuckled. "Are you worried I am going to harm them, Emil?" He leaned back and placed his hands on his chest. "What type of monster do you think I am? I only wish to talk to them. That is all."

Emil nodded, and Konrád knew the man didn't believe him. Yet he also knew the man didn't have a choice. "I know there are many refugees, but this beautiful woman won't be too hard to find." He leaned back even more in the chair, letting it rest against the wall, and laced his fingers behind his neck. "And also remember they will be desperate. Do not try to be too clever. Instead, just let me know where they are, and I will do the rest."

"And if I can't find them? What if they have not come to Prague? What if they are not even alive?"

"Trust that they are." He leaned forward, reached out quickly before Emil could pull away, and squeezed Emil's shoulder with a vise-like grip, causing him to wince. "Because only when I find them can we even begin to discuss your freedom. And it would be sad to have to inform your sister that you would be unable to join her after all."

"And the husband?" Emil leaned closer to the first photo, taking in the view of the man. "Should I expect to find him too? Or has he already left with a work visa to England?"

"Oh, her husband. It is very bad news. He is already dead. I took care of that myself."

The color drained from Emil's face, and he nodded. He stared at the image of the man's smile as the news sunk in. "Can I ask what the man did...why you killed him?"

Konrád returned all four of the chair's legs to the ground. He shrugged. "He robbed from me, and I robbed from him." Konrád laughed. "Yes, I robbed him of his life. It was a theft I'd been contemplating for most of my growing up years. It's a new world, Emil. A world where only the strong survive."

— FIFTEEN —

Prague, Czechoslovakia
Saturday, December 24, 1938

With Andrew by her side, Amity spent three days visiting the various refugee centers around the outskirts of Prague. With Emil's translation help, they discovered that a few of the parents had enough money to help with their children's travel and care. Yet too many more didn't even know where their next meal would come from. Amity's goal was to help them find the best way to get their children out of the country, but gathering all the information was not proving to be easy.

Every night a taxi carried Andrew and Amity back to the heart of the city. It was easier to get a good night's sleep at the hotel. Those who stayed at the relocation center and took over caregiving responsibilities got little rest as refugee children cried and their mothers and fathers pounded on the office doors at dawn. Amity had never seen such a dedicated bunch of volunteers. Many, like Emil and Marek, had heard about the need and had simply stepped forward to volunteer their time.

Sometimes when they arrived at the hotel, Andrew and Amity wouldn't go in right away. Instead, they walked along the long stretch of Wenceslas Square or strolled over to the astronomical clock on the Old Town Hall to watch the figures of the twelve apostles take their nightly stroll upon the full hour.

This night they did the same, and as midnight approached, they waited. Small groups of men, women, and children gathered around them with candles in their hands. The candlelight flickering on smiling faces was uplifting, compared to the anguish and tears they'd witnessed over the past few days.

At the stroke of midnight, the two doors above the clock face opened, and the little wooden men rode on a track out one door and in through the other. The twelve apostles exited in twos and traveled from the left to the right window. As soon as the apostles finished their rounds, a gilded statue of a rooster in the upper part of the tower started to crow. And on the left side of the clock face, a wooden skeleton came to life, tolling a funeral bell.

"A skeleton. Of all the things, I don't understand that one," Amity stated.

"He represents death, reminding viewers that death will come to everyone."

Amity wrapped her arms tighter around her. "It's not something one is likely to forget around here these days."

At the same time the clock struck midnight, the church bells erupted from every direction around the city. "What is that? Why are the church bells ringing?"

"They are welcoming in Christmas. That's today, you know."

"Oh, yes, I forgot." It was easy to forget everything except the sad stories of the people they were trying to help. An image of her previous Christmas with Celia and Clark flooded her mind, and an ache of longing filled her chest. She tried to push the longing down but was unsuccessful.

Tonight, as they walked back to their hotel, they talked about the people they had met that day, but mostly they talked of home—of England—and the ache developing in Amity for Celia.

"She's a beautiful young woman. She has her father's dark eyes, good looks, and charm. Sometimes I feel guilty for taking Clark's money to teach her. His daughter is bright, just like him, and witty. I've never met a father and daughter so similar."

Andrew smiled. "It sounds like you care for Clark very much."

Amity's stomach tightened hearing Clark's name upon her brother's lips. "No…uh, I spoke of Celia."

Andrew cast a sideways glanced at her, the moonlight reflecting off his face. "Oh, yes. I'd forgotten."

"I sent a telegram, you know, a few days ago. I sent a message to Clark to tell him I'd be longer—until the end of January. I asked if I can have an advance on my next paycheck too. Although who knows when I'll return to earn it. I haven't heard back yet. I hope I'll still have a job when I'm through."

"I thought you signed a contract for two more years?"

"I did, but I'm not really keeping my bargain, now am I? I was supposed to return by the first of the year."

"I don't think Clark will get rid of you so easily. He's a very levelheaded fellow."

The softest flakes of white fell from the sky, and Amity lifted her gloved hand to catch them. "You know who I'd really like to know better is Emil. He's a fascinating man. I mean, how many young men his age would volunteer their time for a social organization?"

Andrew cleared his throat, and Amity could tell from the look on his face that he didn't agree. "Emil is young and seems a bit flighty. I'm surprised he's stuck around as long as he has."

"You were young and flighty once too, remember? First traveling to New York City and then to England. You wanted to see the world, and you weren't going to let anyone hold you back."

"You're right." Andrew scuffed his leather shoe on the ground, kicking up a clump of fresh snow. "And now, just think, I'm working for the British Home Office. It's amazing the English trust me with their borders, especially since my passport is American."

"Yes, but you attended university there. And who knows, maybe an American passport will be even more valuable than a British one someday." Amity took her brother's arm in her grasp, and they began their walk back to the hotel.

"Besides, what's not to trust about you, Andrew? I trusted you enough to come, didn't I? But it's Christmas, let's not talk about work, shall we? I think I'll burst into tears if I have to remember the look on that woman's face when she handed over her infant son today." Amity lowered her voice. "She confessed to living and working on the streets. I asked her to stay. I told her I'd find a way to help her, but she refused. From the look in her eyes, it appeared she'd already died, as if she had no hope."

"Either hopeless, or trapped in her own little inner world. It's what people do, you know, to survive. They escape into themselves and lock out their emotions. It's better not to feel than to ache. People do what they have to at times like these. These transports, with parents leaving children behind...it's unbearable. And when children have to leave their parents to survive...well, I can't imagine which one is worse. I think not knowing how your loved one is doing would be the hardest."

"But if we can save their lives, it will be worth it, won't it?" She sighed. "Yet all this paperwork is getting in the way—not to mention all the competition between the different agencies who have the same goal. It's not getting anyone anywhere. Every committee believes its cases are the most urgent. But surely they can see there is no movement without order. I wish we could just get them to understand that."

Amity thought again of the large clock tower, remembering the various parts. Some dials told the time, others the season. Some gave a chart of the stars in the sky. And all of it had been brought together in perfect harmony, with each part doing its unique job. But she realized that in the center of it all was a simple glass face. Did the one piece of glass know that for hundreds of years it would be the center of so much movement?

They turned down a narrow cobblestone road, now void of any autos or people, and Amity thought again of all the clock's moving parts. Each part had its own job, but its design enabled the parts to move together.

Every part of these refugee organizations is moving, but not together. If only someone took the time to create a great design from all the parts...

They'd strolled only ten yards down the quiet street when Amity paused. Andrew did too, and he looked over at her curiously, clearly wondering why they stopped. She tried to snap her fingers, but her gloved hands made it impossible.

"That's it!" she cried, grasping Andrew's shoulders.

"What?"

"The clock. It all makes sense now."

He chuckled. "Did you just now realize what all the hands and dials mean?"

"No, I'm thinking about the transport list."

"I don't understand." He led them to stand under the light of a streetlamp and waited for her to continue.

"I have an idea. We can create one master list. We'll start with a blank page and add names of the most urgent cases we've interviewed. Then Emil can call the committees and invite them to submit their most pressing cases to be added to the list."

Andrew stroked his chin, listening, but she could tell he was already doubting this idea would work. "And why would anyone allow *you* to create this list? To oversee it?"

"Because I'm your sister. You work for the Home Office. You, more than anyone, know how great the burden is to work with so many different agencies. We will help them see how this will expedite the process in London. Don't you agree that it will be easier for officials there to work from just one master list, thereby helping the agencies in Czechoslovakia get more refugees out?"

Andrew's eyes brightened, and Amity could tell he was starting to understand. "Yes, we do spend so much time responding to different agencies, trying to keep everyone updated."

"See, it makes sense. One list will help those who are working on the transport papers. Things will move quicker." A chill raced up her spine, and she attempted to ignore the doubts that yapped at the edges of her mind.

Andrew nodded, and a smile touched the corners of his lips. "I do think it will help."

Amity clasped her hands together. "It's worth a try then, isn't it? We can let all the other agencies know that unless the other lists are received within twenty-four hours of the deadline, their refugees will not be included."

"Instead of everyone fighting for the same spots and holding up the process, we can work together," Andrew said. Then tenderness filled Andrew's face, followed by deep concern. For a moment Andrew was no longer representing the Home Office.

Instead, he was simply a big brother worried about his little sister. "But are you sure you can handle this, Ami? It's a lot to take on."

"I'm not sure, but it's worth a try. Emil can help me."

"Of course, Emil is your answer." Andrew laughed. "Good ol' Emil."

Yet Andrew's face brightened as the idea took shape in his mind. "I'm heading home on Tuesday. I keep pushing back the date, but I'm told there is no pushing it back this time. And I have to keep this job. The people here are counting on me to spur on the Home Office from the inside."

He paused and looked up to the starry sky, and Amity knew he was thinking over the details of this master list.

"You do what you said—start that master list—tomorrow. When I return to London, I'll let everyone at the Home Office know that we will only have to work from one list from now on. Yes, Amity, by God—I think you're on to something. Or more likely *because* of God. I think He gave you this idea. It's nearly the new year, and I have a feeling 1938 will be the last one of freedom that Czechoslovakia can claim for a while."

— SIXTEEN —

Prague, Czechoslovakia
Sunday, December 25, 1938

The notice of the money wire from Clark had arrived on the day before Christmas when Amity had been away. When the notice had arrived at the front desk, the clerk of the Hotel Evropa had gone to the bank himself and had tried to talk the bank manager into allowing Amity to come by the bank at nine on Christmas morning to withdraw the money. The hotel clerk had pleaded, stating that he knew she would be using part of the funds to take gifts to the refugee children. Still the bank manager had refused. He, like everyone else, would be spending time with his family.

"Not everyone," the clerk, Yuri, had protested. "All these families are away from their homes. Some have lost their family members. And what a shame that an American must do for our own refugees what we are not."

It was that last line, Amity had been told later by the excited Yuri, that had gotten the man's attention. The manager stated that he did not have the authority to open the bank, but he did something even better. He promised to call all around the city to friends, asking them to sacrifice and provide what they could to the refugees. Amity hadn't known the night before that many had promised to bring gifts and supplies to the lobby on Christmas morning. And it was this happy scene, with boxes and packages piled all around the hotel lobby, that Amity found after descending the stairway that morning.

Seeing her, Yuri rushed to her with arms open wide. "These are for you! These are for the refugee children!" It was then he told her the story. Amity stood amazed as Yuri handed her the notice, and they watched in gratitude as more families entered with items.

Tears filled her eyes, and she thanked those who'd come out on their Christmas morning to give. Then she rushed to the small office just a few blocks away.

Andrew was sitting in the back room talking to Emil. Their chairs were scooted together, and their heads were nearly touching as they spoke.

"Well, there you are—just the two people I wanted to see. You will never believe what just happened. First, I have money coming in for our work that I can pick up at the bank tomorrow. My employer sent it to me. But more than that, we have deliveries to make—wool for knitting, medical supplies, books for the children, warm clothes. Do you think we can get a driver to take us out to the villages?"

Instead of being excited, the men cast a glance at each other and then looked back at her. With a forced smile, Andrew attempted to join in her joy. It took longer for the tension to ease from Emil's face.

Amity knew she should ask them what was wrong, but she didn't want to. She didn't want to hear any more bad news.

"Yes, I believe we can call around for a car and driver or taxi," Andrew finally stated, rising from his place at the table. "Especially if we promise the driver a bonus since it's Christmas Day." Emil didn't move from his chair.

"What's happening?" she finally dared to ask. "Is something wrong?"

Emil shook his head. "In this world there is always something wrong. There isn't much right, is there?"

"But something is different. I can see it in your faces."

Andrew looked to Emil, and another knowing look passed between him. Then he turned back to her. "We were just discussing Christmas, wishing we could do something to help some of the families." He sighed. "I'm thankful for everyone's generosity, Amity, but even with what's been gathered it will only go so far."

"I know. We can't do something for everyone, but we *can* do what we can to help a few," she said in defense. But even as she said the words, she wondered who. Who, out of everyone, would they pick to receive the gifts?

The men rallied, and their excitement grew over the deliveries they could make that day.

As the two men put on their jackets and scarves, Amity again wondered if she should press to know what they'd been discussing, but in the end she decided not to. Today was Christmas, and the hard truth would come out soon enough. She didn't want bad news to ruin her day of gift-bearing.

Two hours later, with arms laden with gifts, Amity and her brother walked up the worn steps of what had been a grand staircase of a former private school on the outskirts of Prague, lit by the light of a single oil lamp. A once opulent land, and the seat of the Austro-Hungarian and Holy Roman Empires, the crumbling buildings were evidence of how far things had fallen.

Andrew and Amity had chosen this location to deliver the

presents because they'd been there in the last week, and the needs of the people, especially the children, had not left Amity's mind.

They entered the room with arms laden with gifts, and it was a subdued scene that met them. The large open area, which had been a reception area for a fine school, was set up as a sleeping area on one side and an eating area on the other. Some of the local villagers had provided old mattresses, but most refugees had created beds out of old bedding. Worn tables and benches from the city park had been brought in to be used for meals, which Amity heard happened once a day, twice if they were lucky. Mothers' and children's faces turned their direction, and everyone was silent, as if trying to understand what they were seeing.

One young boy, standing within arm's reach of Andrew, jumped to his feet. He called out something Amity didn't understand. His mother patted his back, her eyes wide, as if waiting to hear the response.

Emil smiled and answered him, sweeping his arms toward everyone else in the room. Smiles broke out, and Amity stepped closer to Emil, eager to find out what was being said.

Emil turned to Amity and laughed. "He was asking if those gifts were for him...at least one of them."

Amity smiled and looked down at the boy. Emil continued, "I told him we have something for everyone...even him...even if it is just a small gift."

The mothers and their little ones were overjoyed to see the gifts. Each one waited patiently while the items were passed out. Everyone was thankful for what was given to them, no matter how small. Amity was pleased to see that the women were most excited about the wool yarn. She imagined them knitting hats and mittens for their children.

They passed out all the items, but before they left, the woman who was overseeing the refugee center pulled Andrew and Amity to the side. Her hair was tied back from her face, and her weariness was clear. One child clung to her leg, and a baby could be heard crying from a nearby mattress. No mother rushed to the child, and Amity guessed that this woman was the only caregiver the child had left.

The woman grabbed Andrew's arm in desperation. "We have children we need you to take—tonight, if possible."

Andrew's brows furrowed. He rubbed his forehead. "What do you mean *take*?"

"We have no place for them. Some have been abandoned. Some are lost. There are two who need special care. There are some with parents in jail."

"But we have no room for them and no one to care for them. In fact, I'm heading back to London in just a few days. There are no other places to take them. Can't you care for them? The best thing we can offer is to—"

"To add them to the list. I have heard that so many times. Just last week I gave you their complete files and photos, but what difference is it making? No one has left. When are these transports going to take place?"

"We are working on that." Andrew sighed. "Like I said, I'm heading home the day after tomorrow to find more sponsors."

The woman's hands were trembling now. Her eyes were filled with tears. "I hope you find them soon. I—I'm just not sure how much more we can handle."

Andrew nodded his acknowledgment, and as he gave one last look around the room, his eyes widened. He sighed. "Why does it seem like every time I come there are more children?"

"Seem to be?" The woman scoffed. "There *are* more children."

Emil finished passing out the last of his presents, and with heavy hearts they hurried back to the car. Snow was falling harder now, and it was bitter cold.

"Did you see how their faces lit up?" Amity tried to keep it positive. "I am glad we could give them even a small bit of joy today. I imagine they are all thinking back to how things were last year, though, when they all still had families and homes."

Emil nodded, but his usually bright smile had been replaced by a sad scowl. "I was talking to one of the workers, and she told me about a diphtheria epidemic in one of the other camps. Four children died. And more are going to die."

Amity didn't argue with him. She didn't remind him of the plan of the new master list. *We simply have to keep believing, keep trusting*, she told herself.

As they entered the city again, Prague was so beautiful in the snow that the gentle white eased her heart. God had to make a way—He just had to. Surely He wouldn't have brought these people so far just to abandon them now.

— SEVENTEEN —

Prague, Czechoslovakia
Monday, January 2, 1939

As expected, Emil loved Amity's idea, and on Monday they worked together to call all the other relief agencies to tell them about the new master list. They stated that if any of the agencies wanted their children on the master list, they must have the children's files to them before nine the next morning. Andrew was leaving by plane Tuesday afternoon, and he would be taking with him all the files of those who still needed sponsors.

The first few hours they received no response. With each minute that passed without word, Amity worried. Had she cut off ties rather than unite the groups? Did they trust her? After all, who was she to take the fate of all these children into her hands? Who was she, a mere volunteer, to try to bully these organizations into trying to save lives by her demands?

Yet they did take Amity's deadline seriously. Throughout the day, representatives from each organization came to her with their lists and files. All the representatives seemed satisfied to see how she was organizing their most urgent cases into one master list. Hope buoyed within them that with Andrew and Amity working together, the transports would soon start in earnest.

With a tearful goodbye, Andrew left by flight back to London Tuesday evening. He left with promises that he'd do everything he could to make the British Home Office work quickly through the master list. And in his luggage were hundreds of photos and details of children who were on his priority list—some files they'd created from the families they'd met and others provided by various organizations.

The week after Andrew left, things progressed quickly. One morning Amity arrived at work to find a young woman who claimed to be a representative of the Swedish Red Cross. With a wide smile and eager exuberance, Märta said she had the authority to arrange the transport of twenty children to Sweden. It didn't take long for Amity to join in Märta's excitement.

With Emil by her side, Amity consulted the master list. "Please, Emil, tell me that woman in the front foyer is real. Please tell me that some of our children will really be getting out."

Emil did one better, wrapping his arms around her in a large hug. "Yes, Amity." He lifted her off the ground and twirled her in a slow circle. "It *is* happening. You did it. Just think, instead of living in refugee camps, twenty children will soon find themselves sleeping in real beds and waking up to the faces of their new parents."

At the mention of new parents, Amity's heart stung. For the first time she understood even more what these mothers faced. Not only would they have to worry about their children being taken care of in loving ways, they also were heartbroken at being replaced. Having a child's love seemed like the greatest gift, and now that would be shared with another. Amity's lower lip trembled. Her great success meant that others would be facing their greatest pain by sending their children away into the arms of another.

With both joy and a touch of sadness, Amity consulted her master list and contacted the various agencies, telling them to have their children ready for transport by the following Monday, January 16. Some agency workers were thrilled like she was, but she didn't receive the same response from all.

"I have heard of this Red Cross worker," one man explained with annoyance in his voice. "I have it on good authority that Märta can't be trusted."

Amity held the phone receiver tighter to her ear and turned her back to Emil. "What do you mean?"

"I mean she's working for the Germans. Maybe they think that you are a fool to believe her, but we are not."

Anger rose with Amity, and her heart pounded a steady, heavy beat within her hollow chest. Sensing something was wrong, Emil placed a hand on her shoulder, and his fingers felt as cold as ice. Not able to explain to him now—or hold back her anger—Amity quickly brushed off his hand and tried to control her voice as she spoke into the phone. "I'm not sure *if* Märta is working for the Germans or not. I'm not sure *why* she'd be undercover for them, rescuing children. But from what I can tell from the information I've been given, a transport *is* going to happen. These children from the master list *have* been chosen, and they *do* have sponsors waiting for them. If you do not want your children included, I am willing to cross those children off and move down the list."

"Please, no." The man's tone softened. "If that is the case—if you say the transport will happen—our children will be there."

Not too many days later, the representative stood beside Amity's side at the airport. Together they watched as the transport left with twenty children. Märta joined them as they flew away. Joy flooded Amity's heart, knowing those children were safe. For the time being they were far from Hitler's grasp. As the airplane disappeared into the gray and blue horizon, Amity said a prayer over each one.

"Still, it was only twenty," she complained later when she arrived back at the office to check on Emil and the others.

With a frown he grabbed her shoulders. "*Only* twenty? Do you hear yourself, Amity? Because of your hard work, twenty children now have the chance at life. They have a chance that they wouldn't have had if you hadn't come."

They stood there for a minute, face-to-face, and she allowed the joy of his smile to seep into her heart. Emil was right. With God watching over them, hopefully those children would grow into men and women who would have children of their own.

You are rescuing generations, God spoke in the quiet of her heart.

Please help me save more, she pleaded. Deep down, she knew the hard work had just begun.

In addition to organizing the master list, Amity also worked with Emil, Madeline, and Marek in their continued effort of interviewing families and preparing children's files.

The days flew by, and as the second date that Amity had given Clark for her return neared, she knew she could not return to London as promised. Although she missed Clark and Celia, and wondered how things were in London, she knew she had to stay. The work was too much for Madeline, even with Marek's and Emil's help. Also, Amity was the person the other agency organizers now trusted. She couldn't risk everything falling apart if she left.

Amity knew she had to write yet another letter to Clark and Celia. But before that, she decided to pay a visit to Mr. Gibson, the passport control officer for the British legation. She wore her best suit and joined him for tea. Yet instead of asking her about the work she was doing—or even about the recent transport—Mr.

Gibson chatted on about all the historic sites that might be of interest during her stay. He also carried on about his longing to see friends and family back in England. The whole time he prattled on, Amity wanted to interrupt their talk.

Don't you realize how many children are in need just beyond the city gates? Let's hurry and get down to business, she wanted to say.

When they did finally come around to the worries about refugees, Mr. Gibson was all too happy to keep the responsibility heavy on her shoulders.

"I am glad you are getting some headway with a master list," he declared, pushing his spectacles farther up on the bridge of his nose. "We are thankful to have you working so hard for this cause, Miss Mitchell. I am not certain what we would have done had you not come."

Amity left the meeting disappointed, but it was just another confirmation that she was doing the right thing by staying longer. At least the agencies were working together now. It was a step in the right direction. And thankfully her new friends at the British legation trusted her opinion. Even if they weren't willing to go into the streets and do the hard work themselves, they were now willing to follow her recommendations for the transports. And deep down she understood. The government officials had enough worries about what Hitler was up to next. The fears had increased within Prague. Every person seemed to be walking on pins and needles, waiting for Hitler's next move.

Just two days prior, Czech foreign minister František Chvalkovský had traveled to Berlin to see Adolf Hitler, who made a series of harsh demands. It was all the radio spoke of. All the people could talk about.

Czechoslovakia was ordered to quit the League of Nations and drastically reduce the size of its military. Hitler was also twisting their arm, instructing them to pass German foreign policy and anti-Semitic legislation within their borders. This was not good news for the Jewish families trapped in the refugee camps. Now was no time to leave her work half done. That would only mean hardship and possible death for those unable to escape the borders.

By the time she got back to her hotel room and sat at the desk, Amity's feet ached. Kicking off her shoes, and taking a deep breath, she sat down to write the words she knew her employer didn't want to hear.

23 January 1939

Dear Clark,

I've been in Czechoslovakia for only a little over a month, but it seems as if I can't remember a world beyond the troubles here in Prague. I'm staying near Wenceslas Square, and if I had stayed in this touristy part of town the whole time and avoided the newspapers, I never would have known there is so much heartache in this land. Here, people are still shopping and going to cafés. They have afternoon tea and attend the opera. It's only when I head to my office or travel outside the city and meet the refugees that I understand the real struggle. I hear the heartbreaking stories of Jewish refugees and want to shout them to the world.

Why aren't people in the free world doing more? When will they stir from their comfortable lives and try to make a difference? Can't each person at least help one, sponsor one child? Is that too much to ask? Thankfully, Britain and France have stepped forward and put up extra money for immigration, but what good is it if we have no families to open their homes?

As you can tell, I am passionate about doing more in

the face of this tragedy. These families never wished such loss and heartache for their lives. They are being targeted for reasons that don't make sense. Why should one race be killed by another in the name of racial purity? Why should children be orphaned and forced to face life alone without parents, without hope?

We have been working hard, and the first transport has left with twenty children. I helped to organize a master list for all the various relief organizations, and our hope is that things can work more quickly now—especially with Andrew's help in London, trying to get sponsors.

I am certain by now that you can guess where this letter is heading. Even though I asked for more time, I must ask for the same thing again. There is too much work here for me to return to London. There are too many lives at stake. I still desire to honor my contract for you, but I beg that you will allow me to stay a little longer. Children's lives are at risk. As a compassionate man, I know you understand.

Please tell Celia how much I love and miss her. I rather miss you too. You've always been just as much of a friend as well as an employer. To tell you the truth, I often have wished you were here so I could talk through some of these issues with you, seeking your advice. Please tell everyone in London that I miss them. I especially miss Mrs. McGovern's cooking. When I return, is it too much to ask for a whole chicken and mushroom pie all to myself?

But most of all, of course, I miss the peace of not hearing so many heart-wrenching stories. Sometimes the only way I can remind myself that this world is still a good place is to picture Celia in the conservatory, sitting before the fire with a good book. Oh yes, and to see you, Clark, by her side, looking on with love. Someday I will return to both of you there, but pray that before then God will use me to bring much good to this heartbreaking situation.

With all my love,

Amity

Amity finished the letter and sealed it in an envelope. She'd decided to give Clark no time frame of when she'd return. She did not want to give him a promise, only to have to again tell him she needed to extend her time.

It was hard to do, sending her plea for more time back to two people she cared about so much. How easy it would be to return to London. To spend her days in peace and relative luxury. To put the worries of others behind her. But she knew she couldn't live with herself if she made that choice. Sometimes one had to choose what was hard because it was also what was good.

She'd been thinking about another choice too. A choice she needed to talk to Madeline about. Amity rose and glanced around the luxurious hotel room, her toes squishing into the plush carpet. It was too much. Too extravagant. Especially in contrast with what others lived in around the city.

Andrew had paid for this hotel room through January, and he had given her the money for February too, promising to send more as needed. He assured her that he would pay for the room from his own funds as long as she stayed in Prague, but Amity felt guilty every time she walked into it. Why should she live in such luxury when most of the people she worked with went to bed hungry at night?

She would talk to Madeline. Her friend must know of a small room she could rent not too far from their office. Surely the cost of a few nights in the hotel could cover a simple, rented room for a full month. And then Amity could use the extra money to help pay for the children's needs.

That's what mattered most—the children. Twenty were saved, but hundreds, no thousands, still needed help to escape these borders. They were worth fighting for—her heart told her that every day. And as she looked at each one, she felt a growing love she couldn't explain. Her hope was that the Germans would be kept at bay. And her prayer was that she would be able to get many more children out of this country before it was too late.

— EIGHTEEN —

Prague, Czechoslovakia
Monday, January 23, 1939

When Amity arrived at the office later that day, Madeline was sitting down with a mother and her two daughters, who looked to be about ten and eleven years old. The woman had a round face and rosy cheeks, yet her wide eyes were full of sadness.

Instead of interrupting, Amity sat down. Emil joined them, translating the woman's story.

"She said her husband is in a concentration camp." Emil spoke low near Amity's ear. "She has tried everything to have him released, but it hasn't done any good."

The woman's chin quivered as she spoke. Even though Amity could not understand the woman's words, the emotion was clear.

"The Jewish committee has advised her to send her two daughters to England," Emil explained. "She is heartbroken because they are all she has left. She says that she cannot imagine life without them, but she feels she has no choice."

"That is a hard decision to fall on her shoulders alone, isn't it?"

The mother's face was desperate, and she gripped her daughters' arms as if fearful that at any moment someone would come and take them away.

"She wants to know what else she can do," Emil continued with emotion catching in his own voice. "She says that if they get on a transport, at least they will be safe, even if her husband is not."

The woman released a shuddering sigh. Her hands covered her face and the sobs came. She continued talking, and her daughters cried along with her. Seeing the way the girls clung to their mother, Amity's heart ached. How many similar stories had she heard? Dozens.

Emil wiped his eyes. "The woman says she wouldn't mind if she knew this was a temporary situation. But how does she know? She says part of her knows deep down that she will never see them again, but she still begs Madeline to put them on the list."

As she watched, Madeline did put down both girls' names, but Amity knew there had to be at least five or six hundred children ahead of them. Would they ever get that far on the list? Would they even be able to get any more of the children out? Things were moving too slowly. There were not enough sponsors or funds for even fifty children. Andrew said he would work on it, but still, how much could one man do?

Finally, when all the paperwork was complete, the woman rose to leave. Emil stood and offered to buy the woman and her daughters some lunch. As if on cue, Madeline took a few bills out of her shirt pocket and pressed them into his hand, enough to cover their lunch and a meal for Emil too.

Before he left, Andrew had given Madeline money to help people in such a way, but she guessed that Madeline was also including some of her own funds.

"Make sure they have some red meat and vegetables," Madeline commented to Emil in English. "Their skin looks awfully pale."

"Yes, I will do that." Emil opened the door, obviously telling the trio of the local restaurant he would take them to because happy expressions filled their faces.

The older of the two girls reminded Amity of Celia. Maybe it was the long, straight black hair. If only Celia could see these young women. She'd want to help too.

Suddenly a chill carried down Amity's spine. Excitement stirred in the pit of her stomach, and she knew what she had to do. Even though she'd just finished a letter to Clark and posted it, she needed to write another. She had no doubt that once Celia heard of the condition of these children, she would do all that she could to help their cause.

If Clark was stubborn and determined, Celia was more so, and Amity knew the most important part about dealing with a strong-willed person was to turn them in the right direction. After that, they easily picked up the reigns and joined a cause they felt passionate about, no matter how difficult.

Excitement grew within Amity over the idea of Celia helping to find sponsors for the children. She was young, passionate, and not easily swayed. Amity couldn't think of a better choice to assist Andrew's efforts. She would write a letter when she finished her work tonight. But first, Amity had to talk to Madeline.

Even though the mother and daughters had left with Emil fifteen minutes prior, Madeline still sat in the same position. She was reading over their paperwork again before filing it away. If anyone knew the importance of making sure every box was filled in correctly it was her. But today Madeline looked defeated, drained. All the work and so little movement seemed to be impacting all of them.

Amity sat beside the woman. She took her hand between hers and squeezed. "It's hard, isn't it, day in and day out?"

"Yes, it is hard, but at least they are here. I cannot help but think of all those families who were stuck in Germany or the Sudetenland. What must they be going through? Do they have any hope at all?" Madeline closed the file and turned to Amity. "Before you came in, the mother was telling me that her sister and two sons decided to stay in Germany. They were being hidden away in the basement at the home of a former employer. Another cousin was forced to leave her home because a German family wanted to occupy it. The worst part is that trying to save her daughters, she had to leave behind her widowed mother with some friends. Can you imagine having to make that decision?"

"No. If only there was more we can do. And you have done so much, Madeline. You have given so much." Amity focused on the woman's eyes, hoping to instill courage. "With Andrew in London, I'm praying things can move more quickly, but we will always need more resources. And that's what I wanted to talk to you about. Andrew has me staying in the Hotel Evropa, but it really is too much. I was considering how much money could be saved if I found accommodations elsewhere."

"Like another hotel?"

"Actually, I was thinking of an apartment—or a room I could rent. If you know someone you trust, I would love to be considered. I only need a bed and an indoor toilet."

A smile flashed on Madeline's face.

"What? What do you find so funny."

"Oh, it's just that I've only had an indoor toilet for the last five years, and our weekend house outside the city still has an outdoor loo—isn't that what the British call it? I was just trying to picture you out on our property using the toilet outside at night. I know I shouldn't find it funny, but I do."

Amity returned the smile, happy to again see a brightness to the woman's face. "Yes, that would be quite a comedy, I have to say so myself." She brushed her auburn hair back from her shoulder and raised the pitch of her voice. "An indoor toilet, please. I will not do with any less."

Madeline chuckled along with her and then paused with a new brightness to her eyes. She pressed her lips together as if she were holding in a secret.

"What? What is it?" Amity pleaded.

"Well, I happen to have an extra room in my apartment. Two rooms, in fact. Both of my daughters are married, but I have not had it in me to sell our family home. There have been many times I've considered offering to bring one of these families home, but something inside has kept me from offering. Now I know why. The space was meant for you."

Madeline suggested a price for rent and some meals, and Amity couldn't have been more pleased. "Can I move in the first of February?"

"Yes, of course. And then I can keep a good eye on you." Madeline patted her hand. "I still worry you're not taking care of yourself as you should."

— NINETEEN —

London, England
Thursday, February 2, 1939

Clark shuffled his newspaper and lowered it, picking up his cup of coffee. Beside him Celia was sitting at the breakfast table, but she'd pushed all the food to the side, refusing to eat.

Celia's face was pale, anxious. "I don't understand how you let Amity stay in Czechoslovakia. Have you read the news?"

Clark lifted an eyebrow and narrowed his gaze at his daughter. What had he done except read the news of late? Heaven knew he had gotten little writing done. But at least, after visiting Antonín, he had a story idea and was writing a couple of pages a day. It wasn't close to the pace he'd kept before Gwen's sickness, but at least it was something. It felt good to be writing again, creating again.

The mounting conflict between Germany and Czechoslovakia was enough of a distraction, but the ache was more intense because the house felt so empty without a woman's presence. It had been three years since Gwen's death, and now Amity was gone. He didn't know why he'd let her go either.

When Amity's letter had arrived for him a few days prior, he'd been sitting on a settee in the conservatory, attempting to read a novel, but he hadn't gone through more than three pages. And even though he'd been sitting there for an hour with book in hand, he had no idea what the story was even about.

As soon as Mrs. McGovern had arrived with the mail and he had seen the envelope with Amity's handwriting, he'd guessed the reason for the note. He hadn't been surprised that she'd wanted to extend her stay. What he hadn't expected was how thoroughly Amity had turned her back on her old life with him and Celia.

He took a sip from his coffee and then turned to his daughter. "I've read the news. The world is in a sorry state, and I'm not sure how we'll be able to stay out of a war. I also am just as upset as you are that Amity is in such a dangerous place. But weren't you the one who first said that traveling to Prague would be an adventure?"

"It was just a bit of a joke." Celia took a bite of toast and then dropped it back on her plate. She added a generous portion of marmalade to it and then took another bite, pleased this time.

"I thought for certain that she wouldn't go." Celia sighed. "I did like the idea of her going to help Jewish refugees, but now..." She opened her arms wide. "The house is just so empty without her."

"There are still the two of us, plus Mrs. McGovern, the maids, cooks..." His daughter was right. The place seemed empty without Amity's light and presence.

Celia placed her cloth napkin by her place setting, rose from the chair, and then stamped her foot. It was just a slight stamp, not like when she was three, but Clark clearly saw the child still within her lanky form. "You should have insisted she stayed. Or insist now that she return. All you have to do is tell her you changed your mind. In fact, you can still do that. Send a telegram and tell Amity that you need her back immediately."

"She's my employee, not my daughter. I can't control where she goes or what she does."

"You could have told her that if she went, she'd be out of a job, instead of offering her a contract for another two years."

"Is that really what you want?" He placed his fork and knife on the plate, removed his napkin from his lap, rose, and walked toward the wood burner. There was a slight chill in his bones, but for some reason he had a feeling it wasn't because of the temperature of the room but rather the ache in his heart. "You saw the determination in Amity's eyes once she was packed. Although I'm certain she was worried about leaving us, she was also excited about helping. If I had insisted that she shouldn't go, I'd be placing an advertisement for a new tutor this very day."

Celia crossed her arms over her chest and moved to the window. "Yes, well, can someone stop Hitler's madness? Then maybe Amity will return home. Parliament should be ashamed, conceding to Hitler's demands in the first place."

"So many emotions and worries inside you these days." Clark sighed. "Ever more like your mother by the day. Did I tell you the first time I spotted her twenty years ago? She had drawn the attention of every person at a cocktail party, declaring that it wasn't right that Austria expelled all Habsburgs from setting foot in the country they used to rule. Since it was happening in Austria, most people from Britain didn't waste their time or energy worrying about ousted foreign leaders. After all, we were just happy there was some sense of peace after the Great War. But to your mother it mattered. After all, can you imagine that happening in Great Britain? Can you picture Parliament kicking out King George VI and Lady Mary, and stating they could never set foot in in the United Kingdom again? Your mother thought that appalling."

Mrs. McGovern entered to check on their breakfast. Even

though her lips were pressed into a thin line, the bright cockiness of the older woman's eyes told Clark she no doubt overheard their conversation and had her own opinion, but Clark wasn't in the mood to hear what it was.

"Mrs. McGovern." Celia turned from the window. "I spoke with Father earlier, and we've decided to ask you to limit our desserts, except for Sundays. It really isn't necessary in times like these."

The old woman's eyebrows rose in surprise. "Yes, that is fine... if you are sure. But maybe we should start after tonight. I already had Cook start on a Bakewell tart."

Celia sighed, as if annoyed, but Clark could see from his daughter's eyes that she was reconsidering their optional rationing. "If Cook already started on her bake, I don't want those ingredients to go to waste."

"Yes, that is a wise choice. We wouldn't want anything to go to waste, miss," Mrs. McGovern stated, exiting with some of the dirty plates in her hands.

Clark smiled to himself, wondering what other notions Celia would come up with. She had begun limiting her indulgences as of late, stating that every man, woman, and child in London would be asked to start rationing soon. His daughter realized, just as he did, that war was looming. And he knew that Celia was unable to stand by without taking action—like her mother—and that she would find a way to do more. He just hoped she wouldn't get the notion to start rationing some of his indulgences, like coffee or cream for his afternoon tea.

Celia returned to her seat, sitting down hard, as if all the worries were too much to walk around with. "I don't understand how Neville Chamberlain can be so weak. Hitler isn't bound to stop anytime soon, and Amity..." She folded her hands on her lap and lowered her gaze. "It's a dangerous place she's gone to. There will be many people in need. She'll never return."

Clark folded his newspaper, deciding he didn't want to read another word. His worries were as heavy on his heart as Celia's were on hers, but he didn't let them show. "Even Amity has her limits. She won't be able to rescue everyone. Although I'm with you—I bet she'll try until she gets kicked out."

"I would feel better if she just came home."

"Things are different, aren't they, when someone we love is impacted? And I believe that's why the British Parliament has done what it's done," Clark tried to explain. "They gave Hitler what he wants, knowing it may bring harm to others in a distant land, yet also hoping it will protect those close, who they love."

"Do you believe it will work? Do you believe annexing the Sudetenland will keep Hitler appeased even for a year's time?"

"I shouldn't be discussing such things with a teenage girl."

"Humph. I know the answer then."

Clark was just about to excuse himself from breakfast, and this conversation, when Mrs. McGovern returned with an envelope in hand.

Clark waved her back the direction she'd come. "Go ahead and leave the mail in my office, Mrs. McGovern. I will be there shortly."

"Oh, yes, sir. I have already placed all your mail on the desk, sir. But this letter is for Miss Celia—from Miss Amity, sir."

Clark straightened in his seat, and before he could respond, Celia jumped to her feet.

"Oh, a letter for me! Dad, did you hear that?" She snatched the letter from Mrs. McGovern and quickly ripped open the envelope. Out of it fell a letter and two small photos. They were photos of children.

Celia picked up the photos of the children first. "Who are

these?" She held them closer so Clark could get a better look. One photo was of two young boys. They looked to be about two and three years old. Both had dark, short hair and chubby cheeks. They wore thick sweaters, and a star—labeling them as Jews—was sewn onto each. Neither boy smiled, and the older boy wrapped a protective arm around his younger brother. Seeing them, Celia placed a hand over her mouth in shock. And then she turned to her father. "Are these some of the children Amity is helping? Look at them. They are so young, yet so handsome too."

She looked to the next photo. It was of a young girl about five years old with large brown eyes. Bangs framed her face, and someone had curled her dark hair in ringlets that fell to her shoulders. She wore a white dress, and if it wasn't for the plain, gray metal desk behind her, Clark would have guessed she was dressing for a party.

With shaking hands, Celia opened the letter and began to read aloud to Clark.

27 January 1939

Dear Celia,

I know I've written your father a few times, and I'm sorry that it's taken me so long to write a note to you. There is so much I've been wanting to tell you—so much that I have been certain my heart would burst if I even tried. Well, here I go. For once your tutor is at a loss how to explain everything well!

First, you may be wondering about the two photos. These are some of the children I am trying to help. The good news is that we were able to secure places for a transport of twenty children to be taken to Sweden. The bad news is that there are hundreds more waiting, wanting to escape.

The two boys in the photo are Jakub and Josef. They are brothers, and their father and mother were both killed in Austria. Their aunt was able to bring them to the refugee center, and she is hoping someone in England will sponsor them. They are sweet boys. Josef cuddled on my lap for an hour while I helped to fill out their paperwork. These were not on the first transport of children, but we hope to get them on the next one.

The little girl's name is Ruth. Her mother thought that putting on her best dress and curling her hair might help a family choose to sponsor her. Andrew is trying to find sponsors for these children, but it is challenging. Many Londoners have given to support the Sudetenland refugees already. Some do not have the fifty pounds for the sponsorship. Foster families also must be willing to cover the child's expenses up until the age of eighteen. It's a lot to ask.

But I also know there are most likely a lot more families who would be willing to help if they just knew of the need. And that's why I am writing, Celia. I'd like to ask for your help. I already called Andrew, and he said he'll take all the help he can get. He's in London with hundreds of files with photos of children just like these who need sponsorships. Andrew said he would be willing to bring you some of the files. Would you be willing—with your father's help—to talk to people and find more sponsors? Maybe with your father's connections you can talk to someone at the newspaper. Surely there is a way to help...

Celia's voice trailed off, and Clark knew emotion choked his daughter's throat, making it hard to go on. Tears stung his own eyes as he looked at the sweet faces of the children. *Someone's little ones.*

When Celia finally lifted her eye to meet Clark's gaze, tears filled them. "Oh, Dad, do you think I can help? Amity goes on to include more information about the requirements for the families. Do you like the idea of me helping to find sponsors? Surely that is something I can do."

She placed the photos of the children right in front of him. "Look at them...just look at them. We know a lot of people. Maybe we can find help. Once we get the files, can you help me?"

Clark considered the novel he was supposed to be writing. He knew he didn't have time to add this to his life, but how could he not help, especially when Amity sent photos?

"Yes. Of course. We'll see what we can do. I like Amity's idea of talking to someone from the newspaper. Think of what you'd like to tell them. Write something up, and have Andrew check it when he comes. Then I can pass it on."

"Me?" Her voice raised an octave. "You want me to write something?"

"Yes, I do. Amity wrote to you and asked for help, didn't she?" He chuckled. "It looks like she's given you an assignment from afar. Once a tutor always a tutor."

Celia's smiled at the realization, and then her face sobered. "Yes, but this is not like any other assignment. It's not just about a grade, is it? These are lives at stake."

Clark rose. "Yes, and that's why I also have more work to do to help her. There are a few ways that I've been thinking I could help. I've been putting it off, making excuses, but I think Amity's point has been made. We don't have any more time for excuses, do we? These children are depending on us to put aside our comfort. What will happen to the little ones if we don't?"

— TWENTY —

Prague, Czechoslovakia
Friday, February 10, 1939

Cries of weary children seeped through the thin walls of the office, and Amity was glad Emil insisted she take a break from the interviews for the day. The many people and their stories weighed on her, burdened her.

Like a tightrope walker who had forgotten how to position one foot in front of the other, Amity stared at the scarred wooden desk before her. Then she rose and turned from the desk, looking out the window into the vista of buildings and flats in the distance. The door behind her opened and closed. Too weary to turn, she waited for the visitor to speak.

"Come, you need some time to get out. There is a large city out there, filled with streets and squares, and some quarters older than the bloodline of the queen herself." The voice was a familiar one, but strange in this place. A warm voice. Kind. An English voice.

Amity turned with a start, and she placed a hand over her heart as she saw Clark Cartwright standing there.

"What are you doing here? I don't understand. How is Celia? Did she come?"

"I've come on business. Andrew helped me track you down."

He clicked his tongue. "You do look weary, Amity, but as wonderful as ever."

Fresh tears rose to her eyes at seeing him. She hadn't realized just how much she'd been missing him until this moment. Then, once she saw his smile broaden at the sight of her, she was surprised she'd been able to leave him at all. "You came on business?" She pulled in a deep, shaking breath and felt her body quiver. She hoped he didn't notice.

"Your holiday is turning out to be longer than expected." Clark crossed his arms and leaned against the wall closest to her desk. "Celia misses you. She was worried. She insisted I come to check on you. That's my business here, checking on our tutor. I have to say, Celia's also been busy this past week. You've given her quite a task, but I'll admit it's one she's well suited for."

Clark's white shirt was open at his neck, and he seemed more relaxed both in manner and dress than when they were back in London. Though his smile was wide, Amity noticed weariness on his face, and for the first time she spotted a bit of gray at his temples. His eyes sparkled as he looked at her. "The truth? I had to see how you're coming along. It's a brave fight you've taken on, Amity. A noble cause." His voice possessed a conviction Amity hadn't heard before.

Amity wanted to go to him and be pulled into an embrace. She wanted him to hold her close enough that she could take a whiff of Mrs. McGovern's laundry soap and breathe in the aroma of his familiar shaving lotion. She wanted to feel the warmth of him and his strong arms around her. Heat rose to her cheeks thinking of that.

She had worked for Clark for two years, and although she'd always found him to be attractive, Amity had never felt her heart pound so heavily in his presence. He looked like safety and strength—two things she longed for right now. She again held herself back from running into his arms. Clark, too, took a step as if wanting to move toward her, and then he paused.

"Is your daughter the only one who missed me?" They were the only words she could think of.

Clark tucked his hands into the pockets of the thick traveling jacket he still wore. Then he moved to the chair across the desk from her and sat. "No, Mrs. McGovern asks of you too." A grin spread across his face. "And I have to admit—"

The squeaky hinge of a door opening behind Clark interrupted his words. Like a puppy eager to find his master, Emil entered with quickened steps. He strode past Clark as if he weren't even there and moved straight to Amity.

"Amity, it is working! I just received a call from Andrew. We can start making plans for our first transport. We have enough sponsors now. I have a list of the children who will be included."

Amity's already pounding heart jumped and danced in her chest. She stood to her feet. Her hands clapped together, and she let out a little squeal. "Is that really so? We have enough sponsors for a transport?"

Without hesitation, Emil swept Amity into an embrace, lifting her off the ground. His arms were strong around her, but even within his embrace Amity longed for the arms of another. With another whoop of excitement, Emil lowered her to the ground.

She giggled, stepped from Emil's embraced, and snagged the list from his hand, turning to Clark. "This is what we've waited for. Our first transport! Just think, all these children will soon be safe."

Clark smiled, but she could see he felt unnerved by Emil's presence. And although her mind spun with details it would take for their first transport, Amity's heart fell as the joy disappeared from Clark's gaze.

She pressed the list to her chest. "Emil, can you please look up all the contact information for these refugee families? Tell them we will be working on a transport date, but have them start packing and preparing. Oh, I can't imagine what joyful yet painful news that will be."

Emil nodded. He looked at Clark from the corner of his eye as if he were a fly that needed to be swatted. "I will have to deliver some of the news in person. And I will send the information to the other agencies too. Would you like to come with me and help? I think you, of all people, should be there to share this news. It has been because of your hard work."

Amity looked from the list to Clark again. Of course she could ask him to come. Of course she would love to be there when the families were told of the news, but more than that she wanted to sit across from Clark and catch up. There would be plenty of work to do tomorrow and the day after that.

Amity looked up into Emil's face. "Any other day I would have loved to join you, but please ask Marek to help today." She pointed to the back room where Marek was sorting files. "I have a dear friend who has just arrived in town. I thought he might like some lunch."

Amity swept her hand to Clark. Emil paused, turned in his direction, and really looked at him. Emil's eyes widened as if seeing the man in the traveling suit for the first time.

"I am sorry. I have not used any manners." Emil extended his hand. "I am Emil."

Clark stood and shook Emil's hand. "And I am Clark. Clark Cartwright. I have come to Prague to check on a dear friend of mine." He gave an uneasy chuckle. "And I can tell from the look of things she's become a dear friend to you too."

Emil smiled and puffed out his chest. "Yes, I would say that.

She is a good friend indeed. She's a friend to many. We wouldn't be where we were, concerning Jewish refugees, without her."

Amity didn't like the way the two men looked at each other. It was almost as if they were two cocks, sizing up their competition. Frustration caused the hair on the back of her neck to stand up. Enough was enough. She wanted to really talk to Clark, to catch up, and she wasn't going to allow Emil to ruin their reunion.

Amity moved to retrieve her coat from the hook on the wall and then warmed herself by the wood-burning stove. "Please let me know how everything goes, Emil. I am certain the mothers will give a sigh of relief to know their children will soon be sent to safety. You shouldn't delay, though. There are many agencies to contact and people to visit."

Emil's smile faded, and if Amity wasn't mistaken, there was even a hint of jealousy in her Czech friend's gaze. "Yes, of course. I do understand." He offered a quick bow. "I will get Marek, and we will do all we can to start informing the families. I will let them know that if they have any questions, you will be available soon. Available tomorrow, yes?"

"Yes, tomorrow. That will work." She slid on her coat, started to button it, and then paused. "But, Emil, I am thrilled that all *our* hard work has paid off. It hasn't been easy getting here, has it?"

"That is the truth." Emil forced a smile. "But when we receive word that the children are safe in London, it will be worth it all." Then with one last sideways glance at Clark, he moved into the back room where Marek was working.

Oh, I hope Emil doesn't carry on like this too long. With a sigh, she wrapped her scarf around her head and then put on her gloves, preparing for the bitterly cold air outside. If she and Clark had been back in London, Godfry could have driven them anywhere in the city. But since they were here, and she knew where she wanted to take Clark, Amity hoped he was prepared for a good walk.

Thankful that they would now have time to catch up, Amity approached Clark and placed a hand on his arm. "I hope you haven't eaten yet. I know of a wonderful place we can get lunch. Oh, I still can't believe you're here, and I have to know how Celia's doing. I was excited to hear from Andrew that they'd already made a connection and that she was helping immensely."

"She has a fire under her, that is for certain. But truth be told, the more she worked on finding sponsors, the more I knew I couldn't stay there. I had to come here and do my part. Celia gave me her blessing to come." Clark opened the door. "She wants me to help you on this end...and to find her a baby brother."

"A baby brother?" Laugher spilled from Amity's lips. "Is she serious?"

Clark nodded. "She is, but I am not...not yet, anyway. I told her that every boy and girl needs a mother. And until our home has one of those we'll just do our best—"

Clark's words were interrupted as Emil strode through the office. Clark jumped back to let Emil pass. Without a word or a look in their direction, Emil exited, slamming the office door as he exited.

Amity's head whipped around, surprised. Her mouth dropped open. "I wonder what that is about?"

Clark chuckled. "My guess is Emil fears competition."

"Competition? Whatever do you mean?" she asked, even though Amity could guess.

"Competition for your heart, Amity. Because truth be told, I've come to roll up my sleeves and do something about that too."

— TWENTY-ONE —

Amity took Clark to Old Town Square for lunch, and even the walk was delightful due to unexpected sunshine. In her favorite café, she requested a window table with a view of the astronomical clock. She smiled as she sat, and Amity was sure that her feet hadn't touched the ground the whole ten blocks it had taken them to get there. She and Clark had walked side by side with her arm linked in his. Had Clark really said he'd come all this way not only to help but also to try to win her heart? Her heartbeat quickened into a fast flutter to think of him leaving his home, his work, his daughter, and everything else in London to come to her—to be with her.

They both chose the lunch special, thick goulash and dark rye bread, but for the first time Amity couldn't finish her meal. Her stomach was a ball of nerves.

Equally confusing was Emil's reaction to Clark's appearance. Why had he been so upset? Was it because after all their hard work, she had not gone with him to tell the families of the upcoming transports? Yes, she imagined that could be enough to fluster him. After all, he'd been volunteering his efforts for months—they both had. They'd both given so much in working toward a transport together.

But then again, could it be something more, as Clark suggested? She thought about all the quick hugs Emil had given her. She considered how easily he shared his joys and concerns. Did Emil think of her as more than a friend—had that possibility been on his mind? If she were honest, she believed that he did.

Yet as much as she enjoyed spending time with Emil—and appreciated all his help—it was Clark's voice that had caused her heart to dance. Sitting across from her now, it was his presence that made everything feel right with the world, even though she knew it wasn't. Knowing that he'd be here tomorrow caused a knot of excitement to grow in her stomach, and an ache of expectation quivered inside her.

As they ate their simple lunch, Clark filled her in on all that had been happening at home.

"Celia has been making appointments to sit down with everyone we know. Godfry has been driving her, and Mrs. McGovern has assigned Bonnie to be her chaperone." He chuckled. "Bonnie thinks she's pinched herself and gone to heaven. She told me she feels guilty since all she has to do is visit with fine folks at fancy homes and enjoy afternoon tea. She almost didn't let me pay her because she hasn't been cleaning or serving."

Amity laughed, picturing that conversation perfectly. "Oh, I can imagine. And what does Mrs. McGovern have to say about that?"

"Well, she told Bonnie not to get too comfortable on that high horse, lest she fall all the way back to chambermaid."

Amity gasped. "Mrs. McGovern wouldn't!"

She couldn't remember the last time she'd laughed in such

a way. It was as if a few hours in Clark's presence had eased two months of worries she had been carrying around her heart.

After they discussed more about what had been happening around the house, Amity turned her attention back to her work in Prague.

"Clark, I was wondering...when you return to London, could you help me with something? Andrew says they have started up a new department called the Movement, which will help the transports happen faster. Do you think you could stop in to meet the people in that department, share your experiences here, and urge them to issue permits more quickly? You do have a sort of fame in London that might help our cause. Then there are the travel arrangements that must be made on that side—"

"Ami, please...you are talking so fast." He shook his head. "I beg you to slow down and allow me to take notes. I will try to do my best for you—of course I will—but I hope you don't think so highly of me that I fall off *my* high horse."

"I know there is a lot to take in, and I wouldn't bother you so if there weren't such urgent cases."

He reached across the table and took her hand in his, stroking the back of her hand with his thumb. "I'll do what I can *when* I go back. But..."

A quick glance to the side and hint of a smile, he gripped her hand firmer, clueing her in to the weight of the words to come. "But I will return only when I know I've won the lady. Not a minute before." He chuckled low. "Well, unless Hitler kicks us both out."

The sensation of his grip, mixed with the intensity of his words, caused tingles to move from her hand up her arm. She couldn't help but smile, and heat rose to her cheeks. She waved her free hand in front of her face, hoping she hadn't already turned three different shades of pink.

"Well, I will say that puts me in a dilemma, now doesn't it, Mr. Cartwright? Should I really tell you how your presence is impacting me—give you a hint of the pounding of my heart?" She tapped her chin with her pointer finger, as if trying to make a decision. "Or should I act as if it has no effect on me whatsoever so you'll try harder and stay longer?"

He smiled. "You're clever, aren't you? But just so you know, I already told Celia I'm staying for the month. So, my dear Miss Mitchell, don't feel as if declaring your love to me will send me away on the next train."

"Ah." Amity's heart leaped at his words. He was staying. Clark was really staying. Tears rimmed her lower lashes, but she quickly wiped them away. Then, taking a deep breath, Amity offered him a coy smile, tilting her head to the side. "That's good to know. I am glad you're staying." She sighed. "Relieved, really. As I tell all those who work with me at the office, we need to be caring but honest. People need to know where they stand so they know how to plan." She stirred her teaspoon in her tea cup. Her heart ached thinking of all those poor souls, the joy of the moment faded slightly. "Of course, for those who come to us, *we* are their plan, England their last hope."

Sadness filled Clark's face, and he released her hand. Amity hadn't meant to darken their mood with her words, but she did.

"Will they return?" He looked out of the café window toward the sidewalk. A mother with blonde hair and a light complexion walked by, pushing a pram. A mother and child who were safe and had no worries about Hitler attempting to snuff out her child for the sake of racial purity. "When we get them to England, will these children ever come back here? Will they ever get to know their country?"

Amity looked out at the cobblestone roads, the medieval towers, the clock. There was so much here she'd grown to love. So much she'd miss when she left. So much these children might never learn about their home country once they were sent abroad. "Your guess is as good as mine."

"Maybe I should sponsor a child or two? Like Celia said, she does want a baby brother."

Weary laughter spill from Amity's lips. "Well, sir, you must gather personal references covering your character and your financial stability," she said in an official tone.

"I am an author, remember? There is nothing stable about my income, and as for my character…it depends on who you ask."

Amity smiled, wishing she could spend time like this with Clark every day. She missed talking with him. "Surely you have enough friends who know you not quite well enough who can write a reference letter."

He winked. "An acquaintance? Now that makes more sense. I'll see what I can do."

Amity put her spoon on the saucer. She folded her fingers together, placing them on her lap. Even though they'd been playful about why he'd come, she had to know the truth. "Clark?"

"Yes?"

"One more thing."

"What is it, Amity?" He pushed his bowl to the side and leaned his elbows on the table, his full attention on her.

"We've known each other for two years. I have grown to care for you, and sometimes I've hoped you felt the same. But why now? After all this time, why did you decide to come here now—to travel to Prague—and tell me how you feel?"

"There are two reasons, really," he said without hesitation. "First, with you gone, I've realized how much I really love having you there."

"And second?"

"Well, it's the way you ended the letter you wrote to me. For so long I worried that our age difference would be a problem. I hoped you could overlook it, but then I felt like a fool for expecting you to. Twelve years..." He let out a low whistle. Clark paused. His eyes reflected tenderness and respect. "Then you signed your letter 'All my love, Amity.' I dared to believe that was true and those weren't just words. Having just the smallest bit of faith that you truly cared for me brought me here."

Amity nodded. She placed a hand on her heart. "I can't tell you how much that means to me, and...I signed it that way because... well, yes, I do care. And I've never been too concerned about your age." She tilted her head slightly. "I even like that touch of gray I see."

His laughter filled the room. "Well, I suppose that's good to know."

"But..." She let her words trail off. Then finally she got the nerve to speak what she knew she had to say. "But while I'm here—while we're here—we need to focus on the children. I'm so thankful we had this time together, but things are going to get busy with this transport—and hopefully more transports will follow soon." Then her thoughts flipped from the relaxed lunch to the list of things scrolling through her mind that she had to do. "We should get back. I need to make a call to a Prague travel agency that I've been working with. Special trains will be needed for the transport. I just hope we will have enough money to cover everything, although if Andrew says we will, then I have to trust that everything will be taken care of."

Clark nodded and listened, allowing her to process what was to come in the upcoming week. As she continued to talk, he paid the waiter for their meal and helped her with her coat. As he led her back the way they'd come, Amity paused her talking long enough to send up a quick prayer of thankfulness for his presence.

The Nazis may rattle the gates of the city. The needs around her may be mounting, rather than lessening. But suddenly, with Clark by her side, Amity knew she would do her best to get more children to England. Some say that courage is something one carries within, but on this day—with the unexpected sunshine warming her shoulders—courage was someone who walked by her side.

TWENTY-TWO

Madeline was waiting when Clark and Amity returned to the office, and she insisted that Clark not stay in a hotel but in the third room of her apartment.

"I will be out tonight meeting friends, but there are some things for dinner on the kitchen counter. Feel free to make yourself at home."

"Thank you." He glanced over at Amity. "Celia will be thankful that I'm keeping an eye on you. She's been so worried." He stepped to the door. "Should we get a taxi?"

"A taxi?" She chuckled. "And not take the beautiful stroll? You won't want to miss this." Then she led him onto the chilly sidewalk. Those leaving work walked with purpose to their apartments. A mix of automobiles and wagons clogged the street. Amity swept her hand toward the medieval city, which seemed to sparkle with a million diamonds from the lights of buildings and monuments. The view never ceased to take her breath away.

Amity was eager to show Clark the apartment she'd been living in for just over a week. "I thought I was making a big sacrifice when Madeline offered me an extra room in her flat. The Hotel Evropa was beautiful, but truth be told, I'd rather stay at Madeline's any day."

They strolled together, taking in the sights through Old Town Square and through the narrow, winding lanes that led to the Vltava River. Tall buildings rose on either side of the road, ancient buildings of stone and brick. Antique doors, vine-covered walls, and narrow balconies reminded them that in some parts of the world, the past was still very much a part of the present.

The narrow lane opened up to a busy street where autos, buses, and the occasional wagon passed. A traffic officer waved them across, and they moved toward the medieval tower that led to the Charles Bridge. Clark slowed his steps as they walked onto the stone bridge. Statues of saints rose up as dark gray shadows and seemed to hover in the thick fog hovering over the water. The warm sun had slipped away hours ago and was now replaced by a misty rain as faint as dust.

Walking along the sidewalk, Amity paused ten yards onto the bridge so Clark could fully appreciate the views of the medieval Malá Strana district with its red tile roofs, the castle on the hill, and the spire of the Saint Vitus Cathedral just behind the castle roof.

"So," she said with a whispered breath. "There are many beautiful places in London, but nothing like this, is there? What do you think?"

He pulled a small notebook and pencil from his coat pocket and began to take notes. After a moment he glanced up and looked at her, as if remembering she was there. "Oh, what do I think? I think this would make the perfect spot for a murder."

Laughter spilled from Amity's lips, and she looked around at the other pedestrians passing by. "Good thing they most likely don't understand English. Otherwise someone might be calling the police."

He nodded, again lost in his thoughts, and moved to the edge of the bridge. The only thing stopping them from falling into the water below was a waist-high stone barrier. Clark leaned over, looking down at the dark, murky waters below.

"I imagine if someone weighed down a body and tossed it over the edge, it would never be seen again."

"Clark!" She playfully slugged this arm. "I'm horrified by your talk." She glanced at the water, following his gaze, and then to his bright face. "But I'm also excited because it seems as if your writing muse has been tickled. I suppose I shouldn't be surprised after reading your novels."

"You've read my novels?"

"Every one. At least three times."

"And you still agreed to live in my house, knowing how my mind works?"

She shrugged. "Well, the more sinister the villain, the more exciting when the mystery is solved, isn't that right?"

They continued on, and Clark kept his notebook out, taking notes as he walked. She could tell his mind was spinning, no doubt considering plot ideas. She'd never seen him like this, and she found this new side of Clark thrilling.

They crossed the bridge, passed over Kampa Island, walked up a few long city blocks, and then turned to the left, moving away from the business district to an area with nice apartments, established in one of the oldest parts of the city. Grassy parks with tall trees and a scattering of benches separated the buildings, giving the area a peaceful atmosphere. She imagined it must be a beautiful place to go for an evening stroll in the spring or summer. Would she still be around to discover if that was true?

Clark let out a low whistle as he looked around. "Madeline lives in this area?"

"Yes, I was surprised too. She told me this part of town was built in the sixteenth century. I can imagine the fair ladies and nobles walking the streets, can't you?"

"And knights jousting on the castle grounds. Wasn't Prague the imperial seat of the Holy Roman Empire then?"

"Very good, Mr. Cartwright. You get a high mark for your history."

They walked until they came upon a large baroque house that appeared to have been split into apartments. It was painted in soft green and cream in a highly ornate style. Heavy, dark wood made up the thick doors and framed the windows. Intricate cream and gold designs also framed the windows. They walked up five stone steps to the front door, and Amity pulled a heavy key from her pocket and opened the door to a front entrance hall. A spiral staircase led upward, and to the right an arched doorway led to a sitting and dining area and kitchen beyond.

"It's not a large place, but I love the beamed ceilings and the leading in the windows. I find it so comfortable here." Amity led him through the kitchen to the small room behind it. "Madeline and I have rooms upstairs. That's where the bathroom is too, with a tub. I assume this is the room she intended for you. It appears to have been a room for a cook or a maid, but at least it has a window."

There was a simple twin bed in the room and a stand with two drawers. "It looks fine. My suitcase is being held at the Hotel Evropa. I had made reservations for the night. Is it far?"

Laughter spilled from Amity's lips. "We should have stopped by first and brought the suitcase with us. It's on the other side of the city. We'd better call for a taxi after all." She moved to the kitchen and noticed the fresh bread on the counter and a few potatoes and onions next to it. "Ah, I have found Madeline's dinner plans."

Clark smiled when he followed her gaze and sighed. "Things are simpler around here, aren't they?"

"Yes, and I have to say I've enjoyed doing life without all the fuss—at least for a while. Give me a few minutes to fry up these potatoes and onions, and then we'll be off for your suitcase."

She made a simple meal, and they found a taxi to take them to the hotel and back. Night had completely fallen by the time they returned home. Madeline still hadn't come back yet, so they set the suitcase inside the doorway and then settled onto the cold steps outside, taking in a view of the twinkling lights of the city and the stars.

They sat side by side with their legs stretched out in front of them. The soft wind tossed her hair about her face, and Amity brushed it back.

Looking around, Clark took out his notebook and wrote a few notes.

"More ideas for your novel?" she whispered.

"Yes, and it's about time. This will be my first book set outside of London, and I believe this trip so far has been just the inspiration I needed."

"Good. Just as long as the heroine has auburn hair."

He glanced over at her and winked. "I wouldn't have it any other way."

"And a unique name. Something no one will forget."

"Like Amity?"

"Yes, that's unique, but you can't use it in your fiction, or all your readers would know she was based on me. I've yet to meet anyone else with the same name." Amity thought for a moment. "Hmm...maybe Anja?"

He nodded. "I think I like that very much." He made another note. "You know, when I first met your brother, I asked him about your name. He told me I'd have to ask you about it. He said something about being sworn to secrecy."

She raised her hand vertically, palm out, as if making a pledge. "Yes, I made him solemnly swear, because the story was embarrassing to me when I was a little girl."

"What do you mean?"

"Well, after I was born, my mother decided to name me Jane, after her mother. Just to be a jokester, my father called me Calamity Jane after the American frontierswoman and scout. Andrew was only four years old at the time, and he didn't pronounce his words very well. For the first few days he tried to call me Calamity Jane, but he ended up just calling me Amity, which means friendship. My mother liked that, and when it came time to be discharged from the hospital a week later, she put my name down as Amity Jane on the birth certificate."

Laughter burst from Clark's lips. "I won't call you Calamity—unless it's called for—but I will call you friend." His voice was husky, full of emotion. "And hopefully someday it can be more..."

They looked at each other and smiled. Amity let off a slight laugh to release the tension, and then they grew silent. Amity felt hopeful and uncertain. She was very aware of his closeness and was thankful for it, and she hoped he was too.

The silence of the night was broken by the sound of voices. Three male voices and a female. They were arguing about something. The woman's voice carried down the street, and Amity could tell it was Madeline. Even though they couldn't make out the words, Madeline sounded upset.

Clark stood to his feet. "Should I go check on her?"

Amity rose, standing by his side. She watched the small group who stood just beyond the light of the streetlamp. Amity was about to encourage Clark to go check on her friend, but Madeline broke away from the huddle of men and hurried toward them. The older woman was halfway down the street when she noticed them on the steps and slowed her stride. Amity watched the men hurry away in the opposite direction. One of them seemed to have the stride and cadence of Emil, but she couldn't be certain.

"Madeline, is everything all right?" Amity called out.

Instead of answering, Madeline motioned for them to go inside the apartment. It was only after they'd all removed their coats and were seated at the small kitchen table that she dared to speak.

Madeline's hands quivered as she placed them on the table. She moved them to her lap.

"I am sorry you saw that. My friends sometimes are fools. Everyone knows that our city soon will be under German control, but many of us believe differently how we should handle things. Some people want to fight..." The clock in the other room struck the hour, but Madeline stayed silent.

"And you?" Clark finally asked.

Madeline shrugged. "We have a saying—'*Kdo nemá v hlavē, musí míti v nohou.*' Basically it means, 'Who falls short in the head must be long in the heels.' I'd rather think things through. I don't believe it will be too hard to outthink the Germans. We won't be able to stand up to them with weapons, that is for certain, but not every idea is one we have to pursue."

Madeline rose and began to heat water in a teakettle on the stove. She opened a tin from the windowsill, and the aroma of herbs wafted through the room. "Would anyone like chamomile tea? I know it will help me sleep tonight."

Amity moved to the cupboard for teacups. "Yes, please. Clark?"

He nodded and then focused on Madeline. "If there is any way I can help..."

She fixed her gaze on him and nodded once. A look passed between them. Did Madeline have something in mind? Amity wouldn't guess, wouldn't ask. She had enough worries just thinking about the upcoming transport and all the children who needed a way out.

Amity placed the teacups on the table, and she noticed Clark's eyes were fixed on the painting on the wall. It was an image of a snow-covered Charles Bridge with patrons walking on it and peasant men pulling heavily loaded carts through the snow. A solemn statue of a saint, with lifted hand and snow-brushed shoulders, appeared to be praying a blessing over those who passed. And in the forefront of the painting, a young boy walked with hands in pockets and scarf blowing behind him. His head was turned, and he looked ahead as if looking into the kitchen where they sat, hungry for its warmth.

Clark studied the boy and then pulled out his notebook again and started writing. Amity noticed that something about this place brought him to life. The pain, the heartache, the desperation...she supposed these had a way of making one realize the contrast between powerlessness and power, and one's need to find a place in the struggle between the two.

TWENTY-THREE

Prague, Czechoslovakia
Monday, February 20, 1938

Pavla told herself she wouldn't cry again in Radek's presence. After caring for her family for two months, he was weary from her tears, but she had not been able to keep her word.

They had traveled overnight from Brno to a village just outside of Prague. Pavla had had no intention of staying two months with the farmer's family, but events had transpired to keep her and her children there. After Klára recovered, Ondřej became ill, and then she had too. Their saving grace had been the money Abram had left them. The money had helped pay for all their expenses, and she had been able to give a little more to Radek and Emílie for their trouble.

Thankfully, whatever illness her family had didn't spread to Radek, Emílie, and their seven-year-old daughter, Jana. Emílie believed the illness had come from their hearts more than their bodies. She'd claimed that once in a safe place, their bodies, minds, and souls finally had a chance to grieve. Pavla had nodded as

Emílie explained, but she believed that their illness had come for a different purpose. It had kept them there, surrounded by a different kind of faith than she'd known before.

Even though Radek and Emílie had no idea they were being watched, Pavla had witnessed what it was like to be a Christian. She'd listened as Radek read Bible stories to little Jana at night. And for the first time, Pavla, Ondřej, and Klára had celebrated Christmas.

Hearing the story of the baby Jesus born to the virgin Mary had filled Pavla's heart with joy and her mind with questions. She'd been told her whole life that what the Christians believed was a lie, spread by Christ's followers who did not want to admit they'd followed a madman. Growing up, her parents had spoken of how Christians had persecuted Jews throughout history. And as they escaped Olomouc in the night, she believed that was happening again. Yet what had been done to their home, their business, and their family should in no way be linked to Christians, she realized now. Hitler's dictates had come from his own evil heart.

What Pavla had seen from Radek and Emílie was different. They were not perfect. They still grew angry and often fought, yet they had welcomed three strangers into their home. They shared what little they had. They loved when it was not required. Seeing this love in action touched her heart and stirred her soul, wanting to understand this Jesus they served.

Pavla and her children were well enough to make it to the refugee center, but tears had filled her eyes when she didn't find the help she had hoped for. They'd walked up the wide steps of the former municipal building, and a weary-looking woman had been standing at the front door. She had a toddler on one hip and a baby on the other. They clung to her, and the woman, thin and frail, bounced softly side to side, attempting to sooth their soft whimpers.

"Where have you come from?" she asked, seeing Pavla, Ondřej, and Klára with the small carpetbag standing on the threshold.

"We are Jews from Olomouc," Pavla had explained, touching the band on her finger. She balled her left hand into a fist and felt the rubies against her palm. "My husband and his parents were killed in November. We fled for our own lives, but we've been sick on the journey, so we stayed in Brno for a time." Pavla had forced a smile. "But I hear there is a place for us here. I have also heard they are setting up transports for children—so they can escape to England."

Pavla had shivered in the doorway, wishing the woman would let them in so they didn't have to talk in the cold. She glanced back at Radek, who was still waiting with his oxcart with more of their things. She knew he was tired and cold and just wanted to get home, but she held up one finger to wait just a moment. Frustration was clear on his face, and that's when her tears had come. Would things be like this for the rest of her life? Would she always be dependent on the kindness of strangers and begging for someone to listen to their plight?

Pavla turned back to the woman, and the cries of the two little ones in her arms increased—probably from the cold coming in through the open door. The woman called to someone, and a girl who looked to be about twelve years old came and took the two little ones from her arms. Still the woman did not let Pavla and her children inside.

"Yes, there are transports," the woman said in frustration, tucking her thin sweater tighter around her. "A small flight of twenty children left in January. Another—a train with a few hundred children—leaves a few days from now, but there is no way you will be able to get your children on the list."

Emotion knotted in Pavla's throat. She placed one hand on Ondřej's shoulder and another on Klára's, wishing that she'd left them back in the cart. Wishing they had not heard this. Pavla leaned closer to the woman. "Why did you say there is no way for my children to get on the train?"

"The list is long." The woman frowned and spoke in her normal volume, seemingly unconcerned if Pavla's children overheard. "There are hundreds of children already on the list. You cannot begin to understand..." The woman threw her hands up in the air. "It is taking too long." Her voice quivered. She placed her hand on the door as if she were about to shut it. "You listen to the radio, don't you? Hitler is preparing even now to invade our country. And then what? What will happen to all of us?" The woman sighed. "We've been here waiting, pleading, and *you* think you simply can waltz in here and get on the list?"

Pavla wanted to drop her head. She wanted to apologize for bothering the woman. She wanted to turn and walk away, but instead she lifted her chin and focused on the woman's eyes.

"But there is a list, correct? Then I will try to get my children's names on it until they kick me out the door. If you let us in, we won't be a burden. I simply need to know where to go. What do I do to get my children on the list? Even if it's at the end, with a thousand names before them, I want my children on that list. Who do I talk to?"

The woman shook her head. "You do not understand. We have been waiting here for months." She ran a hand down her pale face. "There are so many hurdles. Every week new decrees, more documents required. It seems as if nobody knows what's happening. Some mothers have given up."

"Given up? But we're trying to save our children's lives."

The woman said nothing but instead looked off in the distance, almost as if she could read the future in the clouds. "I said that some have given up, but not me. I will stand in as many lines as possible. At least my children are on a list."

Pavla jutted out her chin. "Tomorrow I will find a line to stand in."

The woman nodded, but it was obvious she had no hope for Pavla or her children. She barely had enough hope for herself.

Pavla dared to take a step closer to the door. "And tonight... can I stay here?" She knew what she needed—a place to stay and information. And from the hollow look on the woman's face, Pavla also knew what the woman needed—food.

"I do not come empty-handed. I have...uh...purchased some supplies. Things I thought we would need as we wait." She lifted up her carpetbag. "There is food in here, and there are two small suitcases in the back of the oxcart with a few more things." She leaned close to the woman, as if sharing a secret. "I have a loaf of bread, baked just yesterday, and my friend gave me plum jam as a parting gift."

"Plum jam?" The woman whispered the words, and her face brightened. She took a step back, making the space between her and the door wide enough to pass. "We do not have much to share. We do try to help each other. I will be willing to share my bed and blankets with you and your children—at least until you have time to go into Prague and check on those lists."

"Thank you." Pavla released the breath she'd been holding. "That is just what we need. Thank you." Then she placed her hands on Ondřej's and Klára's backs. "Take my carpetbag and go inside. I'll be right in."

Klára didn't hesitate. Hearing the voices of other children, she ran right in. Ondřej, on the other hand, hung back and hesitated.

"It's all right, my son, just step inside. I will be right there."

He looked up at her, fear filling his eyes. Suddenly she knew why. Ondřej had heard them talking. He now knew she would not be joining them to the end of their journey.

"Please, Ondřej," she urged again. "I just need to go get our things."

He nodded and stepped inside the door, carpetbag in hand, watching her every move.

She hurried down the steps to the oxcart. Seeing her approach, Radek pulled the two small suitcases from the back. They were light, but Pavla was thankful for the clothes Emílie had passed down for her children and the few things she'd purchased at the store for Pavla—things the children would need for their journey.

With a suitcase in each hand, Pavla lifted her chin to look into Radek's face. She was surprised to see tears in his eyes.

"Thank you—both you and Emílie—for all that you have done for us. We would not have made it this far if it hadn't been for you."

Radek nodded. "We will continue to pray. We will continue to hope that you find safety." He swallowed hard and looked up at the open doorway. "Ondřej is going to be a fine young man," he said with emotion, and Pavla knew he was thinking of his own lost son.

"This world is full of pain..." Her words came, and she didn't know what she meant by them except to acknowledge that even though she and her children were the ones in hiding, he, too, had experienced great loss.

"And there will be a day in eternity when the pain will be no more." His voice was gruff. "There will be a moment when our last tear will be wiped from our eye...or at least that's what my grandmother used to tell me. She would sing hymns about a place Christ is creating for His people. And on days like today I hold on to that truth."

"Yes," Pavla said, for the first time realizing she did really hope that was the case. "Yes, I want to hold on to that as well."

TWENTY-FOUR

Prague, Czechoslovakia
Wednesday, February 22, 1938

Pavla dressed deliberately for the occasion. She did her best to smooth the wrinkles from her best dress, yet when she put it on she was disappointed by how it hung on her frame. With gentle strokes she brushed out her thick brown hair and pinned it up on the sides. She smiled at her reflection in the mirror, but it did little good. Her cheekbones protruded, and her face looked pasty white. Her reflection reminded her of her aunt who had stomach problems and whose body couldn't absorb nutrition. She smiled again and pinched her cheeks, but it did little good to give her enough color.

Since a child, she'd always been considered bright and charming by those who'd known her. Her mother said she'd been quick to laugh, but now Pavla looked at the shadow of her former self and told herself not to cry. With a sigh of resignation, she turned each cheek carefully to the mirror to ensure not a hair was out of place. Her stomach balled in knots. The lives of her children depended on her performance today.

Two hours later, Pavla strode up to the woman as the desk

inside the municipal building, head held high, and placed the two small suitcases at her feet. Ondřej did the same with the carpetbag, placing it right before him.

The young woman's hair was swept up into a loose chignon, a beautiful reddish brown. Her skin looked pink and healthy, and for a moment Pavla looked at her and wished she could be as beautiful again.

The woman's head remained down as she frantically scribbled notes on a paper. Ondřej glanced up at Pavla. Questions filled his gaze. *Why has this woman not acknowledged us yet?* his look seemed to say.

Pavla patted his head, offering reassurance. Then she brushed her fingers through his dark, unruly curls. He needed a haircut, but that was the least of her worries now.

Ondřej fidgeted nervously while Klára stood on Pavla's other side and sucked her thumb. Any other time, Pavla would have scolded the girl, telling her to pull her thumb from her mouth in public, but not today.

The young woman looked up from the desk, weariness heavy on her face. Then she smiled. It was a warm, reassuring smile—one that put Pavla's heart at ease.

The woman said something in English, words Pavla didn't understand. Then her voice rose, and she called to a man across the room. He approached, rubbing his brow. He was a young man, handsome too. He seemed to be even more relaxed and happier than the woman, and Pavla wondered what could make him so happy in a place like this—a place where mothers had to make plans to be separated from their children.

"I am Emil."

She sighed a sigh of relief when he spoke to her in Czech.

"I'm sorry, my friend only speaks English, and she is trying to finish up travel arrangements in the next hour. How can I help you? Did you receive one of our telegrams about the transport?"

For a split second, Pavla considered lying and stating that she had indeed received a telegram. Would that get her children on a transport out of the country sooner? But no, she couldn't do that. Instead, she gave the man what she hoped was her brightest smile and told the truth.

"Yes, Emil. I have come to put my children on a list for transport. I hear there are those who are caring for them in England."

He shook his head. In an instant the smile turned to a frown. Sadness filled his gaze. "I am sorry. Our list is full. There are more children than sponsors. We have been turning people away for the past two days. I am not even certain how you were able to get inside. I told Marek to keep everyone away except those who are on an upcoming transport."

By prayer, she wanted to say. *By hope and determination. That is how I got inside.* "I understand there is no room." She clasped her hands in front of her, fingering her ring with her thumb. All morning she'd been planning and preparing for what she might have to do.

He raked a hand through his hair, and Pavla knew he was about to dismiss her, so she hurried ahead with her words. "But my husband was a shopkeeper in Olomouc. We had a very nice place. Yes, you understand? I will do whatever it takes to save my children." Pavla's voice quivered, and she told herself to remain strong. She fingered her ring again.

The man listened to her words, and at first it seemed he didn't understand. His eyes moved from her face to Ondřej and then to Klára, and then his eyes brightened. With a sigh he took a step forward and kneeled before the children. He took Ondřej's hand in one of his and Klára's in the other.

"Oh, you have such a good mother, yes? It is clear she loves you so much. I imagine you have faced so many hard things—"

The door opened behind her, cutting off the man's words. Emil looked up in surprise, and she turned to see the man she'd first met outside in the foyer area—Marek, she supposed. He was the one who'd let them in.

Marek approached and placed a hand on Klára's shoulder as he looked to his friend. "This poor woman and her children have had a difficult trip here. I know you said not to let anyone else inside, but wasn't it just this morning that another mother came and removed her two children off the list? Surely these two can take their place."

Emil's eyes narrowed at Marek, and his displeasure was clear. "It is not your position, friend, to make those decisions."

"A *maybe* is better than a no, correct? Imagine if you were in their place."

Emil sighed and stood. "Yes, but we will have to find sponsors for them. And there is paperwork. It's not easy to just replace two names with two others."

Marek didn't budge, didn't back away. He calmly stroked Klára's hair.

Pavla didn't speak. She closed her eyes and held her breath, waiting—praying. She heard Emil release a frustrated sigh and then opened her eyes, fixing them on him. "I will do anything," she said again.

"Perhaps we should get photos today," Marek cut in. "With beautiful children like these, finding a sponsor should not be a problem."

Emil ignored Marek and looked to her. His gaze narrowed on Pavla's, and then he lifted an eyebrow. "I know what you say is true. I know you will do whatever it takes to save your children. The problem is what I can do..."

With the slightest movement, Pavla turned her ring so that her rubies faced out, glimmering in the light. Emil spotted the ring, and even though he attempted to hide his interest, she saw it on his face.

Over the last few months she'd used most of the money Abram had left her to buy food and supplies, but she'd saved her wedding ring for such a time as today. For such an opportunity as this.

He nodded once in acknowledgment. "And your husband?" the man asked as she turned the rubies back around.

"Dead." Her voice was no more than a whisper. "They took him on *Kristallnacht*."

"I see."

Emil placed his hand on the American's shoulder and squeezed it gently. She looked up at him and offered a weary smile. There was a tenderness in her gaze, yet for some reason seeing it caused a heavy rock to grow in Pavla's stomach. This woman cared for this man, she could see, but just from the few moments she knew him, Pavla questioned whether Emil could be trusted.

He said something in English, and the woman released a heavy sigh, answering him.

The young woman looked at Pavla and smiled. "Beautiful children. *Krásné děti*," she said in Czech, and then she went back to the work at hand.

"Amity is in charge here. She says we can add you to the list, but there are no guarantees. Surely you understand. Since a woman took two children off this list, we can add them. This is highly unusual but..." He didn't continue, and Pavla understood. *He wants my ring. He won't ask for it now, but he wants it.*

"Yes, I understand, but if I know their names are on the list..." Overwhelming joy flooded her heart. "That is all I ask for."

Emil nodded. "They will be. For that you have my word." Then he motioned to a gray metal desk. "Please come, sit. There is paperwork we need you to fill out."

She followed him, and only then did she look to her children to see their response. Klára was smiling, but Ondřej wore a frown. They were both so well behaved. She only hoped this man liked what he saw. That he'd remember them. She only hoped their future mother would see their picture and...

The tears came then, but she quickly blinked them away. She refused to let them flow. Not here, not now. She had to stay strong for these children and for this man.

Pavla swallowed down her emotion and sat in the wooden chair. She picked up the fountain pen and only then realized her hand was shaking. Ondřej stood beside her, straight and tall as a soldier, no doubt understanding the importance of behaving. And young Klára curled next to her side. "*Maminka*, I'm thirsty."

"Shh. After we finish here we can get you something."

Emil rose. "I will get some water."

"*Danke*," she said and watched as he walked away. And for the briefest moment, as she watched him pouring a cup of water from a pitcher on the back table, she wondered if she'd been mistaken concerning him. Maybe he was just like the rest of them, struggling with his place in all this and weary over not being able to do enough.

She filled out the paperwork and turned it over to him.

"We need photos of the children. If you will follow me to the next room."

They took a photo of Ondřej first, and thankfully he smiled. But as Klára stood before the desk she pouted. "I do not like this dress, *Maminka*. I want my red party dress for my photo."

"I'm sorry, Klára, we cannot go get your red dress. We left it in Olomouc, remember?"

"I want to go get it." Klára stomped her foot.

"Not today. But..." She clapped her hands together, trying to distract her daughter. "Remember the large clock I told you I would take you to see? After your picture, we can walk there."

Klára folded her arms over her chest so her dress could not be seen, but at least she smiled for the photo.

Pavla did not know whether to laugh or cry as she left the building. Her children were on the list, but she had no idea where to go now or what to do. They had brought their carpetbag and suitcases with them. It had been too risky to leave their things unattended, especially in desperate times such as these, but it was getting late, and she had no way to get back to the refugee center.

Dear God, if You can help me find a way...

Her children were on the list. She had done it. They had traveled so far. Maybe soon they would be safe. As hard as it would be to let them go, at least they would be well cared for and far away from the Nazis' threat.

Her hands tightened around her children's, and her mind moved to the next problem. She said they would go to the clock, but they needed food first. Surely every café around Old Town Square would be expensive. She decided to walk in the opposite direction to find a small market stall instead.

Pavla was turning the corner onto a busier street when she heard quickened footsteps behind her. She tightened her grip on her children's hands.

"Ma'am?" a voice called from behind.

She turned. "Yes?" And then she remembered. *The ring. He wants my ring.*

It was Emil. His cheeks were red, flushed. "If you do not have a place to go, may I suggest one? There is an old school that we've converted into housing. We just got permission to use it so we can better gather people together for our transports. It isn't much, but we have a few extra cots, and after tomorrow—when the next train goes out—you will have the whole place nearly to yourself... until we start gathering people for a new transport, that is."

She nodded as he spoke and then waited, waited for him to ask for the ring. Or to ask for anything else he might require. But the man said nothing else.

"You say we can stay there for *free*?" She placed emphasis on the last word.

"Yes. I thought it would be one less thing to worry about. Unless you have someplace else to go, of course. I saw you listed no address on your paperwork."

She offered Emil a cautious smile. "We don't have anywhere to stay. Anything would be helpful. We don't need much, a place to lay our heads. A little food."

"We do what we can. And we can point you to other places to get food too." He pulled out a slip of paper with an address. "And when will you come?"

"Today. We will come tonight."

"I will tell them to be expecting you." Then, with a glance and a smile to the children, he walked away.

TWENTY-FIVE

Prague, Czechoslovakia
Thursday, February 23, 1939

Amity reached over and took Clark's hand as they stood side by side on the train's platform. A line of children stood in a long row—173 of them. Each wore a label, prepared by her helpers, tied around their necks. Adventure shone in their gazes. Their parents had said their goodbyes, and most of the children had no idea of the reason for their journey. "A happy adventure," their mothers had told them. "Nice people will care for you, and I will join you soon."

Everything was ready for their journey. Sack lunches had been stored on the train in large boxes. Amity, Clark, and Madeline had awakened early and had spent a happy hour packing food in Madeline's kitchen for the children. Then they had hired a taxi to take the food to Wilson Station.

The children's luggage had been packed in the belly of the train. Each child had two labels on their suitcases—one sticker stating the station they were leaving from and another stating the one they'd be arriving at.

Amity thought of all that was packed inside those suitcases:

shirts, pants, dresses, socks…love. All the love a parent could pack for the journey. Only love would make such a sacrifice. Sending their child away was the hardest part, trusting that others would provide the love and care they needed.

Amity was thankful to have Clark with her in Madeline's house. As he had been in London, he was a gentleman in every way. He also came upon more ideas for his novel each day. Amity fell asleep at night as the pounding of typewriter keys drifted up from the kitchen bedroom. That was always a good sign.

Standing next to her at the train station, he placed his hand on her back. With a friendly smile, she marked off each name as the child passed and boarded the train.

The line of labeled children represented many hours of work and just as many hours of prayers. Then she marked off the names of the adult workers. One woman—a Londoner who'd come to accompany the children on their journey—paused before her and opened her arms for a hug. Amity offered her one.

Clark grabbed the woman's hand and gave it a firm shake. "Have a safe journey, and thank you for caring for the children."

Immediately the woman's face brightened. "It's my honor. I am certain the children will be just fine. It is an exciting adventure, after all." Then with quick steps she hurried into the train car and found a seat next to a cluster of young girls.

When the last child entered, Amity released a breath. "I cannot believe this is happening. I cannot believe these mothers have trusted us with their children's lives. It is such a huge responsibility."

"It's your smile, Amity, that puts these mothers at ease. They needed someone here like you. Andrew is a wise man. He made a good choice. Since they trust you, they feel they can trust the families who are waiting. Your smile is saving these children's lives."

Seeing the children onto the train was the easy part. Harder had been watching the goodbyes of the parents—mostly mothers. All of them arrived with brave faces, but Amity took note of their splotchy skin and red-rimmed eyes. Had they slept at all last night, knowing that it would be the last time they would see their child for a long time—most likely years, if not forever?

Amity placed a hand over her heart, suddenly longing for Celia. At least she knew Celia was safe and happy. She had no doubt that she would see her again.

Clark stood with a hand on her shoulder as she watched the goodbyes. Madeline stood next to her too, listening to the mothers' words.

"Watch your brother."

"Try to stay together."

"Be a good boy and girl. I will write and think of you. I will be coming for you very soon."

"See, this is a good and kind woman. She and her friends will take you to England."

One small girl, with dark hair in a perfectly neat pony tail and blue bow, clung to her mother's waist. "*Maminka*, no. Do not make me go. I promise to be good. I promise never to be bad again. I won't cry anymore for my things back home. I promise."

Hearing the girl's pleas broke her heart, and Amity looked at the mother's face. Her eyes were wide, frantic. Amity saw the woman needed help, lest she take her daughter's hand, turn, and walk away. Yet the great love the mother had for her child led to this moment. It was loving enough to realize that her child was safer in the arms of another.

Amity called Madeline to her and asked her to translate.

"Let me see what I can do," Amity whispered, with Madeline translating. She wiped a stray tear from her own face and then leaned down.

Amity reached her hand out to the young girl. "I know it's hard to leave your mother. Would you like me to go with you to line up with the children? They are nice boys and girls. I know you will find friends."

The small girl hesitated. Finally, with a sad smile, small fingers wrapped around Amity's larger ones.

"Ready?"

The young girl gave the slightest nod and then released her mother's hand. They moved forward, and Amity turned to tell the girl's mother that all would be fine, but the woman had already turned and rushed away. Amity understood. If she did not leave the girl now, maybe she never would.

Government officials checked all their paperwork, and then sooner than expected, the train pulled away. Amity heaved a sigh as she watched it leave. They'd done it. All those children would soon be safe in England.

She stood at the station for another fifteen minutes, making sure the train didn't return for any reason. Looking around, she noticed Madeline was already gone. After getting a cup of coffee inside the station, she and Clark caught a taxi.

The office was strangely quiet when they entered, and then she heard voices in the back. It was Emil and Madeline. She wondered if it was a repeat of the conversation they'd had on that dark street a few weeks ago, if that had indeed been Emil in that group of men.

With quiet steps she moved to the back office. Clark followed. She paused outside the door, and it was Emil's voice she heard.

"I do not know why you are so upset. They made it on, did they not?"

"Yes, Emil, but they have not got to the border yet. It is a risk you should not have taken. It could have ruined—"

Not able to stand by and eavesdrop any longer, Amity opened the door and rushed in. "What is this?" She looked to Madeline. "You have to tell me. What's going on."

Madeline pointed a shaking finger toward Emil. "It is him. You should be thankful, Amity, that the train left at all."

"What do you mean?"

Emil turned his back on her, running his hand through his hair. "Everything is fine. She didn't even need to know." Then he turned around and looked at Clark.

Amity was confused. She turned to Clark, standing next to her. "Do you know anything about this?"

"Me?" Clark laughed. "Why would I know anything about this?"

Emil crossed his arms over his chest with a huff and leaned against the wall. "All right. If you have to know, I snuck two adults onto the transport."

Amity's mouth dropped open. Her eyelashes fluttered. "What?"

"They were two artists. They'd already been arrested by the Germans in the Sudetenland, and we managed to get them out of jail there." He flung his hands into the air. "I promise you, Amity, if we did not get them out of the country they would have been the first to be rounded up and sent to a camp. Or worse, killed."

Arms quivering, she stepped forward. "Artists? What do you mean by artists?"

"Jewish artists." He shook his head. "They are very well known, which is exactly what Hitler hates. You would know them—"

She raised her hand. "Please do not tell me. The less I know, the better." She pressed her fingers to her forehead. "I do not want to know their names. I do not want to know how you managed to get them out. I assume you sent them as adult leaders but...no, please do not tell me."

Amity turned back to Clark, who was being strangely silent. She eyed him closer. "And do you have anything to say?"

Clark looked to her, and again she could see the wheels turning in his head. Instead of the anger she felt, she could sense excitement in his gaze. "Can I tell you my guess? How I plan to write *this* into my novel?"

As much as she didn't want to, Amity couldn't help but smile at his lighthearted take on the situation. She placed a hand on her hip. "Well, tell me, Mr. Cartwright, how are you going to write this into your novel?"

"My character is going to add two extra children to the sanctioned list. They will have forged papers, of course, but no one will need to know this." He glanced from Madeline to Emil and then back to her again. "Then, when the names are transposed to the final forms—filled out at the train station—with the final total number of refugees leaving, I would make a 'mistake' and have only the passport numbers and names listed for two of the *children*—ages omitted. No one will notice at the station, and no one would care about the ages of the adults at the border."

Nodding, she turned and strode to the door. She placed her hand onto the doorknob and paused. Part of her wanted to be mad at them for doing this behind her back, but the other part of her understood. What would she do to save a life? Would she bend the rules? She wasn't sure.

Amity cleared her throat. "I don't need to know if that's how it was done or not. Let us just say that this is a *fictional* plot idea we were discussing." She opened the door again, urging herself to remain calm. She had to remember that lives were at stake. She had to remember all the time both Madeline and Emil had given to this cause. No one would have left the station today if it hadn't been for them.

Desperate times lead to desperate measures. Amity released a sigh.

"Please, from now on let's think of the children first," she finally said. It was all she *could* say. She just hoped Emil was right—that they would make it across the border without a problem. Then, hopefully, they could move past this little incident and not think of it again.

TWENTY-SIX

Prague, Czechoslovakia
Friday, February 24, 1939

They had purchased a few things at the store for dinner and were walking back to the school where they were staying when Pavla noticed a man approaching, his eyes fixed on them. From the way he looked at Pavla, it was as if he knew her. He was a short man with a thin frame. She gripped her children's hands and urged them to walk faster, but then she paused and eyed the man, realizing she did recognize him after all.

He offered a quick smile as he neared, and Pavla remembered where she knew him from. He was Marek, the man who'd let her into the back room at the refugee office. The one who'd urged Emil to add her children to the transport list. If it hadn't been for him, her children would not be on the list now. And because he'd urged Emil to consider them, they also had a place to stay.

The old school wasn't comfortable. They slept on thin, donated mattresses on the floor. The windows were cracked and broken in some places, but at least they were out of the cold. At least they were safe. Emil also knew how to find them when the time came from their transport. Pavla hoped it would be soon.

Marek's cheeks were flushed, as if he'd been walking quickly and had just recently slowed. His eyes were gray-blue, like the color of the sky after a storm. There was something about the man that reminded her of her father. Maybe it was the knitted sweater and the thick scarf knotted neatly around his neck. Her father used to wear a sweater and scarf like that. Even on the coldest of days he'd rarely put on a coat. She clutched her grocery bag tighter to her as he neared.

"Pavla. There you are. I had been watching from my window." He pointed up to a nearby apartment building. "I was wondering what was taking you so long. There must have been long lines at the store. It's nearly dark. You shouldn't be out this late. Not with the children."

Her brow furrowed. He'd been watching her? Watching them? Something felt odd about that, and strange chills moved through her body.

"There is enough light yet. We are not worried. It is not far to where we live."

"Yes, the school is a good place. Hopefully there will be more families coming soon. It must be quiet being there are all by yourselves." He glanced down at Klára and smiled.

Klára looked away, whimpered, and curled to her mother's size. Ondřej squared his shoulders, as if attempting to make himself taller. Pavla patted his arm, hoping to calm him. The last thing she needed was for him to lash out.

"We have no problems where we are staying, but thank you for your concern. There is a Czech policeman who comes by several times a night," she lied. "He makes sure everything is locked up tight. He always checks to make sure we are well."

Marek nodded and ran his hand down his neck. "Good. That is good." He flashed a smile. "There are so many people taking care of you, aren't there? People who make sure your children have a place on the train. I am certain you wish you could reward each of them—"

"My children do not have a place on next train yet," she interrupted. "Or at least not that I've heard."

"*Ne.* Not yet. But they will. Emil says it is so, and we must trust that. He made a way for your children, didn't he? It wasn't something he had to do, but you were so convincing."

The man looked to her hand, and then she understood. Even though only the slightest band of gold could be seen, she had made a promise to them. She had offered payment, and it had been accepted. Why had she dared to allow herself to hope it wouldn't be? From the moment of the Munich compromise, when the Sudetenland was handed over to Germany, she had no rights. Her children had no rights. She clenched her fist and felt the rubies—Abram's rubies—press into her hand one last time.

Not allowing emotion to overtake her, Pavla lifted her left hand, extending it toward him. With a knowing smile, he pretended to shake her hand and ever so nimbly slid the ring off her finger. She had lost so much weight, it slipped off easily.

With one quick motion, he dropped the ring into his pocket and then brushed back dull hair from his face. His smile was even more broad than before. Pavla clenched her teeth and pressed her lips into a thin line. It took every ounce of control she had not to slap him. Not to tell the man he should be ashamed of himself for robbing her of such a special memento, but to do so would risk her children losing their place.

"It was nice catching up with you. Have a safe walk home. And be sure to thank that police officer for taking such good care of you." The man winked. "And to think in other parts of this country that would not be the case."

Voices rose from down the street, and a group of young men rounded the corner, walking in their direction. They wore the uniforms of German officers, but as they approached she could tell they were only young men playing dress-up. Still, she didn't want to know how those young men would treat them once they realized they were Jews.

From the corner of her eyes, Pavla noticed Ondřej lift his face to her. He frowned. She placed her hand back on his shoulder and gave him a firm squeeze, urging him not to speak.

She smiled at Marek one last time and started to walk, urging her children forward. "It was nice meeting up with you. I look forward to hearing from Emil soon. We must excuse ourselves—my children need dinner."

Pavla didn't wait for the man to respond. She lowered her head and quickened her steps. Thankfully, her children did the same. Hurrying to the end of the block, they crossed the street to put distance between them and the group of boys, but it did no good. The boys noticed them and started shouting racial slurs. Pavla walked even faster, wishing her children didn't have to see such things, hear such things, and praying yet again that a transport would come. They needed to leave as soon as possible. She was doing her best, but with each passing day it was getting more impossible to protect them.

TWENTY-SEVEN

Prague, Czechoslovakia
Monday, March 13, 1939

It seemed impossible that spring would ever come. Winds blew from the northeast, and the gray sky seemed to mourn with the city. Amity's feet crunched on the snow as she walked from Madeline's apartment to the small office. The world around her seemed dark, depressing, so she looked to the gilded cupolas, baroque towers, slate roofs, and sacred spires to remind her of what beauty remained in this world.

It had only been eighteen days since the last transport, but after talking with Andrew, she knew they could waste no time arranging for the next one. Rumors were circulating that Hitler was preparing to move beyond the Sudetenland. They had to move as quickly as possible.

She hung up her coat and settled down at the desk, glancing over at Madeline, who sat in the next desk over. "How are things going?"

Madeline sighed. "Too many refugees, too few travel documents, and only weeks away before the jackboots will be marching on the streets of Prague."

"Oh, don't remind me. That's all I hear about. Every café and bar is filled with whispered reports of the German invasion."

Madeline wiped her brow with the back of her hand. "Oh really. So you've been hanging out at all the bars listening to the news, have you?"

Amity chuckled. "Oh, Madeline. You know what I mean."

She'd walked to the office by herself that morning. Clark had already extended his time there, and just last night he'd let her know that he would be heading home in a few days' time. He had to check on Celia. He also had a novel to finish writing. The deadline neared, and for the first time in years Clark had hope that he actually could make it this time. He'd gone to the train station to buy his ticket, and knowing that she'd be alone again left an ache in her heart.

Since the first day of Clark's arrival, Amity had not gone out of her way to express her love. Neither had Clark. Instead, they had settled into a gentle routine of showing care and affection for each other in small ways. It was as if they both knew that this season of their lives was a waiting season. A time of waiting for the paperwork for more transports. A time of waiting for Hitler to make his move. A time of waiting until things got too dangerous for her to stay. And then, after she returned home, it would be a time of waiting for life to settle down enough for them to put time and attention into what they both knew their relationship would require. Waiting was never easy, but waiting to allow herself to fall in love was one of the hardest things she'd yet to do.

Amity settled into her desk and pulled out her to-do list, reminding herself of the tasks that needed to be tackled today. Just then, the door opened, and Marek rush in. He hurried straight to Amity.

Marek pointed his thumb behind him. "A messenger has just

arrived, Amity. They are asking you to come and see them over at the British legation."

Hearing those words, her stomach fell. She turned to Madeline. "What do you think it means?"

"It means all those rumors that everyone has been hearing are true."

Amity rose and reached a hand to her friend. "Madeline, would you come with me?"

"Do you think I should? There is so much to do around here. I'm waiting to hear about some of the travel documents."

Marek stepped forward. "I can stay. I can wait by the door and answer the phone."

"All right then." Madeline rose and moved to the hook for her coat. Her steps were quick. Her shoulders were pulled back as if she were already steeling herself up for the hard news they were about to receive. "Truth be told, I am glad you asked me to join you. I am tired of these rumors. They're putting all types of knots in my stomach. I supposed we will both discover the truth now."

Less than an hour later, they were sitting in the office of Mr. Stopford with the British legation. He appeared calm with a hand in his jacket pocket as he stepped aside and invited them into his office, but the *click, click, click* of his fingernail fiddling with a matchbox cover gave away his nervousness.

He motioned for them to sit, but stood silently, staring up at the ornate wall feature. Finally, he turned to them, defeat clear on his face. "I have to warn you, ladies, that we've gotten reports of Hitler assembling his troops, preparing to head this way."

"Already?" Amity placed a hand on her stomach, urging her breakfast to stay put.

Madeline gasped. "So the rumors are true."

"That they are, unfortunately."

"Will you be leaving?" Madeline dared to ask him.

He pulled his hand from his pocket and used both hands to ease himself into his winged back chair. "I will be, although some of my colleges are staying."

Madeline turned slightly toward Amity. "And should she leave?"

"We are recommending that anyone who doesn't have to stay here leave. If your position isn't vital—"

"But mine *is* vital." Amity straightened in the chair. "We have so many transports to get out—the kindertransports. Do you think we'll be able to?"

He shrugged. "Your guess is as good as mine. If it's anything like the Sudetenland, the Germans set up quickly, but still, they allowed people to get out. Let's hope that will be the case here too."

"Yes," Amity gasped, "but where can these people go now? How many can leave who haven't already tried?"

"That's what I've come to tell you. Do what you can to get refugees out by any means necessary. I had already cabled London to tell them the situation is desperate."

"I have been helping with another transport," Madeline said. "My friend Dorothy has been organizing it—she's with another organization, but I am sure you have met her. It's a group of mothers and children for this transport—families whose husbands have gone ahead. They have been told to stand by, but we're just waiting on travel documents from London."

"Go ahead and gather the travelers. Do you have trains prepared?"

Madeline ignored Amity and stared straight ahead, focusing on Mr. Stopford.

"Yes, the trains are ready. The families are ready. It's just the last of the paperwork."

"I will make a call. Waiting for those travel documents is no longer an option. Go ahead and send telegrams to all the camps. Tell the families to be at Wilson Station by tomorrow evening. I don't know how we will make this work, but tell all the women that a train will be standing by with all the travel documents." Mr. Stopford pounded his fist on the glossy top of the wooden desk. "We cannot allow Hitler to claim any more victims."

Amity looked to Madeline. Is that why Madeline had come—to get an audience with Mr. Stopford to discuss this other transport?

Amity blew out a quick breath of frustration. While she was thankful for that transport—for all those who would be able to get out—she worried about her master list with the children. Hadn't she been the one Mr. Stopford had sent for?

"Sir?" Amity scooted forward so she sat on the edge of the seat. "Do you know just how close they are...when the Germans will be here? Do we have time to organize another kindertransport too? I have...we have..." She glanced at Madeline. "We have all the paperwork in place for a children's transport too. All these children have sponsors, sir. We are simply waiting for their travel documents to come through. Although I admit they were submitted later than those others..."

Mr. Stopford rubbed his brow and sighed. He walked to the window and stared down at the street below, as if expecting German tanks to roll down the avenues at any moment. And she guessed that as part of the British legation, these transports were just a small part of his worries. Still, Amity wasn't going to back down.

"I cannot tell you what day the Germans will arrive. I have heard they already occupy the towns on the Polish border. I will ask London about your travel documents too and send you word.

But for now let's concentrate on these women and children. We have to get them out." He returned to his chair and sat with a heaviness that told Amity that the weight he carried overwhelmed him.

Mr. Stopford turned to Madeline again. "How many did you say there were?"

"Five hundred, sir."

"Five hundred!" He shot to his feet. "And you think you can gather everyone? Can you get them to the station by six tomorrow night?"

"I will do my best."

"I will help." Amity placed a hand on Madeline's shoulder. Even though this wasn't officially *her* transport, these lives mattered. Five hundred of them, to be exact. "We'll go to the office and get the names from Dorothy. I'll run to one telegraph office and you to the other. Then Dorothy can work on getting the trains and all the supplies ready in the next thirty hours."

Relief flooded Madeline's face. "Thank you, Amity." She smiled. "And I know when the time comes, Dorothy will help you."

Amity stood. There was no time to wait. She glanced at her watch. "It's still morning yet, but let's get as many women as close to Wilson station as we can."

"I agree."

Amity walked to the door. "Why don't we take them to the school we've acquired? There is plenty of room."

The next day and a half passed by quickly. It was a time of making contacts, arranging transport to Prague for women and children, taking some families to the school, and finding hotel rooms by Wilson Station for the rest of the women and children. Yet they did it, and by six o'clock, five hundred refugees sat in the train as it waited at the station. Outside the train, Amity, Madeline, and Madeline's friend Dorothy waited for any sign of Mr. Stopford.

"He said he'd have all the paperwork here, correct?" Dorothy asked. She was younger than Madeline, with brown curly hair that fell to her shoulders. She wore a traveling suit, as if she, too, were going on the journey today, and looked every part the schoolmarm as she directed the women and children with efficiency. "Do you think he traveled to London himself? Maybe he took a flight to get him there and back."

"No, I don't think he went to London," Madeline sighed. "I'm just not sure whether we were supposed to wait here with the train or go there. Maybe one of us should go to his office."

The words were barely out of Madeline's mouth when a black automobile pulled up. A man stepped out and walked toward them with brisk steps. "Mr. Stopford sent me. All the clearance came though from London." He turned to Dorothy. "We just need you come to our office so we can check your lists."

"Yes, of course."

Amity and Madeline promised to wait with the train. Two hours later Dorothy was back. There was only one last hurdle. All the passengers had to be checked.

Amity crossed her arms and nibbled her lower lip as she waited inside the train station with Madeline. Would it be all right? Emil hadn't tried to smuggle anyone else through, had he?

Finally, at eleven o'clock, Dorothy exited the train with all the passport control officers following her. Minutes later the train pulled away, and Amity sighed another breath of relief. The train had made it out. Another five hundred souls saved. Yet what would happen from here? Would the Germans really allow them to continue the transports as Mr. Stopford had believed?

~

They arrived at home by midnight, and Clark was waiting. Worry filled his face.

Madeline closed the door behind her, locking it. Then she moved to the sofa and motioned for Amity to sit beside her. Weariness weighed Amity down as she moved to the sofa and sat. Clark scooted an armchair closer to them and did the same.

Madeline shook her head. She patted her coat pockets, as if looking for a cigarette. When she didn't find one, she crossed her arms over her chest. "Amity, you are not safe here. I appreciate all you have done, but it is time for you to go. You, too, must flee this city."

Amity looked to Madeline. She refused to look at Clark for fear of the worry she would also see in his eyes. "But don't you understand what just happened tonight? All those women and children were able to get away. What will happen if I go? I cannot just abandon these refugees when there is still so much work to be done."

"No! This is not your fight." Madeline turned sideways and gripped Amity's arms. "You have a choice. You can leave. You don't know what the Germans will do to you. If you think you will be safe because you're an American, you're wrong. Do you think they will like it if you are helping their enemies out of the country?"

She turned to Clark. "Tell her...tell her I have to stay. You understand, don't you?"

Instead of answering, he ran his hand through his hair, nearly causing it to stand on end. Amity had seen him this frazzled only a few times, and usually it was when he'd sat down to write and no ideas had come.

"I'm afraid time has run out." He stood to his feet. "They are keeping the train station open all night. The lines are growing with the rumors of the Germans at our borders." He sighed. "It's time to make a decision. Are you going to come home, or are you going to stay?" His words were brusque, but there was compassion in his gaze. The situation was urgent, and there were no easy answers.

Madeline released her grip, and Amity rose. It wasn't what she'd expected Clark to say. She hadn't expected this from Madeline either. If anyone understood the needs of the refugees, it was Madeline.

Amity stood and paced back and forth in the small living room, wishing for space. Wishing for time. "I really should talk to Andrew. I'm not sure. If there was some way I could talk to him...This is all *his* work."

Clark also stood, and she paused before him. "Why are you thinking that?" His voice softened. "Don't you realize that this is *your* work?"

"But he's the one who saw the need. He's the one who started this."

"And you're the one who is *doing* it. Which also means it is up to you to decide when it's time to go home."

Madeline rose and moved to the stairs, slowly walking up them toward her room. Amity knew the older woman was turning this conversation over to Clark now, but the worry was clear on her face.

"The truth is, Amity, that I came here because I was worried about *you*. I came because I wanted you back with me. Back with Celia. I wanted you safe. Now that I've been here, I see all that you're doing, and it's wonderful work. But I also believe that you will not be safe when the Germans come. I agree with Madeline. As much as I approve of your work, I think it's time for you to come home." He sat down on the sofa and lowered his head and sighed. "I wish there was another way."

Tears filled her eyes, and she pulled her coat tighter around her. "I need to go for a walk. I need time to think."

Clark stood and placed a hand on her arm. "Is it safe...for you to go walking alone?"

Amity offered a soft smile. She cocked her eyebrow. "It's a mounting war out there, Clark. Nobody's safe, are they?" She placed her hand on his. "But don't worry. I'll be fine. I've been walking these streets alone for months. Nothing has happened yet."

He squeezed her arm and then took a step back. "I'll have to trust you on this."

Amity pulled her scarf out of her pocket, wrapping it around her neck. She brushed a strand of auburn hair from her face and then stepped out the door and onto the sidewalk.

Out of habit, she moved her gaze to the place where she always did, to the distant hill and the castle that sat on it. In a strange way, living under the shadow of that castle all these months had given her a sense of peace. As long as the castle wasn't under Nazi control, she was safe. But soon that would no longer be the case.

Amity walked on, hands in pockets, moving to the bridge. Before the global spotlight had been drawn to Czechoslovakia, what had this country meant to her? Nothing. It was a land of castles, marionettes, and Good King Wenceslas. To the major powers in the West, Czechoslovakia was not worth fighting for.

Amity's feet moved swiftly over the cobblestones, and soon she was standing on the Charles Bridge. Even at this midnight hour there were others walking along with her, but it was almost as if they, too, were just part of the landscape. Everything around her was still a dull gray.

She'd heard that within a matter of months the aroma of fragrant blossoms of the linden trees would burst forth, filling the air with a sweet scent. But as she considered that, Amity knew she would never see them bloom. A man walked by, eyeing her, and Amity quickly looked away, instead peering into the river below.

Fear grew within her by the moment. She'd expected Madeline to tell her that everything would be fine. She'd expected a tender hug with a whisper that they'd be able to continue their work side by side despite the hardship. Instead, all she could think about was Mr. Stopford's words: *"We are recommending that anyone who doesn't have to stay here leave. If your position isn't vital..."*

Out of all those who wanted to leave, she could. And as she walked back to the apartment, Amity knew what she'd tell Clark. She'd tell him she was going with him. Together they'd walk to the station to buy the tickets. Together they'd get on that train tomorrow and return to Celia, to home.

— Twenty-Eight —

Prague, Czechoslovakia
Wednesday, March 15, 1939

Amity turned over in bed, clicked on the radio, and tuned in to the BBC. "Today at six o'clock German troops crossed Czech borders and are proceeding to Prague by all routes," the announcer said.

It had come. The day of German occupation, and she was still in the city. A twinge of fear touched Amity's heart. She looked at the suitcase at the end of the bed—the one she'd packed in the early morning hours after returning from the train station. Fear had led her to that decision.

Yet that had been last night. Now, new hope had somehow found itself in her heart in the morning. New courage.

Amity turned off the radio and closed her eyes. Even though the feather duvet was light, the weight on her chest felt as if a two-thousand-pound elephant sat on it. The burden for those children had not released yet. No matter the fears that chased her like hounds, she was not free to go.

I can if I stay, maybe I can help more...

The rumble of trucks on the road outside told her what she'd heard on the radio was indeed reality. Amity climbed out of bed and slipped her feet into her slippers, wrapping her robe around her. She moved to the window. There, on the gray streets below, the first convoy of ice-covered jeeps and trucks rolled into town. They slithered like cold-blooded gray snakes around the curving, cobblestone streets toward the castle. The men on the open trucks wore wool coats and steel helmets. Soon the streets would be full of German soldiers. Would there be any fighting? Were the Czechs simply going to let them come in and take over? It seemed impossible.

The aroma of coffee drifted up the stairs to her room. That ordinary scent—and the sound of a child's laughter filtering through the thin walls from their neighbor's apartment—told her she wasn't dreaming. It was no nightmare, although everything within Amity wanted it to be. She wanted to fall back asleep and wake up in a world where the Germans were still at arm's length and she still had time to try to get more innocent people out of the country.

Movement on the streets caught her attention. People poured out from the surrounding apartment buildings. Men in overcoats and women with thick shawls wrapped around their shoulders stepped out to watch. Many had looks of disbelief on their faces. Other faces were contorted in anguish. Although she could not hear their muffled moans, she saw women crying into their hands. A few young men shook their fists at the Germans in anger, and she wondered how long their innocence would last. Whether they liked it or not, the Czech people would be drawn into this conflict. Amity couldn't help but think of her father's stories from the last war. How many of those young men would be dead before this conflict was through? And how long before the refugees she couldn't help would be shipped off to Hitler's camps?

Most of the people, though, stood tall, looking straight ahead in stony silence. The Czech people had pleaded for help from the Western world, and no one had responded. Instead, those who'd declared themselves to be allies had turned their backs and refused to lift a finger to help.

"Would you have been like Pope Leo I?" she remembered asking Celia. *"Would you have been willing to stand up to the Hun invader?"*

It was Celia's answer that resonated with her now. *"I suppose if I knew God was on my side I would dare stand up to a Hun invader."*

The Huns had come, but who would stand up for the innocent now? These questions weighed on Amity's heart as she gathered fresh clothes and hurried to the bathroom.

She ran a bath, as hot as she could stand it, and stepped into it, sinking down. Steam from the hot water caused the stray strands of hair that she had not pined up to curl around her cheeks. With weariness she closed her eyes, and for a moment she pretended she was back in London. She imagined Mrs. McGovern making breakfast and Clark at the table with his newspaper and coffee. She imagined Celia curled into one of the large chairs in her father's library, lost in a book.

The steam pooled onto the walls and ran in rivulets down the walls. With Hitler's entrance, blood would flow as freely. No Jew in Czechoslovakia would be safe now. Her eyebrows shot up and then folded into a frown. Was it indeed God's will that she stay? Was God on her side? He had strengthened her when she felt weak. He had given her wisdom and favor. She'd seen numerous trainloads of children carried away to safety and put into loving homes. *If God is with me, who can be against me?*

I need to trust that. I have to trust that. There are people who still need me. I can't run.

Amity drained the water, dried off, and dressed quickly. She re-pinned her hair and then glanced at her cheeks. Was that really her with the intensity in her gaze and her jaw set with determination?

With quick steps she moved toward the bed, unlatched the suitcase, and lifted it up, turning it over. Her countries, the United States and Great Britain, had done nothing to help these people, but she wouldn't let her own fears keep her from her work. She was here. And Clark was right. She had already been doing it. She would stay until it was impossible to save another child or until she felt God releasing her to go. She would not run in fear, abandoning these people like everyone else had done.

Amity moved to the mirror and looked into her face with a mixture of exuberance and worry. "You have always felt inferior to your brother," she whispered into the mirror, "but God has a unique role for you." She straightened her shoulders and imagined that while she was still in London, sitting across the table from Celia and reading British fairy tales, God saw her there. God saw her now too. Had God seen the warrior within, one she couldn't have imagined until now? That thought brought a smile to her face.

Amity looked to the traveling suit that she had laid out the night before. She had no intention of wearing it now. Instead, she slipped on a simple gray dress.

With soft steps she walked down the stairs. There was a single figure at the table. He looked up at her, and she paused at the last step. Clark didn't seem surprised that she wasn't wearing her traveling suit. Two train tickets sat on the table before him. He had gone out and purchased one for her the night before.

"You're staying?" he asked, his words no more than a whisper.

"I have to. I can't leave them. I have to do more."

He turned away from her, brushed the tickets aside, and then stood.

"I had a feeling that with the dawn you would think differently. Do you want to go to Wenceslas Square with me? It's history in the making."

"History that could have been avoided if—"

Clark took quick steps toward her and placed a finger on her lips. "Your words won't make a difference, but your actions can. I also hope you will be able to do more. Even though Celia will still be worried—I will be worried—I am proud of you." Then, with a tender touch his hand moved to her cheek. He stroked it slightly before lifting her face to his. For the briefest moment Amity was certain Clark was going to kiss her. Then he removed his hand from her face and stepped back. Color rose on his cheeks. "I'm sorry. I...we...this is not the time."

Amity released the breath she'd been holding. "I...I understand." Her brow furrowed. "Tensions...emotions are high." She turned, swallowed the lump in her throat, wishing she could stop the butterflies that danced in her stomach. "It seems we all try to find a bit of comfort in times of pain."

But even as she said those words, Amity wondered if she was happy or sad that he hadn't kissed her. A tender love had been growing in the years they'd both been caring for his daughter, but it was a love that would still have to wait. *Now is not the time.*

Amity placed a hand on her stomach, took a deep breath, and then finally turned. "Yes, I think we should go to Wenceslas Square. You're right. This is history, and we are part of it now."

The streets of Prague had transformed overnight. Large snowflakes dropped from the sky. Steel-helmeted soldiers marched through the city, taking control of the baroque palaces. German university students paraded around in Nazi uniforms. Amity wanted to march up to them and shame them for joining the Germans, but she knew it would do no good. The truth was, not all Czechs were sad about their lost freedom. For some it was just what they wanted.

Local Germans also marched through the street, screaming, "Heil Hitler!" and waving paper swastikas. As they went along, they saw more men and women gathered into small groups, weeping.

Some young men threw snowballs at tanks and armored cars, as if that would do any good. Others wore Czech flags on their buttonholes.

They overheard people saying that German trains had arrived at the main station, and artillery pieces and tanks were unloaded. Nazi flags and banners were unfurled on the fronts of buildings all over the city.

The narrow streets were packed. It was as if every city building had emptied onto the streets. The heart and soul of the capital city poured out in the form of mourning people. People who'd been abandoned. People who attempted to be brave with their unity and with their song.

It took Clark and Amity more than an hour to walk to Wenceslas Square. Amity heard the raised voices blocks away, voices raised in unity, joining together in patriotic songs. Yet even as the defeated people sang, they were pushed back onto the sidewalks by the approaching German vehicles. Yesterday they were a free people. Today German battalions rolled into the streets. They spread through every narrow outlet of the ancient city, consuming all hope in their wake.

Clark and Amity approached Wenceslas Square and paused. Amity placed her hands over her mouth and shook her head in disbelief. Clark placed a protective arm around her shoulders, and she curled into his side. As the people's voices rose with emotion and fervor, a trembling moved through her body. Clark wrapped his other arm around her and pulled her tight against him as a sign of protection as she guessed he had done with Celia when she was scared as a child. They stood a long time, mourning with these people, until Amity knew there was work to do. She wiped her eyes and pulled back from Clark's embrace.

"I should go to the office—check on things. Madeline is going to be surprised to see me, isn't she?"

"I imagine she will be. I need to get a telegram to Celia too, to let her know that I'll be on a later train." He sighed as his blue eyes pierced her. "I can stay another day, maybe two, but I need to get back."

"A daughter and a deadline. Both need you."

"Yes, I suppose that's right."

It was slow going as they moved through the crowds. The streets were dark, as if night had descended on the city hours before it should have.

Amity glanced around, feeling the gloom pull her down. "It seems as if even the sun is hiding its face today."

They walked to the office, and there were only a few families there. Only a few that had any hope.

They opened the office door, and she rushed in. A joyful gasp escaped Emil's lips. "Look who has returned! Or rather who never left. Let me guess—did you decide you could not live without us?"

She allowed Emil to give her a quick hug. "Something like that."

Madeline sat at the desk, reading over a file. She barely glanced up as Amity and Clark entered.

"Of course, I should ask...Madeline, you don't mind me staying, do you?"

The older woman looked up. Her eyes were red and puffy. Her nose was too from dabbing it with her handkerchief. She narrowed her eyes in anger, but Amity had a feeling it wasn't her that Madeline was angry with.

"I do not understand why you're staying. You are a fool to believe you will be safe here. But I suppose if a fool is still able to pay rent, I will not kick her out into the street."

"Do you really think that with all that's happening in this large city, the Germans will be concerned with me?"

Madeline pointed a shaking finger toward her. "You saying that *proves* you should not stay here. You simply have no concept of what the Germans are capable of."

Amity felt Clark's hand press into the small of her back. At least he believed in her.

"Yes, well, I suppose I will have to face what comes, but for now please tell me how I can help."

Madeline lowered her head again, staring intently at the file in front of her. "There are some papers that Marek needs to pull from the files. I suppose you can help him with that for now."

"What do you mean?"

"Have you not heard?" She cocked an eyebrow. "The Gestapo are sweeping the city for enemies of the Reich. They are depending on lists they had previously prepared. Spies have been in the city for months keeping tabs on their enemies—especially the Jewish refugees who have already fled the Nazis elsewhere." She jutted out her chin. "Mr. Stopford called. He's leaving today. I cannot handle the horror. Lines of people have been banging on the doors of foreign consulates, begging for visas. Some Jews have committed suicide on their steps."

"And what are we to do with the files?" she dared to ask.

"I am not certain when the Germans will be here, but they will. We must destroy any documents that might be incriminating if they fell into the wrong hands...the names of our refugees, their associates, their past histories, any anti-Nazi comments, their reasons for wanting to immigrate—all of those papers must be burned.

Amity nodded and turned to Clark. "I need to help. But I know you have to go..." Deep down, Amity hoped Clark would offer to stay longer. Instead, he offered a reassuring smile.

"I need to take care of a few things, but I will be back to walk you home. I need to send a telegram to Celia. I am certain she will be worried sick. And I need to send one to my editor. Of course, he's going to be thrilled I finally have some ideas for my book. And I also have to buy a new train ticket." He lifted his eyebrows and stared intently at her. "Should I buy one or two?"

Amity jutted out her chin. "You will just need one train ticket, Clark," she said loud enough for Madeline to hear. "I will be staying."

Clark squeezed her arm, and then turned and left. And even though Amity had been working in this office for months, it suddenly felt like a foreign place to her. Emil looked over at her and shrugged. Amity told herself that emotions were high, but it was hard to feel as if she suddenly wasn't wanted, wasn't needed.

Did I stay for no reason at all?

She moved to the back room, where Marek sat in a chair. A stack of files was on the floor by his feet. "So, how can I help you?" she asked before she remembered he didn't speak English.

Still, the thin man seemed to know what she was saying. He pointed to a pile of files and then to the stove in the other room. All those had to be burned.

Twenty-Nine

The fire was blazing, consuming their files, and Amity hoped Marek was being careful. They needed to keep the necessary information for those who still remained, yet they had to destroy all the files of anyone who'd already left. She checked everything they had written in English for the British Home Office, but she had to trust that Marek was taking care of everything written in Czech.

She was feeding another stack of files into the stove when Clark strode into the office, followed by Emil.

Clark rushed up to her side. "I'd just arrived when I saw their car show up."

"Their car? Who are you talking about?" But from the fearful look in Clark's gaze she didn't have to guess.

Emil placed a hand on her shoulder. "Amity, you have been summoned."

"What do you mean?"

"The Nazi high command. They sent a request for you to meet with them. They want you there in an hour's time."

Fear flashed through her, followed quickly by obstinacy. "I don't want to go meet with the German high command. Why would I want to do that?"

Clark took a step closer to her, as if his presence could protect her from what was to come. Amity wished it could.

She put down the files and brushed her hair back from her face. "Me? What ever could they want from me? How do they even know about me?"

Madeline gave her a look that said *I told you so.* "They're already arresting enemies of the Reich. Some of my friends..."

Amity sat down in a chair in misery. A lump in her throat felt the size of a teacup. "Do they consider *me* an enemy?"

"Are you their enemy?" Emil shook his head. "Obviously not. If you were, they would have already arrested you. I would say you are a person of interest. My guess is they have questions about your transports—also, they want you to know they are well aware of your work."

A sharp pain struck her chest, taking her breath away. In her mind's eye she pictured herself standing before a high-ranking soldier. With a snap of his fingers he could end her life—or worse, stop the transports.

"Are you all right?" Clark placed a hand on her shoulder. "Can you breathe? You're not going to faint, are you?"

This is what I was afraid of.

Her eyelids fluttered closed, and she told herself not to get worked up. "It's all right," she managed, breathless. "The pain in my chest is lessening. The worry, not so much."

In all her life she could not have imagined such a thing. She was a nobody. She never stood out in school. She was a simple tutor, never demanding or receiving attention, running from the spotlight. And now, less than twenty-four hours after the Germans had invaded the Czech capital, they had requested *her* to join them for a meeting. Of course, it wasn't a request. And she only had one hour before she had to be there. If she left now, she'd just make it. Yet how could she get across the city with her knees as soft as ice cream?

Clark must have noted the concern on Amity's face. "I will take you. You should not have to do this alone."

Relief flooded over her, followed by confusion. "You don't have a car."

"We'll get a taxi."

"I have a friend who can drive you," Emil piped up.

This brought the smallest bit of a smile. "Your friend will not try to flee the country with me, will he? Actually, I will be grateful for a ride. I am thankful you have people to turn to."

"When you live in such a city, in such turbulent times, you have to know who can help when you find yourself in a bind."

"I'll accept your offer then—both of your offers. Give me a minute to freshen up, will you?"

"Yes, of course," Emil said. "I'll be back in ten minutes."

"Thank you. I...uh...just thank you."

Amity rushed into the water closet and placed her hands on both sides of the sink, attempting to stop their trembling. She had read about the German high command on the BBC, and none of it had been good. Would it be possible not to go to this meeting? She didn't think so.

As promised, Emil was waiting outside with an automobile. Clark opened the door for her. She paused before getting in, pointing a finger at him. "If you try to take notes..."

He shook his head and climbed into the backseat beside her. "Of course not. I would never."

Emil drove her to Prague Castle and parked outside the main gates. Amity released a soft breath seeing that the Czech castle guard still stood at attention in their sharp blue uniforms. At least not everything had changed overnight. Yet beside the castle guards stood German troops, and from the windows Nazi flags had been hung.

She opened the car door.

"Do you want me to go with you?"

Amity shook her head. "No, although I will take note of details for your novel."

"I don't need that. I just wanted to support you."

She smiled. "I will be fine. I'm sure of it."

"Yes, but remember to answer only the questions he asks you. Don't elaborate."

"Thank you." She climbed from the car. "I will remember that."

Amity approached the front door, gave her name, and was ushered inside. She was led down a long hall to a room on the ground floor. The office was fully furnished. *Who occupied this room just yesterday? Are they still alive?*

The assistant who'd led her inside didn't offer her a chair, so she stood tall in the middle of the room, her fingers threaded together in front of her.

A few minutes later she heard the sound of a man's footsteps coming down the hall and striding through the door. She continued to face the desk as he entered. With a smile he approached.

He was a young man with spectacles and had a stocky build. His hair was so blond it was nearly white. She would have considered him handsome if it hadn't been for these circumstances.

"Well, so you have come." He spoke in perfect English, which surprised her. He waved a hand to the small wooden chair beside the desk. "Please, have a seat, Miss Amity Mitchell."

She did as she was told. "And your name?" she dared to ask.

"*Oberleutnant* Klaus Böhm, but from now on I will be the one asking the questions. Do you understand?"

"Yes, *Oberleutnant* Böhm. Please excuse me."

The *Oberleutnant* sat in a high-backed chair. He picked up a file, looking through it.

They have a file on me? The Germans have a file...

"So, they tell me you are with the British government?"

"Oh, no, sir, that's my bro—" She paused, remembering what Clark had said. "I am just a tutor."

"A tutor? In a school?"

"A private tutor. For a family. I just have one student."

The man adjusted his spectacles. "And who is your employer?"

Amity paused. She was fine revealing information about herself, but now she was bringing Clark into this.

The man concentrated on her face without flinching. Did he already know the answer and asked this just to test her? Amity guessed that was the case.

She forced a smile. "His name is Clark Cartwright."

"And his work?" The *Oberleutnant* again flipped through his file.

"He's an English novelist and academic. He writes crime fiction. I believe he currently has nine novels in print."

The officer nodded to himself, as if something in his mind had been confirmed.

"Yes, a few of those novels were translated into German. I greatly enjoyed his main character, Sir Henry Wilson, an inspector at Scotland Yard. Amazing what one can learn from fiction."

"I also enjoy his work."

"Has Mr. Cartwright been enjoying our city?"

So he knows Clark is here too.

"I believe so."

"Good. A shame he will be leaving us so soon. I imagine he has conducted excellent research for his next book. Surely Mr. Cartwright has good connections here."

"I am not certain of that, sir. I really don't know. My main job is to make sure his daughter finishes her math homework."

The German across from her laughed appreciatively and then leaned forward. "I am not here to cause any problems, Miss Mitchell. I am not here to interrogate you. My job is simply to make sure you follow rules. *Our* rules. You have my interest, and you will keep that interest until the day you leave our protectorate."

Amity knew what he was saying—that she would be watched—but she didn't want him to know she was worried. She crossed one leg over the other and relaxed into her seat. "I am thankful to know I can feel safe here under your protection. With all the people in this large city, it's an honor that you're taking time for me."

Amusement brightened his face. "I have my job. You have yours." Then he stood. "Can I have someone drive you to your hotel? It is usually a safe city, but with all the refugees, I am worried there could be a problem."

"Oh, no. I have a ride waiting."

His face brightened. "Is Mr. Cartwright in the vehicle? I would love to meet him."

"Yes, he is."

She stood and led the way. Her soft-soled shoes barely made a sound down the hall, but his boots reverberated loudly. From the other direction a small group of Germans in uniform walked slowly, admiring the art on the walls as if they were appreciating a great museum.

Just like that, this is all theirs now.

Clark must have seen her descending the steps with the *Oberleutnant*. As the German officer approached, Clark stepped out of the car and extended his hand.

Amity smiled. "Clark, it seems you have a reader who would like to meet you."

"A reader…is that right?"

"Only a few of your volumes. I'm waiting for more to be translated into German."

"Well." Clark stroked his chin. "I'm unsure whether that will happen now. It might not be a priority for my publisher. Although your English seems good."

"Not good enough for reading in English, but I thank you." He cocked one eyebrow. "But if you do write a novel of the occupation of Czechoslovakia, can you name one of the characters *Oberleutnant* Böhm?"

"I could, but he would most likely be one of the villains."

The *Oberleutnant* smiled wickedly and nodded his head. "*Ja!* Of course. *Gut!*" Then with another firm handshake, he strode away.

Madeline was waiting for them when they arrived back at the small office. Her face was white, and if possible, she looked even more tired than she had earlier that morning.

The woman glanced up at Amity with a weary gaze. "Well, how did it go?"

"He didn't say much. The *Oberleutnant* simply encouraged me to follow their rules in all we do. Oh, and he made it very clear that I am being watched. He had a file on me. A real file…and he asked to meet Clark. It seems he knows of his work."

Madeline gasped. "He did not."

"Oh, he most certainly did. He is a fan…and he asked if Clark could use his name in an upcoming novel."

Madeline turned her gaze to Clark, eyes wide.

"I suppose you did not understand just who we had in our presence," Amity said.

But instead of a smile, Clark's mouth turned into a frown. "I know it sounds like a good time was had by all, but this makes me even more worried. What else does he know about us that wasn't revealed today?"

"Well, just as long as we can continue taking children to safety, I don't really care what he knows." Amity slipped off her sweater and placed it on the back of the chair. She tried to act as if it really hadn't bothered her to be interviewed by the Germans. Or that she was being watched.

My every move has been recorded. And that had happened before the Nazis had invaded the country. What would happen now that they were here and in control?

Unwilling to think about that anymore, she turned to Madeline. "Let me guess, the travel documents for the children haven't yet come in?"

Madeline let out a long, frustrated sigh. "No. What is the Home Office thinking, that we're all on holiday around here?"

Amity had barely sat down when she rose to her feet again. "I suppose this warrants another call." She slipped her sweater back on and turned to Clark. "Do you wish to come with me? They still let me use the phones at the Hotel Evropa. I don't feel safe using the lines here anymore."

He opened the office door for her. "Yes, of course."

She glanced back at Emil and Madeline, wishing she knew what Emil was thinking. He'd been silent on the ride home from the castle. He'd been quiet since they'd entered the room.

"Wish me luck," Amity quipped.

"You'll need all the luck you can find," Madeline mumbled under her breath. "I imagine every hotel lobby will be full of new German soldiers. They are taking over every space available. You'll spend an hour waiting for the phone at least."

Amity and Clark discovered what Madeline said was true. Making an urgent phone call in the lobby was now more difficult with the presence of noisy *Oberleutnants* phoning their wives. She'd finally gotten through, only to discover that Andrew was not there. But she received even worse news as she and Clark walked back to Madeline's house.

"I have to tell you, Amity, that I have a train ticket, but it is for tomorrow. The ticket office said they could not guarantee anything beyond that with circumstances as they are."

"Yes, of course. It makes perfect sense. I'm glad, though, that you've been here, especially the last couple of days. I needed you by my side."

They passed the Church of Saint Salvator on Křižovnická Street by the bridgehead, and Clark paused and pointed. "Amity, look."

The church was completely full. No mass was being said, but everyone was kneeling. Amity's chest ached as if thorns were being pressed into her heart.

They continued on to the Charles Bridge, and they discovered yet another German convoy was heading into town. As soon as the trucks and tanks passed, they had to stop on the bridge itself to let a line of infantry march across. The soldiers' boots pounded on the stone roads in a heavy staccato beat. And then almost in defiance, cathedral bells from all around the city chimed out, drowning out the sound.

Tears came to Amity then. She hadn't cried all day, but hearing those bells stirred her deeply. She tried to keep her sobs quiet, but one broke through. Clark paused and wrapped his arm around her shoulders, pulling her close. His frozen breath puffed from his mouth and filled the air between them.

"What's wrong?"

She laughed, a sad laugh. "What isn't wrong?" She pointed to the white slopes of Petřín Hill. "They are deploying field guns on the slopes, but that's not why I'm crying." She sighed. "The bells—they reminded me that God *is* still here." She placed a hand over her heart. "The enemy can come, but God is still here for those who believe—for those who kneel before Him."

As they neared Madeline's house, they noticed groups of soldiers attaching loudspeakers to lampposts and trees. And not too many hours later, voices came over the loudspeakers. Martial law was declared and a nine o'clock curfew was announced. Joachim von Ribbentrop, foreign minister of Nazi Germany, had also commandeered the main radio stations. Czechoslovakia had ceased to exist. Bohemia and Moravia would be incorporated into greater Germany. The government, now a protectorate, would take orders from Berlin.

"What do you think they will do about the transports? Do you think they will allow us to continue?" Amity dared to ask Clark as they sat at Madeline's table drinking a cup of tea.

"I suppose you can only keep going until they tell you to stop."

You. The word hung in the air.

"You will leave in the morning?"

He picked up her hand and stroked her fingers. Then he placed them to his lips and kissed each one. A shiver traveled up Amity's arm, and she was certain of another thing too—when it was time for her to return to London, she would have Clark's love waiting there.

"I will be leaving in the morning, but I will make you this

promise. You continue to do what you're doing here, and Celia and I will find as many people as possible to take the children."

Amity couldn't hold back her emotions any longer. She rushed to him, falling into his arms, and then pulled back. "I will say goodbye now, Clark, because I'm not sure I can handle it in the morning."

"Yes, of course. At least I leave knowing one thing."

"What's that?"

"I know I have, indeed, fallen in love."

"I love you too, Clark." The words were unfamiliar on her tongue. She'd never spoken them to anyone besides her parents and brother.

She embraced him again, allowing him to pull her close.

She listened to the beating of his heart, and he placed gentle kisses on the top of her head.

Finally, she pulled back. "Thank you, Clark. Thank you for believing in me. Thank you for urging me to come here. I needed to remember that there are things—people—worth fighting for."

Pavla lay beside her children and stared at the broken window, realizing her heart had been shattered into pieces. Her children slept, and she decided not to wake them. Only sleep kept their hunger at bay. Only sleep kept her fears at bay too. Yet sleep had evaded her most of the night.

And not long after dawn she'd heard the voices of fellow refugees talking in the halls. After the last transport, there weren't many of them left—only her and her children and a few other women and children who had been too ill to travel.

The news wasn't what she'd wanted to hear. The Nazis had come, and they would not waste any time bringing their new protectorate into line with the laws and policies of the Third Reich. A black shroud had descended upon Prague, and soon it would reach its fingers of death into every village and hamlet.

Slowly, quietly, as to not wake the children, Pavla sat up and wrapped her arms around her legs. She placed her chin on her knees. Her lips pressed into a line, thin with emotion, and she blinked dangerously fast, attempting to hold everything inside. She couldn't cry and wake the children.

She was just about to lay back down and attempt sleep again when a soft whimpering met her ears. She stood and walked to the door of their room, which had once been a small classroom. Then she left the room and moved down the hall.

The whimpering came from the door next to her, and Pavla knocked softly. She heard shuffling inside. The door opened, and a small boy sat there. He looked to be no more than three years old. Pavla knelt before him.

"Are you all right?"

"*Ne.* I am thirsty."

Pavla looked into the room. The curtains were shut tight, and it was too dark to see anything. "Does your mother know?"

He wrapped his arms around her neck. "She no wake up."

A sinking feeling came over her. Pavla pulled the boy into an embrace and stood. "Come. We have water in my room. Then I will check on your mother, *ano*?"

The boy yawned and then nodded. His eyes fluttered closed. She took him into their room and poured water into a tin cup. He drank it thirstily.

"What is your name?" Pavla asked, taking the cup from his hands.

"Michal."

"Well, Michal. You stay here, and I will go check on your mother." She squatted down and patted the place on the bed next to Klára. He ran over, curled up, and soon his eyes fluttered closed again.

Seeing that he was taken care of, Pavla took a deep breath and headed back. She stepped inside the door, sucked in a deep breath, and moved to the curtains, opening them wide. Golden light flooded the room. Pavla's eyes moved from the pair of child's shoes, to the small suitcase, to the bed. And that's when she saw the boy's mother. The woman was so thin, so frail, that she looked not more than a twelve-year-old child herself in form, even though her face revealed she was Pavla's age.

Her cheek rested on the pillow, and her dark hair partially covered her face. She had fine crafted features, reminding Pavla of an angel statue. Pavla watched closely, looking to see if the woman's chest rose or fell. She saw the slightest movement.

"Oh, thank goodness," she muttered.

The woman's eyes fluttered open. Pavla took a step back. "I am sorry. I did not mean to wake you. Your little boy—he was crying."

She lifted her head and looked around. "Michal?"

Pavla pointed to the doorway.

"He is in my room. He was thirsty, so I gave him water." She smiled. "I'm Pavla, by the way."

"And I am Maruška Tesařová." The woman's head lowered. The softest cry escaped her lips. "I am so sorry. I was in so much pain. I took the last of my medicine from the doctor. I had been saving it for months."

Pavla sucked in a breath and waited for the rest.

The woman offered the slightest smile. "I have been saving it to allow me rest without pain, not to die, yet that will come soon enough too."

The woman sat up, and Pavla could see that took effort. Maruška rubbed her eyes. "I am sorry Michal woke you."

Pavla wanted to tell the woman it was no problem. She wanted to go to her room, lift the sleeping boy, and bring him back to his mother, but something stirred within. Compassion for this woman overwhelmed her. Instead of simply returning the boy, Pavla moved toward the bed. Maruška patted the place beside her, and Pavla sat.

"What do you mean that death will come soon enough?"

Tears filled the woman's eyes. She covered her face with her hands and slightly shook her head.

Pavla wrapped an arm around the woman. Maruška's shoulder blades sharply protruded.

In a moment, the tears stopped. Maruška lowered her hands and attempted a smile.

"I was diagnosed with cancer of the pancreas a year ago. My mother died of the same condition when she was my age. I had hoped the cancer wouldn't find me." She gave a harsh laugh. "Or I was hoping that if it did find me, my husband would be there for my son. But the Germans took my husband. It was then I knew our only hope was to get on a train to England. I was put onto the list with women and children, but when the train left, I wasn't allowed on it. My health...I am worried my health will make it so my son can't go to England. What will happen to him then?"

"Have you talked to the volunteer working on the transports?"

She nodded. "Since my son already has his travel documents, they said they can put him on the next transport—the one with the children."

"Well, that is good then..."

"*If* the transport happens, now that the Germans have arrived." The woman laid down on her side again. "And if I make it that long. If not, who will care for my son until then?" The woman's eyes fluttered closed as if holding them open was just too much work, and soon she'd again fallen back into her drugged sleep.

"I will," Pavla dared to whisper. "I will."

— THIRTY —

Prague, Czechoslovakia
Wednesday, March 22, 1939

A week had passed since Czechoslovakia had come under German control, and the only thing noticeable at first was an increase of military weapons and men around the town. That and the addition of a small boy to Pavla's room and to her heart. Dark-haired Michal reminded Pavla of Ondřej when he was younger. Thinking of that, she smiled softly to herself. She and Abram had been talking about having another child just a year ago, but then the world turned upside down and they decided they could not bring another child into the madness. Could either of them have imagined all that would happen? Thankfully no. Even with the looming threat, though, they had enjoyed their life together. Enjoyed being a family. Enjoyed being in love.

Pavla lay on the sagging mattress and pushed the curtain to the side to look out at the city that had become home. The yellow morning light bounced off the red tiled roofs and streamed through the window. For the first time in months, she'd woken with a smile. The dream had come as a gift. She was back in the forest again, running through the leaves and rolling down the hills, gathering speed, laughter escaping her lips. She had spent her childhood playing in the Bohemian woods with friends, and her favorite days were sunny ones like today.

She'd also met Abram on a day such as this—a day when bright sun had come after days filled with gray clouds. She had traveled to Olomouc for her cousin's wedding. Her parents had urged her to attend the wedding even though she didn't know her cousin very well. She'd seen Abram then, so handsome and friendly. And then just a few weeks later there was his family at the synagogue.

With his tall, thin frame, dark hair, and easy smile, Pavla had been attracted to him immediately. They used to go for walks in the sunny woods on days like today.

All these thoughts were on her mind when a soft knock on the door to their room caused her to jump. She threw her coat over her dressing gown and hurried to the door. Emil stood there.

"We received news. There will be another transport next week."

Pavla gasped. "So soon?"

"Yes, and your children will be on it."

"They will?" She clung to the door tighter. "How did this happen?"

"When I explained your situation to Amity, she called her brother. Andrew called the family who had sponsored those other two children whose mother had taken them off the transport list. He explained the situation, and they agreed to take Ondřej and Klára in their place."

She glanced back at her children, and sudden panic overtook her. She had been with them since they were born. There had been only a few times when she and Abram had left them in the care of his parents. Maybe this was a mistake after all.

Pavla felt his touch on her arm, and she jumped. "I am so sorry about all this. About your husband, and now your children..."

She turned back to him and nodded. She pictured them leaving on the train, and blinking back tears, she knew it would be the most loving thing she'd ever done for her children. More than reading bedtime stories or bandaging knees, her true test of a mother's love had come down to this.

God, please help me go through with it.

Pavla was determined to take the next step forward, no matter how hard it was. She wanted to tell Emil she appreciated his kindness, but she knew in truth that it was her wedding ring that had moved them to the top of the list. She also knew if she tried to speak now, tears would overcome her words.

Instead, she simply smiled and brushed a wet strand of hair behind her ear. Tears rimmed Emil's eyes too, and then she thought of Marek's prideful face. Maybe Marek had kept the ring. But she would not mention the ring at all. She didn't want to do anything to risk her children having a spot. "Thank you. I suppose I need to talk to my children today...to prepare them."

"I know it won't be easy." He looked at his watch. "I need to get going. There are other families I need to inform."

"I won't be the only one with an aching heart that day, will I?"

"No," Emil whispered. He cleared his throat. "And as for the details." He straightened his back, as if remembering he was there in an official capacity. "Each child is allowed one suitcase. Only clothes."

"Only clothes, but—"

"Only clothes. No photos or toys," Emil interrupted. His voice was stern, but there was also a tenderness there.

She was about to tell him that there was no need to worry

about that, since her children had neither. "And food?" she asked.

"We will make lunches to send." He turned to walk away, and she reached out her hand and touched his arm. "Sir..."

Emil paused and turned. "Yes?"

"The photos that you took of my children..."

"Yes?"

"Is there any way I can get a copy of those?" She felt pressure on her chest and placed a hand on her heart. "I had to leave so quickly from my home, you see. I do not have any photos. Is there any way..."

He nodded. "Yes, of course. I did not think of that, but I understand. I will see what I can do."

"Oh, one more thing," Pavla dared to call after him.

"Yes?"

"What about Michal? Will he be on the transport too?"

Emil scratched his head. "I am not sure who you are talking about."

"There is a mother and son in the room next door. They were supposed to be on the last transport—the one with mothers and children. She is ill, and they were left behind, but the boy has all his paperwork done...at least that is what his mother said."

Emil pointed to the door, and she nodded. "Yes, that one."

"For some reason I have not heard about this. I will talk to her." He tucked his hands into his pants pockets, lowered his head, and moved to the next door, knocking. Pavla heard Maruška's voice, and she was thankful the woman was up and around today. Pavla just hoped she wasn't in too much pain.

Pavla shut the door behind her and returned to the creaky bed and sat, waiting for her children to wake. She watched them sleep, forcing herself to remember this moment, remember their gentle breathing and the soft rise and fall of their chests. How many times had she watched them sleep like this? Many times, but it suddenly wasn't enough.

Klára woke first, her eyes fluttering open. She looked up at her mother and smiled. "I dreamed we were eating birthday cake."

"Oh, that sounds like a wonderful dream. Did it taste delicious?"

She nodded her head and then pouted. "We don't have any birthday cake, do we?"

"No, not today. But as soon as Ondřej wakes up, I have exciting news."

Klára tried to be patient, waiting for her brother to wake, but her singing and running back and forth across the room made it impossible for him to stay asleep.

After he was awake, they made a picnic on the floor, eating the bread and cheese she had purchased the previous evening. Her funds were running short, but she had enough to last until the children left. After that, she didn't need to worry. That her children had enough was what was most important.

"We are going to move again, but this time we can't all go together. I will go to a different place, but you two get to ride on a train. It's going to be a long journey."

"How far? Can we bring our suitcases?" Klára asked.

"*Ja*, filled with all your things."

Ondřej scowled. "Just our things? What about your things? Why can't you go too?"

Pavla forced a smile. "My things. They are staying with me for now. I will not be joining you on the train to England. I have to stay back to clear up a few matters of business."

Ondřej crossed his arms over his chest. "Then we will wait for you."

"*Ne.*" Pavla's voice was stern, startling her children. "You do not know how hard it has been to get these documents. You will travel next week." Then her voice softened. "It is what your father would want. He wanted the best for you—to protect you—and this is the only way I know how." Tears came then, brushing against her lashes. She told herself not to cry in front of her children, but it did little good. She would cry, and they would see her tears. That's just how things had to be.

Klára's eyes were large and filled with questions. "But you will come to find us?" Her voice quivered.

"There are people who will tell me where you are. In fact, they've already told me you will be in a nice, safe place with a family. You will sleep in a real bed again and be able to attend school."

At the mention of school, Klára's face brightened. She'd only been able to go to school for a few months, and she'd cried and cried when Abram told her she couldn't return. How could Pavla have explained to her young daughter that Jews were no longer welcome? Klára saw herself like any other child. Her light hair made her look more Aryan than Jew, but that did not matter to the Germans. They knew each Jew. They sought them out. They longed to destroy them, just as others through the centuries had tried to destroy God's chosen people.

"So we will go on a train? A real train..." Ondřej fixed his eyes on hers. "To England?"

"Yes." Pavla nodded, trying to be brave. "You have always wanted to ride a train. You will go with Klára. I will need you to do that for me."

He didn't answer, and she guessed he knew more than he let on. He knew about his father and about Hitler. He no doubt knew she would most likely not be coming for them.

Klára wrinkled her nose. "Where is England?"

"Oh, it's a faraway place—a big island."

Klára scratched her head. "The train goes over the water?"

"After the train you will go on a ship too. It will be a wonderful trip." Pavla clapped her hands together and attempted to sound convincing. "Very nice people will meet you. You will stay for a time and...and I imagine you will make so many new friends." She stroked Klára's hair back from her face.

"When will you come, *Maminka*?"

Pavla sighed. She furrowed her brow and feigned anger. It was easier to do that than allow herself to be overcome by the emotion that built inside. "You know, I am not certain. And that is a cruel trick, is it not? Just pray that *Mutti* will get a ticket. *Ja*, just pray." Pavla shook her head then and swallowed down the emotion.

She reached out to touch little Klára on the top of the head and did the same with Ondřej. *God, who will love these little ones now?*

Ondřej pulled away but didn't respond. She knew he would obey her and go. She just hoped that someday he would understand. These children were all that remained of her shattered life, and it gave her a small bit of peace that they would live on. She and Abram would live on in them.

A rattling of the broken glass captured their attention, and they all looked to the window. Outside the building, on the street beyond, a German tank rolled by. It was emblazoned with the emblem of Hitler's Reich.

"Children, sit on the floor now. Get out of the sight of the window."

Pavla wasn't sure if they could be seen from the outside—or if the Germans even knew anyone was in there—but she didn't want to take a chance.

After the sound dissipated and she knew the tank was out of sight, she allowed her children to rise. Pavla closed the curtain, blocking the view, and they all dressed for the day. They would stay inside as much as possible. It was always a risk to leave now that the Germans had arrived. She had only one duty now as their mother—to get them to the train station safely.

"Promise me, will you, that you will obey the women on the train who will care for you? And stay together. Promise me you will always stay together."

Ondřej nodded, and Klára attempted to smile. "We promise, *Mutti*."

She kneeled before them, her knees pressing into the cold concrete floor. Pavla's arms wrapped around her children, pulling them close. She placed a dozen kisses on their cheeks but refused to allow any more tears to come. Those would come later, after she knew they were on the train. After she knew they were safe. "That's my good, good children..."

It was only after Pavla knew that her children would soon be safe on a transport that she allowed herself once again to remember the night her husband was killed. *Kristallnacht*—November 10, 1938. Had it been just four months ago? The dark of the night pressed around her, and as she listened to her children's breathing as they slept, she allowed her thoughts to take her back.

That night Pavla had believed the worst had come when news arrived that the synagogue was burning. Even though they attended Shabbat services only a few times a year, the synagogue was still the center of their community. It was a place of prayer, study, and education. She often spent time with friends doing social and charitable work, and for her whole family it was a social center. It was bad enough to think of their *shul* burning.

Her knees quivered, and a thousand times she wished she could go back and replay that night. She had been trying to get her children to sleep, pretending all was right in the world, while her husband and his parents discussed whether they should go to the city and see if their business was still standing. She was reading them one of their favorite bedtime stories. Though all was quiet in their apartment, a storm was raging in the center of town, just a fifteen-minute walk away.

The creaking of the bedroom door and the shaft of light from Abram opening the door had first annoyed her. Couldn't her husband give her a few minutes to get the children to sleep? But worry had creased her husband's face, even deeper than it had earlier, causing her to lay aside the book she'd been reading to the children.

"Shh...I will be right back." She'd attempted to keep her voice soft and gentle as she patted her children's heads. And while Klára complained that she'd stopped the story, Ondřej sat up in bed and watched her go. He balled his fists and narrowed his gaze, as if he knew an enemy was waiting not far beyond their home, an enemy he was ready to fight with all his strength. Her poor sweet boy. He had no idea how much fighting he would have to do over the weeks and months to come.

Looking back, Pavla knew his childhood ended that moment. For months he'd overheard their low, whispered tones, probably trying to decipher what had caused his father and grandfather so much angst. *Dědeček* had wanted to immigrate to Palestine, yet it was Abram who had been more reasonable. "Let us just leave the country, Father—to England or even Australia—anywhere to protect our family."

If it had only been her and the children that Abram had been concerned about, Pavla knew they would have left months earlier. They had all heard Hitler's speeches and rumors of Jewish persecution. Yet no one in Czechoslovakia realized Hitler's death grip had already wrapped around their country, just waiting for him to squeeze.

And then the German had arrived that night, taking away her husband and his parents, and the terror of the Nazis had hit home, shattering forever the life they had once enjoyed.

Now, in the abandoned schoolroom, Pavla cuddled closer to Klára. At the thought of both of her children leaving without her, she wanted to curl up and die. She imagined herself finding the shallow grave where Abram was buried and stretching out over it, allowing herself to fall asleep. But even in her despair, something stirred inside her.

Abram gave you love, now you must give him a future through your children. As long as they breathe, they carry on their father's good name and his story.

It was those words that stirred Pavla's soul from the dark cave she'd hidden inside. It was then she knew she only had one mission—to ensure that her children, Abram's children, lived. After that it didn't matter what happened to her. After that she could allow her mourning to consume her.

THIRTY-ONE

Prague, Czechoslovakia
Tuesday, March 28, 1939

Pavla's mouth watered, and her stomach growled as she eyed the two plum dumplings, wrapping them up in two kerchiefs and placing them inside her carpetbag for safekeeping. Each child's suitcase bore two labels: "Wilson Station, Prague" and "Royal Scot, London-Glasgow." Her children's former life and their new one represented by two sticky pieces of paper. And their last gifts from their mother were two delicious treats given to her by a Nazi soldier whose attention she had caught outside a small café. Since her children couldn't eat the dumplings on the train, Pavla's plan was for them to eat them on the walk to the station on Friday—anything to distract them from what was to come.

Earlier she'd left the children in the room with Maruška and Michal. Maruška was up and around today as if she was feeling better, but deep down Pavla worried it wouldn't last. Both Pavla's parents had died from illness, and she knew that often a few weeks before the end of one's life, one often rallied new strength. Strength that soon slipped away until it was gone.

After making sure the children were settled, Pavla had put on her best dress—the one without the yellow star—and walked down the street to the store. Today, she'd decided, she'd shop like every other citizen. She had a few things she needed to buy, and she never would have been able to buy them wearing the star.

But before she shopped, she needed time to think, to pray. She'd walked through the Jewish district, and not a person was in sight. The doors of the synagogue were sealed tight. A silence as empty as death filled the air, almost as an omen of what was to come.

She'd been here before with Abram, and it had been a vibrant area back then. She approached a bench by the Pinkas Synagogue and sat. The last time they'd been here, a few years ago, the streets had been bustling with locals and visitors. Rabbis had walked along the streets with their disciples. *Where are they now? All in hiding? Have some of them already been sent away?*

She knew this synagogue dated back to the fifteenth century. Behind it was the Jewish cemetery with layers of graves, their centuries-old gravestones piled on top, leaning on each other for support. In a way, Pavla knew that when she walked away from this place, she would be walking away from that faith too. She was sending her children away to live with Christian families, and when their train pulled away, she would take steps toward that new way of faith too. It wasn't that she was leaving the religion she'd been raised in. Instead, she was discovering it in a new way by daring to believe that Jesus was, indeed, the Messiah her people had been looking for—that she had been looking for.

When she had stayed at the refugee center, many of the mothers had been upset about being separated from their children. But equally upsetting to these Jewish mothers was that most of their children were going into Christian homes.

"Is it worth saving my child's life knowing she will be raised not knowing the faith of her ancestors?" one woman asked the others. Some hoped that their children would remember the Jewish faith of their early years. Others said that just knowing that their children would live was enough.

For Pavla, maybe this was her children's chance to discover a faith that she and Abram had not given them. She thought of Radek and Emílie and the peace she had found in their home. Maybe, in a small way, this would bring her children the strength for whatever they had to face in their own futures.

She'd left the Jewish district then and had gone shopping in the fine part of town that she remembered so well. After this week, she would not be able to give such gifts to her children, and this was her last chance. She'd made her purchases without a problem. No one had guessed she was a Jew.

Pavla had only been a few blocks from the store when the German soldier approached her, inviting her to lunch. She remembered then that she wore no ring, no star. She was about to refuse, but the rumbling of her stomach caused her to give in. *They have taken from me. Today I will take from them—even if it is only lunch.*

It was the first time she'd eaten inside a café in months. She chatted with the handsome soldier, forgetting for a time he was her enemy, and requested two plum dumplings to go. The man had honored her request and asked if he could meet her for lunch the next day. Pavla offered him a smile and then slipped away, strolling down Malá Strana. The soldier had no idea that beneath her smile were tears, nor that within the shopping bag she carried were the last gifts she had to offer her children—new shoes for their journey. Shoes that would walk them up the steps to the platform and onto the train that would carry them away from her forever.

When she arrived back at the school, Ondřej and Klára were still playing with Michal, running around in their new coats, even though they were inside. Emil had brought the new coats by the day before, and she'd been thankful. Her first winter without her children. Their first winter without their mother. Maruška was sitting in a chair, watching the children play, a soft smile on her lips. If she was in pain, she didn't show it, and for that Pavla was grateful.

Yet even as she sat down next to Maruška she couldn't get her mind off of the coats and the shoes. Her children had what they needed now, but what of the winters after that? Who would make sure they wore warm coats and didn't lose their mittens? Pavla placed her fingers to her eyes and pressed. She couldn't think of that now. She had only to think of the next few days and of getting her children to safety.

— THIRTY-TWO —

Prague, Czechoslovakia
Wednesday, March 29, 1939

Emil had come around to the schoolhouse the night before, telling Pavla to be at the office today to look over her children's travel documents and make sure every detail was correct. Now that the Germans were here, there couldn't be any mistakes.

Pavla and her children arrived just on time, and other women were waiting. When her turn came, Pavla provided their last name, and the older woman with gray hair handed over a file.

Excitement caused her shoulders to tense as Pavla held the document in her hand, reading it to herself. She couldn't believe she had transport papers. She swallowed hard, knowing all the time and effort it had cost these volunteers to get them.

> *This document of identity is issued with the approval of His Majesty's Government in the United Kingdom to young persons to be admitted to the United Kingdom for educational purposes under the care of the Inter-Aid Committee for children.*
>
> *This document requires no visa.*

Listed next was her son's name, his birthday, and the address of the school. He looked older in his photo, more mature than his eight years. Two seals made the document valid. *This is it.* Ondřej would be leaving her.

"And my daughter's papers?" she asked the woman.

The woman, Madeline, glanced up and looked to Klára, offering her a smile.

She began shuffling through the papers on her desk. "Your daughter. Oh, yes. Let me see if I have the paperwork here."

The woman continued looking through the pile of files. "I am certain the file was here. I remember reading her name, and it was such a beautiful photo."

The older woman turned to the younger woman with the auburn hair. They said something in English—something Pavla did not understand, but from the look on her face it didn't look good.

The younger woman hurried over and glanced at both of Pavla's children. She studied their faces and then scratched her head. Then, after saying something else, she turned and hurried into a back office. Was that other man back there? Marek? A sinking feeling plummeted in Pavla's gut.

Pavla's stomach clenched, and she sent up a hurried prayer. What would happen if they only had the paperwork for her son and not her daughter? To know one of her children would be safe but not the other?

Klára looked up at her with large blue eyes. "*Maminka*, what is happening?"

Pavla stroked her daughter's hair. "Nothing, sweetheart. They are just trying to find all the papers we need."

Ondřej's dark-brown eyes narrowed, turning his face into a scowl. "Klára will not have to stay here, will she?"

Pavla smiled down at her son, hoping it was believable. "Of course not, Ondřej. I am certain in just a moment they will find her file too. We just need to have faith."

The volunteers had spent the day turning the office upside down, but they could not find Klára's file. Amity had never been so frustrated. How could a file be lost? A child's future was at stake.

When the day slipped into night, Amity found a ride for them back to the schoolhouse and went with them. She also brought Emil back with her to translate.

Amity watched as Pavla sent the children inside the room. Standing in the hall, she took Pavla's hands into her own. She turned to Emil. "Can you please translate?"

He nodded. "Yes, of course."

"I am so sorry. I am not sure what happened. Even Madeline says she remembers seeing the file. But I am sorry. We have not found it. Your daughter cannot go on the transport in two days."

Emil translated, and Amity's heart ached to see tears in the woman's eyes.

He turned back to Amity. "She wants to know what that means for Ondřej."

Amity released a heavy sigh. "I am so sorry. Pavla will have to make a decision. Does she want to send her son now? Or does she want him to wait with her daughter for the next transport?"

Pavla pressed her fingers to her lips. Amity could see her swallowing down her emotions.

Amity's head throbbed imagining the woman's decision. She placed two fingers to her temple, praying for wisdom.

The woman spoke to Emil, and then she slipped inside the room.

Emil's eyes looked tortured as he turned back to Amity.

"What? What did she say?"

"She says she will send her son. At least—no matter what else happens—she knows he will live."

Amity crossed her arms and pulled them in tight around her. "I just do not understand how that could have happened. This has never happened before."

Emil patted her back in an attempt to comfort her. "I have faith that we will find the file. It has to be around there somewhere."

"Yes, but I think we all have the same question. Will we have an opportunity for another transport?"

Amity's heart was heavy as she stood in the hall, but her work in this schoolhouse wasn't done.

"Emil, can you show me the ill mother and her child?"

"Oh, yes." He pointed to the next door over. "Maruška is inside." He lifted a bag in his hand. "Madeline gathered food and some medicines for me to bring. I am not sure they are going to help."

Almost on cue a boy's cry split the air. Emil knocked, and when there wasn't an answer, they hurried into the room. The mother was sitting on the bed, but she was slumped forward, as if in pain. Emil rushed to her, urging her to lie down.

Amity opened her arms to the boy. He ran to her and buried his face in her neck, his tears wetting her blouse.

"We cannot leave them like this. It is obvious that this poor mother cannot care for this boy."

"Do you have the means to care for a child?" Emil's voice was no more than a whisper.

A voice came from the hall, and Amity looked up to see Pavla standing there.

With quickened steps the beautiful woman rushed into the room. She repeated something, and Amity looked to Emil for a translation.

"Pavla says she will take care of the boy," he explained.

"But how? Why?" Amity couldn't understand.

Now that Maruška was settled, Emil moved to the window, looking out into the night. Amity could see emotion all over his face in the reflection of the window. Then he turned back to her and tapped his chest. "I suppose you don't need anything but what's in your heart to share compassion."

From the sanctuary of Amity's lap, the small boy stopped his crying. Pavla approached, reached out, and placed a hand on his head.

Behind her Maruška had fallen to sleep and was quiet now.

"Is she still with us?" Amity's voice was soft.

"Yes, but I am not sure for how long. When I came by last night to check on them, Pavla told me that Maruška hadn't eaten or drank anything for two days. She said she was up watching the children, smiling, and then—as if air were released from a balloon—she just deflated. It's all happening so fast." Emil took a few crackers from the bag and brought them to the boy, who hungrily ate them. "Thankfully, Michal is on the next transport. At least knowing this, his mother can die in peace."

Amity sighed. "I suppose we can be thankful for that."

Then she handed Michal to Pavla, amazed that when everything was being taken away from her, this woman still had something more to give.

Amity rose. "The next few days will be hard ones. Do you think you can check on them often?"

He nodded. "Yes, of course. As much as I can get away. It seems Marek has disappeared. No one has seen him for days. Yet that's not this woman's problem, is it? Seeing Pavla give of herself to this woman, though she has lost so much herself, well, that makes me want to help her as much as I can."

Amity pointed a finger at him. "I hope you're not getting any ideas. I've seen the way you look at her."

Emil sighed. "Do not worry. I will not ask it."

"Good. And let's hope that the German high command doesn't catch a whiff of your scheme. Then again, it's not your head that will roll, is it?"

— THIRTY-THREE —

Prague, Czechoslovakia
Thursday, March 30, 1939

Amity was slightly less alarmed when she was called to the Gestapo headquarters again. It was now policy that all exit documents had to be stamped in person. Her new contact for all the transports, she was told, was *Kriminalrat* Boemmelburg. She hadn't known what to expect, but when she arrived she was met by an elderly, smiling gentleman.

The *Kriminalrat* invited her to join him for tea and chatted as if they were long-lost friends. He seemed very interested in her project—too interested, as far as she was concerned. Still, she smiled, chatted, and tried to be as vague about her work and life as she could.

"I have so many questions, Miss Mitchell," he said, offering her cookies to go with her tea. "Mainly, why does England want so many Jewish children?"

"They are children. Isn't that enough?"

"There is a big difference between a child and a Jewish child." He sighed. "But I suppose you would not understand."

"*Kriminalrat* Boemmelburg, I have the paperwork for the

transport," she said, trying to steer the conversation in the right direction. "If you would just include your stamp, I could leave you to all your other important work."

He paused for a moment, and Amity held her breath. Then he lifted his gaze and met her eyes. Finally, he looked down and stamped the paper with a flourish.

"Tomorrow my Gestapo clerk will meet you at the station. And the children will be ready?"

"Yes, indeed." Amity didn't wait for the man to continue. She picked up the papers and took a step back. "I don't want to take any more of your time, sir. I appreciate your help."

"Miss Mitchell, one more thing."

"Yes, sir."

Kriminalrat Boemmelburg narrowed his gaze at her. "You have to know that I am trying to be helpful here. Germany has no need for Jews, criminals, or Communists within our borders." A shudder seemed to travel down his spine. "I will do what I can to help you remove these unwanted from our borders. And that's how I see them, as unwanted leeches."

Amity was appalled by the way the *Kriminalrat* spoke of children, as if they were cockroaches that needed to be stomped out. Even while he was conveying such hatred, his expression remained passionless. Yet she detected an underlying rage that she hadn't noticed until now. It hovered there within his eyes, and she had a feeling with the smallest provocation the anger would unleash.

Her knees grew soft, and overpowered by his gaze, Amity returned to her seat and folded her hands together, hoping to hide their trembling.

"As I was saying, we have no need for those children within our borders. But I promise you, if there are any errors on the transport list, it is *you* who will become the criminal, Miss Mitchell."

He leaned forward against his desk and folded his arms over each other. "I have toured a few of the camps, and I have to say they are no place for a lady like yourself. Yet that would be the better of two fates."

She nodded slowly, letting him know she understood. Yet the false papers seemed to burn like fire within her grasp.

"Yes, you hold an American passport, but you are still in our jurisdiction, submissive to our control. Even though it is not public knowledge, there have been quite a few Americans who have disappeared within this city in the last few months. It's so hard to keep track of them—even aid workers—on foreign soil. It's a shame, isn't it?"

Her throat tightened. She sucked in slow breaths, hoping he couldn't see the full extent of the fear that was coursing through her.

His gaze stayed fixed for a few more seconds, and Amity was sure he could hear the beating of her heart. But then, as if a flip were switched within, *Kriminalrat* Boemmelburg leaned back. His face broke into a smile, and he folded his hands on his large middle.

"I believe now that we understand each other better, yes?"

Amity nodded and searched for her voice. She cleared her throat, "Yes, sir, we do."

"Fine then. Continue with your work. You're doing such a fine job for someone your age. I will see you in no more than a month's time with information about your next transport."

"Yes, sir. I will be back." She rose and offered what she hoped was a believable smile in return.

— Thirty-Four —

Prague, Czechoslovakia
Friday, March 31, 1939

Pavla knelt before Ondřej and pulled him into her arms. Ondřej's face was even with hers, and she kissed his cheeks over and over again, unable to get enough of him.

Her son pulled back. "*Mami*, please. I will miss the train."

Pavla laughed through her tears. "I know, it is too much. I will not let you be late, and my friend Amity has promised that Klára will be on the next transport."

Worry filled his large brown eyes. "But, *Mami*, you said I was not to leave her."

"I know, but it is just the paperwork." She spread open her arms and shrugged. "These things happen. But I promise you that when the next train comes, your sister will be there, and some very nice people will bring her to you."

"And you, *Mami*?" Ondřej narrowed his gaze. "Will you come?"

She nodded wildly, hoping that he believed her. Pavla wasn't sure he would get on the train if he didn't. "Not soon, but sometime in the future, Ondřej, yes, I will come."

Pavla bit her lower lip, rose, and took a step back. Was she wrong in telling him that she would come for him? Should she tell the truth—that this was their final parting? No. She couldn't do that. In this moment she'd rather let Ondřej be impatient than racked with grief.

Ondřej leaned in, turning his cheek her direction one more time. Instead of kissing him, she took his chin in her hand and turned his face to her, peering into his eyes. "I am proud of you. Remember that. And your father was too. He was so proud of you, Ondřej." Only then did she kiss his cheek, once, twice, three times more.

Emil approached, carrying Michal. As if knowing what to do, Ondřej extended his hand. "Come, Michal, you can sit with me."

Pavla didn't have to tell him to watch out for his little friend on the train. She knew he would, just as he'd always cared for his sister. She just hoped her son didn't take all the responsibility upon his shoulders for all the other children in the home he was going to. Maybe in England he'd have a childhood once more.

"Will Ondřej be going across the water, *Maminka*? And in a few weeks, will I be going across the water too?" Klára rocked from her heels to her toes and back again as she asked the same question she'd already asked twenty times that morning.

Pavla released her hold on her son, even though her heart ached and everything within her told her to hold on tight.

"*Ano*, Klára. Ondřej will be going across the sea to England. His first time on a train and on a ship."

She smiled at her son, hoping he, too, would see this as an adventure. "Make sure you remember everything so can you write me and tell me about it."

"Yes, *Maminka*," he said. And then with one more quick hug he took Michal's hand and headed to the line to join the others.

~

It took forever for them to get on the train. But once inside, Ondřej found a seat for him and Michal. He sat closest to the window and dared to look outside, looking for his mother.

She stood rigid as a statue, standing on the platform, unmoving. Klára twirled by his mother's side as if she wasn't upset at all that he was leaving. Ondřej waved at her even though he knew she couldn't see him. She was too small to really understand.

Then he waved his hands frantically at his mother. Did she see him? If *Mami* did, she made no sign of it. In his mind he prayed a prayer of protection over his dear mother, just as he imagined his father would have done. Then he thought of his father too.

Táta, I tried to do my best to take care of them, but why do I have to do this alone? Is it wrong for me to go and for them to stay?

The train started to pick up speed, and Michal let out a happy squeal. Around Ondřej, children cheered and sang. To them it was a great adventure. But his poor mother. How could he rejoice to be leaving his mother?

With frantic movements Ondřej reached for the window to open it—to call out to his mother one last time—but the window was sealed. She was just a small gray blur now, and with trembling hands he pressed against the glass. If only there could be a way of escape for her too. How could he live his life without a father and a mother? How could he live without Klára? *O Creator God,* his soul cried, *please help us...*

Ondřej released a breath when the train station was finally out of view. He missed his mother in a way he hadn't expected. Not the mother who'd brought Klára and him to Prague—the secretive one who pretended as if they were not being hunted here in

Czechoslovakia, just as the German Jews had been hunted before them—but the one who used to laugh with them, dance with them, tell them stories. That mother had died the day they left Olomouc, he supposed.

He also missed his father and still felt guilty for leaving. His father had wanted him to be the protector, so why had he run?

For the months before his father's death, they had spent special time together. At least twice a week his father would wake him in the night and lead him out to *Dědeček*'s workshop beyond the garden. Father had told him he'd wished he could protect Ondřej's childhood, but in this world that was not possible.

And as the hours had ticked by and Ondřej had rubbed his eyes, attempting to stay awake, his father had talked to him about the resistance. Ondřej had stayed quiet and attentive during the midnight lessons. His father had spoken of how to survive and how to care for his mother and sister if needed. Ondřej had done his best.

Once, his father had even brought a friend who had taught Ondřej how to resist questioning by the Gestapo. Thankfully that hadn't been needed, yet every night since his father's death he'd replayed all he had learned before he drifted off to sleep. How to overcome anxiety from hiding in a dark space, how to deal with heat and cold, and how to hide in ways one wouldn't be found.

Ondřej hadn't used many of those things, but he *had* remembered where to tell his mother to go for help. He had been able to forage for food while she slept in the shed. He had done his best to help keep Klára distracted so she wouldn't be so noisy.

Ondřej looked at Michal, who stared out the window so peacefully. Ondřej was sure that he wouldn't be so peaceful if he was old enough to understand they'd soon be traveling through the land of their enemies. The land of the dictator who wanted all Jews dead, even light-haired ones like his sister.

Please...let her be able to get out.

Ondřej yawned and stretched. How many hours had they been traveling? He'd lost count.

The scariest part of the trip was going through Germany. In his mind's eye, Ondřej pictured the Nazis boarding and telling them to get off the train, but that hadn't happened. They were nearly all the way through. Now the German-Dutch frontier was just ahead. Or at least that's what the woman in the train car said. She had helped to take care of Michal, who now slept.

The train started to slow, and Ondřej's heart jumped to his throat. They could get out of Germany, couldn't they? There was no problem, was there?

A boy rushed up to Ondřej. "We are in Holland! The Germans are behind us!"

Not too long after that, the train pulled into the first Dutch station. The people looked different here. They looked happy and healthy. Ondřej let out a low whistle. "Look, this is a busy place."

A large number of people were on the platform. The train neared and slowed. People waved. Some cheered.

"Are they cheering for us?" the boy asked Ondřej.

"Surely not. How would they even know?"

But when the train came to a complete stop, they were told they were going to disembark for a time. "Come, children, lunch is waiting. Look at all the people who have come to see you," the woman who held Michal said.

"They are here for us?" Ondřej's jaw dropped opened. His eyes widened. In Olomouc, people had known him for who he was—the shopkeeper's son—but after he left, he was a nobody. Just a person hiding. And among the refugees he was just a face in the crowd. But here. His heart warmed in his chest. He was important.

"If they ask, I will tell them my name is Andrew."

Emil had told Ondřej that Andrew was his name in English. Emil had also said it was the name of the man who had traveled to Czechoslovakia to save the children. Andrew liked his new name, and he also made a promise that one day he would save children too.

— THIRTY-FIVE —

Prague, Czechoslovakia
Saturday, April 8, 1939

Konrád narrowed his gaze at Emil. "Did you think you could escape from us so easily?"

A lone lightbulb hung from the ceiling of the dank basement of the city municipal building that had recently been turned into one of the Gestapo outposts around the city. And under the bulb sat Emil, with hands and feet tied. Konrád felt hurt. He'd trusted Emil to bring him Pavla Šimonová. Instead, he'd tried to escape.

Next to Emil was a table with two items on it. A family photo of the Šimonová family and a ring.

"What a fool, trying to get across the border hidden under a pile of straw. It was smart of you to try to bribe the farmer. Too bad I had already gotten to him first, letting him know if any refugees approached him, looking for a means of escape, that he'd receive a finder's fee. Thankfully my bribe was larger than yours."

In the chair, Emil did not move. He only looked straight ahead.

"Did you think that if you gave all your time and energy to the British cause, they would save you? Sacrificing yourself for others, *ja*, it sounds noble. But did you really think that anyone would be there for you at the end?"

"What do you want from me?" Emil growled under his breath. "I told you I did not see that woman."

"You lie, Emil. If you haven't see her, then why did you have her ring?"

"How do you know its hers?" Email said defiantly.

"It's in the photograph. This very ring is on her hand."

Emil shrugged. "Someone gave it to me."

Heat surged through Konrád. He slapped Emil's mouth with the back of his hand. Emil let out a low grunt, followed by a moan. Blood trickled from his lips.

Konrád wiped the back of his hand across his forehead, no doubt leaving a bit of Emil's blood behind. Not that it mattered. He hoped to be covered with Emil's blood by the time he was finished. "Emil Marek, bookseller of anti-Nazi propaganda. It would be so much easier if you would just tell me where she is."

Emil jutted out his chin. "I will never support your quest. You deserve nothing."

"I have no quest except what will bring me satisfaction. I have told you before that I will not hurt her. I simply want what is owed me."

Emil lifted his gaze again. "What do you mean?"

"I mean that for all my life I had to live with a father who drank every night until he passed out, which I didn't mind, since it brought sweet relief from the beatings I would get with the cane. Yet even as a child I knew it wasn't me he hated, but the Jews who led to our family's destruction.

"We had a beautiful home until after the Geneva Compact. Then we found our German homeland in Czech territory. And my father—a city leader—was out of a job."

Konrád sighed. "Losing his position was hard enough, but after having to sell his property to Jewish vermin, my father was never the same."

Emil sunk deeper into his seat, the hatred clear in the German's eyes.

Konrád took another drink. "Do you know what it's like to walk by your former home and peer into the room that used to be yours? To watch Abram on a bicycle, while my shoes pinched my toes and hunger gnawed at my stomach?" Konrád laughed. "And now the worms are eating his corpse. It is the last thing I think of when I go to sleep. It's the first thing I remember when I wake—a shallow grave in the very forest he used to play in as a child."

"It seems as if you've gotten your revenge."

Konrád smirked and then lifted his revolver from his desk and pointed it at Emil. "Except for the fact that his wife and children got away. And along with every penny the family owned."

Emil's hands were trembling. He balled them into fists on his lap, trying to hide their shaking. It did not help.

Konrád leaned so close, his face was just inches away. He took in a deep breath, smelling the scent of fear each time Emil exhaled.

"And what if I refuse?"

Konrád fixed his eyes on Emil and narrowed his gaze. "I've already strolled around the city. Have you ever been on Petřín Hill? There are dozens of trails, and no one would think much of a shallow grave there."

Konrád could read the thrashing about in Emil's mind. Her life for his. It wasn't a choice Emil wanted to make.

"What if I stand by the story—that I've not yet met anyone with that name?"

"Well, then I suppose you're keen on digging your own grave."

"How long will you give me to find her?" Emil finally asked.

Konrád smiled and patted his shoulder, knowing he would come around. "Tomorrow. You have until tomorrow."

— Thirty-Six —

Prague, Czechoslovakia
Sunday April 9, 1939

The next morning, in his new apartment in a much nicer part of the city, Konrád dismantled his Walther semiautomatic pistol. Piece by piece he took it apart and then meticulously cleaned every section. Today was the day. Today he'd finally discover the location of the treasure he'd been longing for.

Once the pistol had been put back together, he slid it into his holster. He put on the holster and then put his jacket on top. He was going to settle his score, receive his prize.

Finally, Konrád reached into the top drawer and pulled out the dagger, sliding it into the holster in his boot. Even though there were minor skirmishes on the streets of the city lately, the last thing he wanted to do was draw attention to himself. A knife was a much quieter way to kill if necessary. Konrád enjoyed using force in his official duties, but this mission was personal. The least attention he could draw to this situation the better.

Konrád stepped forward and opened the door.

The soft knock on the door woke Pavla from her sleep. She opened her eyes and looked around, wondering what time it was. From the slant of the sun, later than she'd slept in a while.

Yesterday Emil had moved Maruška's bed into her room to make it easier to care for the woman. They had pulled a third bed in too, and that's where Madeline still slept. She'd come to stay the night, certain it would be Maruška's last. After all that Pavla had endured, Madeline said she hadn't wanted Pavla to face that alone.

The knock sounded again, and Pavla pulled her arm from under Klára's sleeping form. Still dressed in yesterday's clothes, she hurried to the door, opening it.

"Ma'am, we have news." She recognized the voice first. Then she rubbed her eyes and cleared her vision. It was Marek. The one who took her ring.

Pavla crossed her arms over her chest. "What do you want?" She thought she remembered something about him being gone, but with her foggy brain she couldn't remember.

He frowned slightly. "Emil sent me. We found your daughter's file."

Pavla did not believe him.

Seeing her uncertainty, the man reached into the satchel. He pulled out some paperwork and handed it to her.

She gasped. Here it was—Klára's missing file.

"And will this cost me anything?" she snarled.

Marek seemed confused. "No, not at all. She has a sponsor. All her needs have been covered."

Pavla flipped through the pages again, making sure he was telling her the truth. Her eyes scanned the papers, and sure enough, it was her daughter's file. There was her name, information, and photo. Also tucked in the back were two extra photos, copies that Emil no doubt had made for her.

A gasp escaped Pavla's lips. "So it's true." Her free hand covered her face. "Dear God, it's true."

"You need to pack and prepare. Another transport has been arranged and will be leaving in just a few days. And there is one more paper we need you to sign, but I forgot it at the office. I will need you to come with me."

He held out his hand, indicating that she should return the file to him. She reluctantly gave it to him. "Yes, of course."

She looked back into the room where both Madeline and Klára were still sleeping. Even though she didn't want to wake her, Pavla went to Madeline's side.

"Madeline?" She barely touched the woman's arm. "Do you think you can watch Klára? I will be right back."

Madeline's eyes opened, fought against the bright morning sun, and then closed again. "I can watch her. Go ahead now. We will be right here."

Pavla left with the man. "Thank you, Marek, for finding this."

"Oh." He smiled. "Now that our business is almost done, you can call me by my first name."

She shivered against the morning cold as she walked. "What do you mean? Isn't Marek your first name?"

He lifted his brow and grinned. "My name is Emil. I thought it would be confusing with two Emils working with the refugees, so I went by my last name, Marek."

He walked with slow steps, which was causing tension to rise within her.

"Yes, that was sensible. We should hurry, though. I must get back to Madeline. I don't want to leave her there too long. I also need time to go buy some things to prepare my daughter."

"Wait." He paused. "Madeline was there? In your room?"

"Yes. It is too much to explain now, and we should hurry."

She followed Marek but was confused when he turned down an alley.

"I thought we were going to the office. This isn't the way, is it?"

"Oh." He waved a hand in the air. "I spent much of my childhood in this city. It is a shortcut."

A strange feeling came over her, and an uneasiness settled in the pit of her stomach. Something wasn't right. This was some type of trick. He'd taken her daughter's file for a reason.

Pavla paused her steps. The man was just beside her, moving toward a doorway. Pavla turned and began to run.

"No!" Marek's voice shouted behind her.

The sound of footsteps pounded behind her. Then she felt Marek's arm roughly encircle her waist. A scream pealed from her lips, and he clamped a hand over her mouth. Then another set of hands grabbed her arms, and a growl sounded in her ear. Helpless, Pavla felt herself being dragged away.

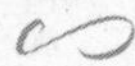

Once they'd secured the woman, Konrád demanded that Marek leave. "You better get back to your work and find some excuse for why you've been missing. But just because I have her doesn't mean I am through with you yet. Keep your mouth shut."

Marek looked to Pavla, pity on his face, and for a moment Konrád thought he might show some type of bravery and try to defend this woman. Instead, Marek walked backward, reached his hand back, and touched the doorknob. Then he turned and ran out the door.

"Just like a coward. Thankfully your Abram wasn't like that. When faced with danger he didn't run." Konrád laughed. "Yet he didn't fight, did he?"

Pavla sat on the cold concrete floor. Her back was against the brick wall. Her legs were stretched out before her, and her ankles were bound. Her hands, resting on her lap, were also bound.

She'd tried screaming, tried fighting, but it had done no good.

"Scream all you want, my lady. There is no one within hearing distance. The factories are all closed today." He shook his head. "Not that anyone would come to help if they knew you were a Jew. I've heard them all mumbling, the people on the streets. They are tired of being overrun by vermin."

She jutted out her chin. "I don't care if you kill me. Do you hear that! I want to die." Her lower lip quivered and some of her bravado faded. "But I have to know. How do you know my husband? How do you know his name?"

Konrád kneeled before her so he was eye to eye. She was a beauty, even though she'd lost so much weight. Her long, black hair was no longer styled as it had been in Olomouc. Instead, it was in a simple braid that loosely hung over her shoulder.

"Are you telling me you don't recognize me? We lived not a half mile apart in Olomouc. I knew you. I saw you often. My mother shopped in your husband's pharmacy. Even though I told her she shouldn't. I told her your family wasn't worthy of our money."

She narrowed her gaze, and he could tell she was searching her memory. "I am so sorry." Her voice was gentle, as if she was trying to appease him. "Olomouc was a large town. There were many people. And I had just moved there not long before I was married. After that I was busy raising children. I'm sure you understand."

"Oh really?" He stood and paced, walking from her to the door and then turning and walking back again. "I assumed your husband would have pointed me out. After all, it was my family who used to own your apartment." He let out a low whistle. "It was a fine apartment, wasn't it?"

She shook her head, and she still looked confused.

"My father used to have an important position," he went on.

"Then everything changed. Although we lived in a German-speaking area, we became part of the new country...and lost everything."

"I'm so sorry." She twisted the ropes on her wrist, as if trying to break out of her bindings. He watched in amusement, knowing she didn't have a chance. "I know nothing of these things. And I don't understand what they have to do with me now."

"Surely your husband told you of the treasure he had hidden. And since all that he had was first mine, I'd like to claim it for myself."

"Treasure? I have no idea what you're talking about. We had nice things, but nothing of great value."

A harsh laugh escaped his lips. What kind of fool did she think he was? He pulled a cigarette and a lighter from his jacket pocket and lighted it, placing it between his lips. He thought he would be able to take it easy on her. He expected her to have a weak will, as thin and frail as she was. The fact that she didn't readily offer the information he needed both surprised and delighted him. He appreciated a worthy opponent. He also greatly enjoyed extracting information from those who did not provide it willingly.

He leaned forward again and blew the smoke from his cigarette into her face. She coughed and turned her head away, but it did little good. With a firm hand he gripped her jaw and turned it back to him.

"Do not think I won't use every resource available to me to extract the information I need." He laughed.

She was silent, and he placed a hand to her neck and squeezed. Her eyes bulged, and she gasped for breath. Her face grew red, her eyes wild. When he finally released his grip, she cried out, swallowing down big gulps of air.

Konrád pulled back and took another puff from his cigarette. "Are you ready to answer yet?"

She nodded and managed to catch her breath. "I do not know anything about a treasure," she gasped.

Konrád laughed and ran his finger down her cheek. "You should not have run away. It would have made things so much easier on me if you would have just stayed."

"Yes," she said louder, finding her voice again, "but what good are scared rabbits huddled inside a cage?"

Konrád reached forward and stroked Pavla's hair. "I am actually impressed by how brave you are." He flicked his ashes to the ground. "Now, where is the wealth your husband hid?"

"I have already told you, I don't know what you speak of."

"Are you saying you have no wealth?"

Pavla held back her shoulders. "From my family I have received much wealth and a priceless inheritance—deep convictions about fighting for what is good and right. I believe in the need to stand up to evil. I believe in the motto of the Czech people '*Pravda vítězí.*' Truth prevails."

Konrád gripped her jaw tighter, jerking it forward and upward. "You speak so poetically, but I don't believe you'll be able to beg for mercy in such an eloquent manner."

Pavla let out a cry. "I promise you I do not know anything. My husband never spoke to me of treasure. I have no idea where you would have gotten that idea."

"Why, I got the idea from your husband myself. He spoke of the treasure he'd hidden just seconds before his death."

Pavla gasped. "You were there? Did you see who killed him?"

Konrád gave her a knowing smile.

Tears formed in her eyes. "It was you! But why?"

He paused for a moment, trying to decide what he should tell her. Trying to decide what information to give her that would extract the information he needed.

"Give me the location of the treasure, and I will tell you about your husband's last moments. I am sure a loving wife like you would want to know of his final words." Konrád offered a half smile. "Maybe he even had a message for you."

Pavla's face scrunched up. She lifted her chin and stared into his face with defiance. "Why are you doing this to me? I do not know of a treasure. You are making this up. Abram would not keep such a thing from me!"

Anger surged through every ounce of Konrád's body. Heat coursed through his veins, and the same rage that caused him to kill her husband months ago now engulfed him.

He reached into the holster and pulled out his pistol, pointing it at her chest. "Your husband begged for his life. He begged that I would allow him to return to his wife and children. He said he would turn everything he owned over to me, including a hidden treasure, but I pulled the trigger too soon." Konrád's hand shook. "I pulled the trigger too soon."

Tears filled her eyes, and she closed them and turned her head away, trying to hide her tears.

"Are you going to beg? If not for you, then for your daughter?"

He had her attention then. Blinking back her tears she looked at him, and for the first time he saw fear there.

"I know where she is. Marek told me. Haven't you figured out the reason he took her file? He wanted to keep her for himself. Though I will take her instead."

"You are an animal if you would dare to kill a child!" Her voice rose with anger.

He laughed. "Oh, if you think that, you think me a fool." He smiled. "I would not kill her, but I have always wanted a daughter. Isn't that the purpose of the occupation? To remove or kill half of the Czechs and Germanize the rest?"

"But she's a Jew. Would you really want to adopt a Jewish child?"

"With her light hair and eyes she looks far from Jewish. Besides, it would give me unique pleasure to raise Abram's daughter as a future member of the Reich."

The woman's shoulders began to tremble, and he was certain she was about to break.

"If you come closer..." she whispered. "I will tell you." She slumped farther down, as though she did not have the strength to hold up her body anymore. "Just please don't do anything that will hurt my daughter." Her voice was low, soft. Konrád was certain she'd come to the end of herself. Excitement built within him. After all this time he would know of the treasure he'd been seeking.

"The treasure..." She lowered her voice even more, and Konrád leaned over her. He ran a hand down her face, wondering how a Jewish woman could be so beautiful.

"The treasure..." she repeated again.

Then with unexpected quickness, the woman's knees pulled back and her feet rocketed forward. Before he had time to jump back, her feet kicked into his gut. The sharp pain caught him by surprise. The wind was knocked out of him. He felt his body propelling back from her, and before he could respond, she kicked him again, right in the upper thigh.

"You can kill me!" she shouted. "But you will not touch my daughter!" Her voice came from deep in her chest, like a tribal yell. And even as Konrád writhed in pain on the floor, he also found pleasure. After all those he'd killed and hunted down, finally someone worthy of a fight.

His stomach felt as if it had been split open, and he let out a low moan. Suddenly he realized his pistol had flown from his hand. He spotted Pavla attempting to crawl on her knees and bound hands toward it on the floor in front of the door.

He forced himself to his feet and staggered in her direction. Part of him wanted to allow her to get closer to the gun, to allow her to put up a good fight. But the other part of him was ready to take her life now.

Don't do it, he told himself. *Don't give in or you will never find the treasure.*

Instead of reaching for the gun, Konrád reached his hand forward and grabbed Pavla's hair, jerking it back.

"Tell me about the treasure. Tell me about the treasure!" he growled.

"You can think what you want, but there is no treasure. Or should I lie and simply lead you on a wild goose chase? How do you know there ever was a treasure? How do you know Abram wasn't simply trying to prolong his life? Don't you think a man seconds away from dying would say anything for one more breath of life?"

Konrád tightened his fingers in her hair, and suddenly he knew she was telling the truth. There was no treasure. Abram had said that to deceive him. All of it had been a lie. All this time. All of it wasted.

Still holding her hair, Konrád reached his hand down and slid his jackknife out of his boot. He pointed it down at her. Then he pulled her head back so she could see it. Her eyes widened, and Konrád could tell by the resolution in her face that she knew this was the end.

He was just about to plunge the knife when he heard the door open behind him.

"Konrád!" It was Marek's voice he heard, but it was an older woman with gray hair who stood in the door. And the last sound, before blackness, was the sound of a pistol firing one round and then two.

— Thirty-Seven —

Prague, Czechoslovakia
Monday, April 10, 1939

A low moan escaped Pavla's lips, and pain shot up her back. Cool sheets were wrapped around her body, and Pavla stretched out her hand, searching for her children's bodies beside her as they had been for the past few months. Nothing but emptiness awaited her, and her eyes flew open. She was in a bed, alone.

It was then that both events of the last week came crashing back. Her son was gone, sent to live with strangers. And she had been attacked by an evil man trying to find a treasure he believed existed and threatening to take her daughter. But after deceiving her, Marek had been flooded with remorse and had gone to get Madeline, who had run to Emil. Pavla remembered seeing Madeline scoop up the gun and fire it at her attacker, and she recalled feeling Emil's arms around her, catching her. The strength of his arms had made her feel safe, but his embrace had brought on a deep ache from within.

In that moment, in his hold, she'd allowed herself to be weak. For so long she'd had to be strong for her children. She wanted to feel her husband's arms around her again, wanted to rest in his protection and love.

But now the reality came crashing in. Where was Klára? Was she safe? And what about her file…had it been lost?

She opened her eyes wider, noting the light flooding into the room. It looked to be a hotel room of some sort, on the ground floor. She could hear the sounds of people and traffic just outside the window. She could hear the voice of a desk clerk in the foyer, not far from her room, welcoming a guest.

Pavla rubbed her eyes and attempted to sit up, and only then did she smell smoke and see a form sitting on a chair in the corner. Her heart began pounding until she remembered that the German was dead and it was her hair that smelled of smoke from the pistol.

The glare of the light from the window blinded her, and it was hard to make out the man's face.

"Careful now, don't overdo it. You have some nasty bruises. I'm surprised that struggle didn't break you in two, considering how thin and frail you are."

She recognized the voice immediately and relaxed. *Emil.* He'd been there to catch her when she fell. He was with her still.

Pavla looked down and noticed she was wearing a nightgown of fine linen like the ones she used to wear as Abram's bride. She didn't want to think about how she got into this gown or where her clothes were. Instead, all she could think about was Klára. Ondřej, she knew, was safe.

"Klára?" she asked.

"With Madeline. She's fine. Madeline is as good at playing paper dolls as she is taking a good shot." He swept his hand around the room. "Madeline's been caring for you too."

"I'm thankful." Pavla smiled weakly. "What time is it?"

"It's nine in the morning, and you've been a sleep for nearly twenty hours. A doctor checked on you. He claims that with good food and rest, you'll make a full recovery."

"Oh, yes, and I am certain that's exactly what I'll be able to get now that the Germans are here. They will take care of it all, right?"

She eased herself back under the blanket, tucking the pillow under her cheek. "I know, I should be grateful..." Pavla's words traveled off.

"You are safe here. You do not have to worry. More than that, your children are safe, Pavla."

He said her name so tenderly that tears came upon hearing it. They came softly at first, but then grew in volume. She should be ashamed of these tears, but she wasn't. She cried until sweet sleep threatened to engulf her again. The pillow under her head made her feel like a real person, and she snuggled down deeper. She drifted off knowing Emil was in the room, and that too gave her comfort.

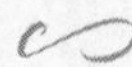

Amity looked down at the little girl's file that she'd spread upon her bed, flipping through the pages one last time. In one last act of decency, Marek had given Madeline the file before he fled into the night. The child would be on the next transport, but what about the mother?

Amity scanned a second file she'd laid out before her. Maruška Tesařová died on Easter morning, knowing that her only son, Michal Tesař, had made it to safety, into the arms of a new family in England. She also died with an exit visit already stamped and ready to go. The only problem was the photo. The slight pixie of a woman looked nothing like the refugee that Amity wanted to get on the next transport.

A shiver ran down Amity's spine as she remembered *Kriminalrat* Boemmelburg's words, *"There have been quite a few Americans who have disappeared within this city in the last few months. It's so hard to keep track of them."* She knew what would happen if she was caught trying to sneak out one Jew on another's paperwork.

Her mind also flashed back to Clark's words as he peered into the dark waters of the Vltava River. *"I imagine if someone weighed down a body and tossed it over the edge, it never would be seen again, would it?"*

Should I do it? Should I use Maruška's paperwork for Pavla? Is it worth the risk?

She thought of a story she had heard since staying in the Czech capital. Václav Wenceslas—whom Wenceslas Square was named after—was a devout Christian, hated by the pagan nobility because of his kindness to the poor. He was murdered by his brother and became Bohemia's first martyr. Good King Wenceslas, he was called. It was a Christmas carol she knew even from the States.

She remembered her mother singing it as she decorated the home with evergreen boughs and poinsettias. When she asked about it, her mother said it's a song about a Bohemian king who went on a journey during harsh winter weather to give alms to a poor peasant on the Second Day of Christmas. During the journey, the king's page struggled to keep up, but he was able to continue by following the king's footprints step by step through the deep snow. Amity softly sang the words.

> *"Sire, the night is darker now, and the wind blows stronger;*
> *Fails my heart, I know not how; I can go no longer."*

"Mark my footsteps, good my page. Tread thou in them boldly.
Thou shalt find the winter's rage freeze thy blood less coldly."
In his master's steps he trod, where the snow lay dinted;
Heat was in the very sod which the saint had printed.
Therefore, Christian men, be sure, wealth or rank possessing,
Ye who now will bless the poor, shall yourselves find blessing.

Why was she thinking of that now? She knew the reason. It was the answer to her prayer. She knew what God was asking of her. It wasn't just a matter of courage. Instead, it was about sacrifice, should it come to that.

What she had to face was something she could not stand up against on her own. The night was too dark. The obstacles too surmounting, yet only one thing was required of her—to walk in the Master's steps and to bless the poor. Or in this case, to bless one poor soul whose life depended on the decisions that Amity would make over the next few days.

Amity put the files on the nightstand, turned off the light, and snuggled under the sheets. She was but a page, stepping in her Master's footsteps. She was but a defenseless pope, standing against a merciless Hun.

She lay in the dark and listened as Madeline's old Chesterfield clock chimed from the downstairs hall. There wasn't anyone else awake in the apartment, and even the streets outside seemed strangely quiet. The German patrols that rumbled through the streets in their armored vehicles or walked in groups of two or three were obviously occupied elsewhere.

Another quarter hour passed and then another. Would she be able to sleep tonight? She didn't know how she could. If things didn't go well tomorrow, tonight would be her last night of freedom.

She sat up and pushed back the covers. Her legs moved over the edge of the high bed, and it took a moment for her feet to find the floor. She ignored her slippers and bathrobe, and instead walked to the window. She placed her fingertips to the window, sensing the cold of the night slip through the glass. Regardless of what the next few days brought, she knew she had done everything God had asked her to do, and because she had been obedient to His call, lives had been saved.

— THIRTY-EIGHT —

Prague, Czechoslovakia
Tuesday, April 11, 1939

With quickened steps Amity strode into *Kriminalrat* Boemmelburg's office. The man sat behind the desk and didn't rise. He was also missing the familiar grin she had been accustomed to. He didn't motion to the chair either, so Amity remained standing.

Boemmelburg wasted no time in telling her the reason that he'd sent for her.

"I've learned that one of the leaders of your last transport was someone who escaped illegally."

Fear seized her, and Amity took a breath, not knowing how to answer except by telling the truth.

"I am so sorry. It was a mistake on my part. It is just that some of these mothers and fathers came to me in such a state of desperation." Her hands began to tremble. "I made a mistake, but I promise not to do it again. I am trying to help the children, but sometimes I wonder why I have taken on this job."

Boemmelburg's scowl softened. "People have used you, and I am sorry for that. But from now on it is absolutely forbidden for any adult to leave the country without a special *Ausreisebewilligung*."

"An exit permit. Yes, that makes perfect sense. Does that include me, sir?"

His gaze quickly flicked up at her. "Are you leaving us now?"

She nodded. "I am sorry. I do not have a choice." Amity quickly looked for an excuse he would understand, and again she decided simply to tell the truth. "As you can see, the pressure has become too great. In order to leave with my honor intact, I must return to England." Her chest filled with emotion, and she guessed he had no idea how hard it was to say those words. But deep down she knew her time had come. She was no longer safe. As hard as it was, there would be others in London who still needed her help.

She placed her exit permit before him and was surprised by how quickly he stamped it.

Then he scanned the list of other names before him. "What about others? Do any of them need exit permits?"

"Only one." Amity urged her heart to stop its wild pounding, but it did no good. "A mother, traveling with her child. Maruška Tesařová—she was unable to make the last transport because she was ill."

"And she is better now?"

"Yes, sir."

Boemmelburg continued to flip through the list "And she is Jewish?"

"Yes, sir."

"And the child, Jewish also?"

"Yes, sir."

Finally, after she'd answered all his questions, he lifted his eyes to her, removed his reading glasses, and smiled.

"You are right to get out now while you can, and you must continue to be careful, even in London. A beautiful young woman like you—people will try to take advantage of you." He sighed.

"And remember, we Nazis will care for the Aryan children. You have no need to worry about them."

"I will try to be more careful—both here and in London. I appreciate your concern."

"Thank you for being honest. There are so few people I can trust these days. It makes my job so much harder, as I am sure you understand."

Without hesitation he stamped the remaining exit papers and handed back the list of children for transport. On the top was Maruška's exit document, stamped and ready for her to board.

Pavla walked up to the train platform. A few days ago she would have considered this to be the scariest thing she had ever done, but after what she'd experienced with the German agent, she realized that carrying false documents took second place. Her head spun. Her heart raced.

Emil, who walked beside her, touched her arm. "Pavla, whatever you do, you can't let them see your fear. Pretend you do not have a care in the world. Pretend you have nothing to hide."

She had used that technique just days ago with that horrible German, but now she questioned whether she had enough strength to do it again. Yet Pavla knew she had to try. If the train attendants saw the slightest sign of fear, they'd look too closely at her paperwork, and she couldn't have that. Not only did her life depend on it, but Amity's did too. And then there were the two hundred children who filled the train to consider, including her sweet Klára.

Without another word, Emil walked away to help the children, and Pavla didn't look back. She moved ahead to the first-class car. They had made these arrangements to give her as much space between herself and the children as possible in case something went wrong.

Even as she walked, she knew that somewhere on this platform, Amity was helping load children onto the train for the last time. She had no choice but to head back to London now. There were too many people scrutinizing her every move.

Pavla walked with light steps toward the train, telling herself she wasn't walking to a train platform. Instead, she was walking to a party, and Abram was waiting for her inside. She was wearing a fine dress that they'd had designed and sewn just for her at the local dress shop. The children were home with their grandparents, and when the party was over they'd hurry home and place kisses upon their heads.

Only after she made it onto the train...only after she exited Czechoslovakia and made it all the way through Germany...only then would she let the truth seep in. She couldn't embrace the reality that she was leaving her home country and all the memories of her life with her husband for good. Not now. Not yet.

A steward approached and offered her a smile. "Miss, may I take your baggage?"

"Yes, thank you, sir." She smiled as she handed over a small suitcase that Madeline had given her.

After passing over the suitcase, Pavla straightened her traveling jacket and readjusted her purse on her arm, and then she continued forward. Eyes watched her, but this time for a different reason. They wondered how a Jew walked with such confidence, and maybe they realized it was because she was leaving this new German protectorate for good.

Pavla settled into the fine crushed-velvet chair and prepared for the long journey, but it was two hours later when her acting skills were truly put to the test.

When the train stopped at the border, two Secret Service operatives in black uniforms with skull and crossbones on their hats, members of the Secret Service Death's Head Brigade, climbed onto the train, asking for documents.

Her spirits sank. If anyone would be able to see beyond her charade, it would be these men. With a smile, she turned over her passport, her Gestapo permit, and her tickets.

"How did you get the exit permit?" one soldier asked.

She cocked an eyebrow, pretending to be offended. Then, seeing that she caught his interest, Pavla forced a shy smile. "If you have any questions, why don't you call your headquarters in Prague and they will tell you?"

"Why isn't your age on this card? Just your name and passport number?"

Pavla folded her eyebrows into a frown. "I'm not sure." She tipped her head. "But if you must know, I am thirty."

"And why are you in first-class?"

She shrugged. "Again, I have no answers, but if you call the headquarters in Prague, they will tell you."

The guards said nothing else. Instead, they just collected the documents and walked back out.

Pavla prayed with their every step and held her breath. Maybe they would just take her, not realizing her connection with the children.

Yet as she watched, the men got halfway to the station, then turned around and came back to the train.

"Heil Hitler. We wish you a pleasant trip," the guard said, tossing the documents onto her lap.

Amity had never heard such a ruckus of excited, eager children in all her days of traveling, but she wouldn't have it any other way. Part of her rejoiced with the children. They would soon be safe. They would soon be able to be children again. Yet she mourned all those left behind. Although Madeline and others promised to keep working on the transports, Amity wondered how many more children they'd be able to transport to safety. Too few. Always too few.

She thought about the morning she'd awoken and had known the time for her to leave had come. It was a gentle knowing, a peace from God that His work with her in Czechoslovakia was done. What she wished she could have done for all, she'd at least been able to do for some. The battles weren't over yet, but she was released from this fight—at least on this side of the transports.

Now she had watched out the window when the train had stopped at the German border. Secret Security officers entered the train and checked all their passports. She tensed as they checked Emil's paperwork, who was sitting next to her. His smile put the officers at ease, and Amity released the breath she'd been holding when the officers also exited first-class and waved the train on.

When they crossed into Germany, the excited chatter faded, and fear was clear on the faces of the children. What atrocities had they already seen committed by the Germans? What nightmares invaded their sleep at night?

The muffled cries of one young woman carried through their train car, but soon a soft humming took its place, and then—nearly as one—the children's voices rose in song.

"What is that? What are they singing?" Amity asked Emil. She had used his real name and almost his real age. The Emil on the exit paperwork was four years old, while this Emil was twenty-four...a clerical error, of course. She just hoped that Boemmelburg didn't figure it out. At least the security guards hadn't.

"The children are singing our country's national anthem—or at least it was."

"The words," she asked. "What do they mean?"

He hummed along and then translated.

Where is my home, where is my homeland?
Water roars across the meadows,
Pinewoods rustle among crags,
The garden is glorious with spring blossom,
Paradise on earth it is to see.
And this is that beautiful land,
The Czech land, my home,
The Czech land, my home!

Where is my homeland? The question caused Amity's heart to ache. They all would have a different homeland now.

Many hours later, after going from train to ship and crossing the English Channel, the children stood on the deck, waiting for the ship to drop anchor, the yellow lights of the ship casting an eerie glow on them. *Ghost children.*

The words of the song sung on the train had filled her mind. The cold sea air hit her, and a shiver ran down her spine. The past lives of the children were dead. Even if they were again united with their parents, the old lives they had were forever gone.

The sea gulls' cries echoed over the water, causing Amity's soul to ache. Just last year at this time these children were running through gardens, chasing butterflies, rolling in the dirt. They had sticky fingers and smiling faces from their mother's treats. Wrestling before bath time with giggles and laughter. But now they had turned into small adults. They had to be responsible. They had to be subdued. Amity still heard their parents' translated pleas in her ears. *"Be a good little boy. Be a good little girl. Obey. See, this nice lady will take care of you."*

Whispered secrets had replaced their shouts of glee, but hopefully not for long. New families would be forming, new memories made.

Amity wanted to say goodbye to Emil, Pavla, and Klára on the ship. Instead of catching the train to London, they would be taking a different train to the countryside, where one of the artists Emil had saved had offered up her summer home for Pavla and her children to use as long as needed. Once they arrived they would send for Ondřej, who was certain to be thrilled to be reunited with them.

As their ship neared the shore, Amity couldn't help but pull Pavla into a large embrace. She considered asking Emil to translate a goodbye but then changed her mind. She did not need to tell Pavla how much she believed that God would give her a good future. God had already saved Pavla and her children.

Then, after she stepped back from Pavla's embrace, Amity bent down so she could look into Klára's smiling eyes. The salty sea air caused the girl's light hair to flutter around her cheeks, and Amity was certain she'd never seen such a look of joy.

Klára was on a ship, with her mother at her side. Few other children had been so lucky, and soon this small girl would be reunited with her brother. It truly was an answer to prayer.

Still, Amity's heart ached for all the other children and mothers left behind. She had helped to get out hundreds, but thousands still waited on the list. *O Lord, be with them now.*

Madeline would continue their work as long as she was able, until either the Germans stopped the kindertransports or war was declared with England. Amity's only hope was that Madeline would be able to get more transports out before either happened.

Pavla said something in Czech that Amity didn't understand, and Klára stepped forward and gave Amity a tight hug.

"Tank you," the small voice whispered into her ear English. "Tank you so mush."

Tears came to Amity's eyes as she heard those words. Emil had taught them to Klára, she had no doubt. Those words sank deep and bounced around every inch of Amity's heart.

She placed a soft kiss on Klára's cheek, feeling the echo of every child on every transport, in those words. But instead of holding on to it, Amity offered the words up to God as a prayer.

"Thank You for choosing me for this work," she whispered. Then she watched as the wind carried away her words on its wings. Carrying them up to the One who mourned with her over all the lost children.

Finally, she looked to Emil. What could she say to him to sum up all she felt inside? "I couldn't have done it without you," she stated simply.

"Nor I without you." He extended his hand, and she placed hers inside it. It was warm, comforting. "I promise you one thing, Amity." He wiped away tears with the back of his hand. "I will live a life worthy of your rescue." He looked to Pavla and placed a hand on her shoulder. "The love you gave all of us will live on."

— THIRTY-NINE —

London, England
Thursday, April 13, 1939

Amity clasped her hands in front of her as she stood on the platform and searched the crowds for the one person she was looking for. As he walked toward her in the yellow glow of the streetlamp, Clark Cartwright didn't slow his pace. If he hadn't been trying to act the part of a perfect gentleman, Amity was sure that Clark would have run toward her. Yet he was an English gentleman, and even that made her smile.

He raked back his hair as he approached her. He was wearing a suit jacket and blue shirt that Celia always told him brought out the blue of his eyes.

He wrapped his arms around Amity, cupping his hand at the back of her neck and pulling her to him. She placed her cheek against his chest and smiled, remembering again how much she adored the aroma of Clark's shaving lotion and Mrs. McGovern's laundry soap.

Clark cleared his throat. "I can breathe now. I haven't been able to for the past few days. I did not know if you would make it, especially after I heard your crazy idea for helping one of the refugees."

Her eyes widened. "But how did you know?"

"Andrew told me." Clark sighed. "He's had many people watching out for you—more than you know."

Amity's eyes fluttered closed. "Her name is Pavla. She is a mother of two children. She was in danger. I had to help her." She bit her lower lip. Had Andrew known about Emil too? She guessed not. But that would be another conversation for another day.

"Of course you had to help, Amity. And that's why I love you so, and I can't wait to marry you."

She sucked in a breath and held it, and she then pulled back and looked into Clark's face. "Can you repeat that? I believe the noise of the train might have distorted my hearing. I thought you said—"

"That I love you," he interrupted. "And that I can't wait to marry you." He winked. "If you would have me, that is."

She pulled back slightly so she could look into his eyes. "Yes, Clark, a hundred times yes."

Then he grinned. "And we will have to go together to pick out an engagement ring. The house has been a little busy, as you will soon see."

He stepped back even more, taking both of her hands. "But before we head to the auto, there are a few things I need to tell you. I didn't realize how much you had become a part of my life and heart until you were gone. And seeing your work in Prague...well, I've never been more proud of another person. And you're here now. And I promised myself that if you made it back I would tell you how much I love you every day of your life." He prattled on with a joy she hadn't seen before bubbling up inside. "You are my friend. You are my hero. You are my muse—"

Amity help up her hand. "Wait. Did you say muse? Tell me, did you finish the novel?"

"Yes, since arriving back from Prague, the rest of it has just poured out. And..." He touched her nose with his finger. "You're going to like this. The main character's name is Jane."

"Jane? A plain name, but I like it." She chuckled. "So, is the hero really a female this time?"

"Yes, and she is strangely similar to you, but with blonde hair and a fiery temper. Someone determined to work with the resistance to smuggle children out of Germany."

Amity blew out a breath. "Oh, Germany, good. I was afraid it would sound too much like me." Then, thinking back over all that had happened in the past five months and realizing that she was finally back, safe on British soil once again, her legs felt like jelly, and she found herself leaning on Clark for support.

"There is so much to tell you, so many stories. I'm not sure where to start, but we must pray. My hope is that Madeline will be able to continue the work and that they will be able to get out more transports. I also have to tell Celia how much good she has done helping to get sponsors. I'd love to find some of the children and see them again." She paused and looked around, realizing for the first time who was missing. "Where's Celia?"

"She is in the car with the little one. Michal fell asleep..."

"Michal?"

"Yes, the small toddler. You told us to find a special home for him, and Celia could not think of a more special home than ours."

Tears came to her eyes then. "His mother, she passed away..."

Clark's own eyes filled with tears. "Oh. I am so very sorry to hear that. How tragic."

"All she had wanted was to make sure he was safe," Amity

whispered, dropping her chin guiltily. "I just wish I could have done more for her."

With the edge of a finger Clark tipped her chin up. "You did all you could. You did *what* you could. You saved her child, and I'm sure that's the one thing she wanted most."

"Yes, it was."

"And by loving him as a mother, you will be giving a gift to her every day."

Mother? Amity didn't know if she'd ever heard such a beautiful word...well, other than *wife*. The thought of Michal running around the halls and up and down the stairs of their London home brought a smile to her face. "Wait, Clark. Does this mean you will adopt the boy?"

"Yes, that is what it means. Celia will be thrilled to have a younger brother."

The generosity of this man overwhelmed her. "I love you, Clark," she told him calmly but passionately. "I am not sure I know what I did to deserve a man such as you."

"Love is not something you have to earn. It's given. You've had my love even before you left for Czechoslovakia. I want you to know that."

She was thankful he said that. It was good to know that she was loved for who she was, not just for what she had done. Amity stepped back from him, realizing for the first time how their exchange must have looked to all those watching. But at this moment it didn't seem as if Clark cared too much about appearances.

"Hurry." She tugged on his arm. "I can't wait to see your daughter..." She laughed. "And your son!"

For the first time Amity noticed that Godfry, Clark's driver, was standing to the side and had already gathered the bags. "Are these all you brought with you, miss? Did I miss anything?"

"That is all, Godfrey, thank you." She laughed. "I'm not sure I'm going to know how to act, being taken care of so well."

Clark took her hand and led her to the car. Celia was watching for them, and after spotting Amity, her face lit up. It looked as if she was fumbling for the knob, and then the door opened and she jumped out, a sleeping Michal curled up on the seat.

"Oh, Amity, you're home. You look so beautiful. A little thin, but so beautiful all the same. Don't worry. It'll only take Mrs. McGovern a few days to fatten you up." Celia's voice was loud and excited, and Michal stirred. His eyes fluttered open, and he looked to Celia first and smiled. Then he glanced over at Amity. With an extra wiggle, he released a small squeal and stretched out his arms to her.

"Oh, sweet boy, look at you." She took him into her arms and squeezed. He smelled of shampoo and warm milk. And Amity imagined he already had the whole staff wrapped around his little finger.

He put his chubby arms around her neck and held on, and then he snuggled his head under her chin and let out a sigh. Her throat felt hot and thick, and she opened her mouth to speak, but no words came out. Pressing her lips together, she blinked back the moisture gathering in her eyes.

"Oh, this child was so loved. You should have seen how well he was loved. We have a big task to live up to, but we will do it. Oh yes, we will do it."

— EPILOGUE —

Ústín, Czech Republic
September 20, 1993

Charles exited the deep well and blinked back the light that burned his eyes. He reached over to the edge of the well and gently set the velvet sack on the ground. He set down the stone with his grandfather's initials right next to it.

His father, Andrew, looked at it, and his features softened. "I remember that bag. It's my father's tallit bag."

"A tallit?" Charles scratched his head. "Isn't that a prayer shawl?"

"Yes, it's worn over outer clothes during the *Shacharit*—the morning prayer. And also during all prayers on Yom Kippur. My father received his as a wedding gift from his parents, although my grandfather was more religious."

"That didn't matter to the Nazis, though, did it?"

"No, to Hitler it was Jewish blood that he despised. But we have had this conversation before, have we not?"

His father eyed the bag but didn't take a step toward it.

Charles climbed onto the ground on the side of the well and undid his harness. He knelt on the ground next to the items, and for a moment it was as if he knelt on sacred ground.

O Lord, thank You for protecting my father, aunt, and grandmother. Thank You for the heritage of faith You have passed down to me. He thought of his grandfather, a man he didn't know, yet whom he felt close to in this moment.

"Even though he strayed from some of the Jewish traditions, grandfather was a man of faith, wasn't he?"

"Faith," his father whispered. Breathless wonder haloed the word. "Yes, he was a man of faith, to prepare me for what might happen. To provide for my mother. To plant this treasure here." His father knelt, but instead of touching the bag, his fingers traced the carved initials in the rock. His chin lowered to his chest. His shoulders quivered. His face grew red, and Charles knew his dad was trying to hold in his emotion.

Charles placed a hand on his father's shoulder. "It's okay, Dad, you don't have to hold it in." Tears came to his eyes and rolled down his face. Soon his shoulders quivered too, and he cried for the grandfather he never knew. He cried for his father, who shouldn't have had to face such horrors as a young boy.

"I have never told this to anyone," his father finally said, his voice croaking out with pent-up emotion, "but I wasn't surprised when that German came to the door. My mother thought I was, but I was just pretending. The truth was, I had been afraid that whole day."

Charles sat and leaned his back against the wooden fence. A fence his father said had been there since he was a boy. How had that fence stood when so much around it was lost or destroyed? It made no sense.

"What do you mean you were afraid all day? How could you have known what was to happen?"

His father swiped a hand down his face. "Oh, I didn't know that my father, grandmother, and grandfather would die that day.

But I did know what was going to happen with the businesses on *Kristallnacht,* the Night of Broken Glass.

"Most people at first believed the riots happened on their own, but now history tells us that they were planned. On the morning of November 10, Joseph Goebbels sent an urgent secret telegram to the *Sicherheitspolizei,* the Security Police, containing instructions about the riots. Police were instructed to seize Jewish archives and to arrest Jewish males to transfer to labor camps. And I knew this..." His voice quivered now.

Instead of turning to his father, Charles lifted his face to the sky, and the white clouds that floated in front of the sun cast a gray shadow. He suddenly was cold all over, and a shiver ran down his spine. His father didn't answer, so he asked the question again. "What do you mean you knew?"

"One of my childhood friends and neighbors, Filip Knápek, had a father in the Security Police. He told me they were going to let the German people loot the Jewish homes and businesses, and he also told me if I told a soul, his father would come to my house and send me to a camp that night."

Charles reached over and grabbed his father's hand, guessing where this story was going.

"After my mother put us to bed, I stayed awake, listening to my parents and grandparents talking. When I heard a knock at the door, I snuck out of bed and saw the German take my father and grandparents away. Then I heard Mother frantically packing. I urged her to leave immediately, telling her we didn't have time. It was good that we left when we did. I have no doubt the German would have come back for my mother. Of course, my mother knew nothing about this treasure, and no one thought to ask me.

"I knew where to run to. My father had prepared me. He was a man of faith. He had faith that we would survive, even knowing the evil that the Nazis were determined to do. And he had faith in me—even as a young boy."

"Speaking of your sister," Charles said, "We promised to call Aunt Klára when we found that treasure. I think I spotted a pay phone down by the pub down the street."

His father wiped the tears from his face, finally turning to him. "You're getting ahead of yourself."

"What do you mean?"

"Don't you think we should see what's inside the bag before we make the call?"

"Does it really matter, Dad?"

"No, I suppose it doesn't." He sighed. "I wish your grandmother had known there truly was a treasure."

"I don't think it mattered to her much either. She got out of the country with what she treasured most."

"With most of what mattered—she never did get used to living without my father. She died the day before his birthday, and she said his name with her parting tears. The doctor said he thought she still had a few more weeks, but she surprised us all, didn't she? I don't think she wanted to live through another birthday without him."

Charles had heard that story many times before, but it was different this time. He was sitting in the yard that his family once again owned. The past and the present intersected in this moment.

Charles smiled, thinking of bringing his own wife and two sons here. And someday, when they got older, he would tell them the story of this day and how their story tied into a greater one.

"We will call Klára tomorrow," his dad said finally. "And for now let us keep this moment for ourselves."

With a tender touch his father opened the top of the bag. He held his breath as he slipped his hand inside. He smiled as he pulled out a small menorah. "This was always in the center of our dining room table. I don't remember it not being there, but my father must have hidden it a few weeks before."

"Is it valuable?" Charles dared to ask.

"It's plated in gold, if that's you were wondering, but probably not worth as much as you might think."

"It was a treasure to him then?" Charlie commented.

"Yes, it was a treasure to him."

His father handed it over to him. It was heavier than he expected.

"The seven-branch menorah that was used in the ancient temple of Jerusalem was gold and lit with olive oil." His voice drifted off. "I remember my mother telling me stories about the temple. Like all Jewish families at the time, we talked about immigrating to Palestine. It was so hard to think of leaving everything behind. My father was especially worried about leaving his parents." He sighed. "It is so easy to look back now and know what could have been done differently. By the time my father figured out what was about to happen, it was too late to get anyone out. He did the best he could."

"There is more in the bag." Charles pointed. "What else do you think is in there?"

His father tipped over the bag and a dozen gold coins fell out. They both gasped and picked them up, turning them over in their hand. "Look at this." Charles placed four coins in his hand. He studied the dates, unsure if he saw them right. All of them were dated 1897 or 1898.

"A treasure indeed."

This was the gift of a father for his family. He wasn't a rich man, but he'd gathered together what he could. Charles could see from his father's face that finding this meant more to him that if he'd found a load of riches.

"Is that all?" Charles picked up the bag and held it in his hands. He plunged his hand into the bag, and his eyes widened as he felt something small and metal on the bottom. He pulled it out and held it on the palm of his hand.

"My...my mother's wedding ring," his grandfather said, sounding shocked.

"What do you mean? Your mother used her ruby wedding ring to get you and your sister on the list."

"Yes, that was the ring I always remembered. I would play with it when she read to me. It was a band of rubies. But when they were first married as poor university students, he'd gotten her a simple band. This is it."

His father held his hand out. Charles placed the ring in it.

"Did you see what was inside?" his father asked. "There is writing in it. Can you read it?"

"Yes, it says, 'Pavla, our Iyar begins.'" Charles furrowed his brow. "Iyar. It's a month of the Jewish calendar, isn't it?"

"Yes, it is. It's the second month of the Hebrew calendar. It's a month of divine healing."

"Healing?"

"Healing that comes from refining. 'These have come so that the proven genuineness of your faith—of greater worth than gold, which perishes even though refined by fire...'" his father said, quoting the contemporary Scripture version from memory.

"You escaped the fire, Father..."

"And I have found something greater than gold on the other side. I have found God. I have discovered what true sacrifice means. And I have seen God's hand upon my life. That truly is the greatest treasure, isn't it? To know that in a world filled with evil there are still those who are willing to stand up for all that is right and good, and shine the light of God in the darkest of places."

Andrew squeezed the ring in his hand, and tears came then. His tears of thankfulness watered the earth that once again would produce fruit—life—for his family. Just as hoped, just as planned.

— Discussion Questions —

1. Amity Mitchell was an American tutor living in London when news of the growing Nazi power was carried over the radio. What unique concerns did Amity, Clark, and Celia have during this time?

2. Amity was plunged into a new world when she visited Czechoslovakia. What did you learn about what was happening in Czechoslovakia during that time in history? What surprised you?

3. Pro-Nazi Czechs were eager to welcome the Germans into their country. How did the mistreatment Konrád faced after the Great War affect the way he treated others throughout this novel?

4. Pavla's life changed overnight when the Nazis entered the Sudetenland. In what ways did this affect her and her children?

5. How do you feel about the treatment of the Jews by the Germans? What were some of the challenges they faced? Did you learn anything new about their mistreatment from this novel?

6. What did you know about kindertransports before reading *A Daring Escape*? What did you learn about them? How would you have felt putting your child on a kindertransport?

7. Part of the story was told through the eyes of a child. How did a child see this time differently than an adult would?

8. Prague is one of the most beautiful capitals of Europe. How did the beauty of the city contrast with the pain of the war?

9. Amity risked her life to help Jewish children. Who in our day are sacrificing themselves in various ways to help those who are in great need?

10. What surprised you about the plot of this novel? Do you think the author pulled off the ending?

11. Who was your favorite character? Why?

12. What did you appreciate most about this work of fiction?

ALSO FROM TRICIA GOYER...

Duty Brought Them Together.
Will Secrets Destroy Their Love?

American Emma Hanson came to England to study at Oxford but joined the Women's Auxiliary Air Force at the height of World War II. She is stationed at beautiful and historic Danesfield House west of London as part of the highly secretive Photographic Reconnaissance Unit.

Englishman Will Fleming is a handsome young artist who has been commissioned by the British government to record the changing landscape in paintings. His path intersects with Emma's when his real mission—tracking Nazi spies—leads him to Danesfield House, the target of a sinister plot.

Emma and Will become friends, but neither can reveal the true nature of their assignment. Can their relationship grow amid such secrecy? And can Will save Danesfield House—and Emma and her coworkers—before it's too late?

HARVEST HOUSE PUBLISHERS
EUGENE, OREGON